Cm Et 3/12   BK 7/20
WW 8/12   Ell 9/20
Ell 9/12   BK 1/23
Char 12/12   WW 2/23
BKO 8/13   Nuill 4/23
Sheatt 5/16 Shatt 4/23
WW 6/16
Ell 7/16 ✓
BK 10/17 ✓
Shatt 2/19
WW 3/19

13/57

THE PARTICULAR SADNESS
OF LEMON CAKE

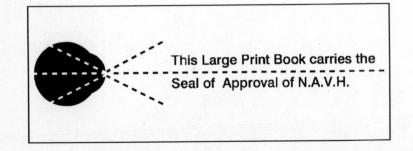

This Large Print Book carries the
Seal of Approval of N.A.V.H.

THE PARTICULAR SADNESS OF LEMON CAKE

AIMEE BENDER

THORNDIKE PRESS
A part of Gale, Cengage Learning

GALE
CENGAGE Learning™

Detroit • New York • San Francisco • New Haven, Conn • Waterville, Maine • London

GALE
CENGAGE Learning

LIBRARY OF CONGRESS CATALOGING-IN-PUBLICATION DATA

Bender, Aimee.
  The particular sadness of lemon cake / by Aimee Bender. —
Large print ed.
    p. cm. — (Thorndike Press large print reviewers choice)
  ISBN-13: 978-1-4104-3064-9
  ISBN-10: 1-4104-3064-2
  1. Taste—Fiction. 2. Family secrets—Fiction. 3. Psychological
fiction. 4. Large type books. I. Title.
PS3552.E538447P37 2010
813'.54—dc22   2010024171

Published in 2010 by arrangement with Doubleday, an imprint of Knopf Doubleday Publishing Group.

Printed in Mexico
2 3 4 5 6 7 14 13 12 11 10

For Mir

Food is all those substances which, submitted to the action of the stomach, can be assimilated or changed into life by digestion, and can thus repair the losses which the human body suffers through the act of living.

— The Physiology of Taste, *Brillat-Savarin*

■ ■ ■ ■

PART ONE:
FOOD

■ ■ ■ ■

1

It happened for the first time on a Tuesday afternoon, a warm spring day in the flatlands near Hollywood, a light breeze moving east from the ocean and stirring the black-eyed pansy petals newly planted in our flower boxes.

My mother was home, baking me a cake. When I tripped up the walkway, she opened the front door before I could knock.

How about a practice round? she said, leaning past the door frame. She pulled me in for a hello hug, pressing me close to my favorite of her aprons, the worn cotton one trimmed in sketches of twinned red cherries.

On the kitchen counter, she'd set out the ingredients: Flour bag, sugar box, two brown eggs nestled in the grooves between tiles. A yellow block of butter blurring at the edges. A shallow glass bowl of lemon peel. I toured the row. This was the week of

11

my ninth birthday, and it had been a long day at school of cursive lessons, which I hated, and playground yelling about point scoring, and the sunlit kitchen and my warm-eyed mother were welcome arms, open. I dipped a finger into the wax baggie of brown-sugar crystals, murmured yes, please, yes.

She said there was about an hour to go, so I pulled out my spelling booklet. Can I help? I asked, spreading out pencils and papers on the vinyl place mats.

Nah, said Mom, whisking the flour and baking soda together.

My birthday is in March, and that year it fell during an especially bright spring week, vivid and clear in the narrow residential streets where we lived just a handful of blocks south of Sunset. The night-blooming jasmine that crawled up our neighbor's front gate released its heady scent at dusk, and to the north, the hills rolled charmingly over the horizon, houses tucked into the brown. Soon, daylight savings time would arrive, and even at nearly nine, I associated my birthday with the first hint of summer, with the feeling in classrooms of open windows and lighter clothing and in a few months no more homework. My hair got lighter in spring, from light brown to nearly blond, almost like my mother's ponytail tassel. In the neighborhood gardens, the agapanthus plants started to push out their long green robot stems to open up to soft purples and blues.

Mom was stirring eggs; she was sifting flour. She had one bowl of chocolate icing set aside, another with rainbow sprinkles.

A cake challenge like this wasn't a usual afternoon activity; my mother didn't bake all that often, but what she enjoyed most was anything tactile, and this cake was just one in a long line of recent varied hands-on experiments. In the last six months, she'd coaxed a strawberry plant into a vine, stitched doilies from vintage lace, and in a burst of motivation installed an oak side door in my brother's bedroom with the help of a hired contractor. She'd been working as an office administrator, but she didn't like copy machines, or work shoes, or computers, and when my father paid off the last of his law school debt, she asked him if she could take some time off and learn to do more with her hands. My hands, she told him, in the hallway, leaning her hips against his; my hands have had no lessons in anything.

Anything? he'd asked, holding tight to

those hands. She laughed, low. Anything *practical,* she said.

They were right in the way, in the middle of the hall, as I was leaping from room to room with a plastic leopard. Excuse me, I said.

He breathed in her hair, the sweet-smelling thickness of it. My father usually agreed with her requests, because stamped in his two-footed stance and jaw was the word Provider, and he loved her the way a bird-watcher's heart leaps when he hears the call of the roseate spoonbill, a fluffy pink wader, calling its lilting coo-coo from the mangroves. Check, says the bird-watcher. Sure, said my father, tapping a handful of mail against her back.

Rah, said the leopard, heading back to its lair.

At the kitchen table, I flipped through my workbook, basking in the clicking sounds of a warming oven. If I felt a hint of anything unsettling, it was like the sun going swiftly behind a cloud only to shine straight seconds later. I knew vaguely that my parents had had an argument the night before, but parents had arguments all the time, at home and on TV. Plus, I was still busily going over the bad point scoring from lunch, called by

14

Eddie Oakley with the freckles, who never called fairly. I read through my spelling booklet: knack, knick, knot; cartwheel, wheelbarrow, wheelie. At the counter, Mom poured thick yellow batter into a greased cake pan, and smoothed the top with the flat end of a pink plastic spatula. She checked the oven temperature, brushed a sweaty strand of hair off her forehead with the knob of her wrist.

Here we go, she said, slipping the cake pan into the oven.

When I looked up, she was rubbing her eyelids with the pads of her fingertips. She blew me a kiss and said she was going to lie down for a little bit. Okay, I nodded. Two birds bickered outside. In my booklet, I picked the person doing a cartwheel and colored her shoes with red laces, her face a light orange. I made a vow to bounce the ball harder on the playground, and to bounce it right into Eddie Oakley's corner. I added some apples to the wheelbarrow freehand.

The room filled with the smell of warming butter and sugar and lemon and eggs, and at five, the timer buzzed and I pulled out the cake and placed it on the stovetop. The house was quiet. The bowl of icing was right there on the counter, ready to go, and cakes are best when just out of the oven, and I really couldn't possibly wait, so I reached to the side of the cake pan, to the least obvious part, and pulled off a small warm spongy chunk of deep gold. Iced it all over with chocolate. Popped the whole thing into my mouth.

2

After my mother quit her job, she spent those first six months or so beautifying the house. Each week, a different project. First, she grew that strawberry plant in the backyard, fastening it on the fence until the berries popped points of red in a wavy row. When she was done with that, she curled up on the sofa in heaps of old lace, placing her best new doily beneath a bowl of fresh-picked strawberries. Then she whipped the cream to put on top of the strawberries picked from the vine and put it all in the ceramic bowl she'd made in college that rested on top of the doily. It was red and white and delicate and elegant but she was always bad at accepting compliments. After the vines slowed for fall, she wanted to do something more rugged, so she called up a friend who knew a contractor and hired him on the promise that she could assist while they installed the side door in my brother's bedroom, just in case he ever wanted to go outside.

But he hates outside! I said, following them into Joseph's room for measurements. Why can't I have a door?

You're too young for a door, Mom said. My brother held his backpack to his chest, watching, and he gave a short nod when Mom asked if the location was okay. How long will it take? he asked.

We'll only work on it while you're in school, she assured us both, pulling out a notebook list of supplies.

It took three weeks of sawing, sanding, destroying and rebuilding, my mother in jeans, her ponytail tucked under the collar of her blouse, the contractor giving long explanations on sizing. Joseph slept under an extra quilted comforter once the wall had broken open, because he preferred his own bed. They worked day after day until the wood was finally fitted, and the window at the top installed, and the doorknob attached, and cheerful little red curtains hung partway down the frame. Mom presented it to Joseph as soon as we came home from school. Ta-da! she said, pulling him by the wrist and bowing. He put his hand on the doorknob and exited through the door and then circled back through the front door of the house and went into the kitchen to eat cereal. Looks good, he called, from the kitchen. Mom and I opened and closed the door fifty times, locking it and pulling the curtains shut; unlocking it and pulling the curtains open. When Dad got home at his usual time, six feet tall and nearly ducking under door frames, he made a few calls in the bedroom, and when Mom dragged him out to see the finished product, he said nice, nicely done, and then folded his arms.

What? Mom said.

Nothing.

It has a key lock, I said, pointing.

Just funny, said Dad, wrinkling his nose. All this work for a door in a room only one of us goes into.

You can use it, Joseph called, from the kitchen.

In case of a fire, I said.

We did so much sanding, Mom said, tracing the new calluses on her palms.

Very smooth, said Dad, touching the curtains.

After dinner, while Dad finished the rest of his work in the bedroom, Mom stretched out on the living-room carpet in front of the red brick fireplace, and even though it was warm out still, almost seventy degrees, she lit a fire using an old pine log she'd found in the garage. Come sit, Rose, she called to me, and we nestled up together and stared as the flickering flames licked the log into ash. I had nightmares that night, since they say you have nightmares more easily when the house is too warm. I dreamed we were plunging down frozen rivers.

My birthday cake was her latest project because it was not from a mix but instead built from scratch — the flour, the baking soda, lemon-flavored because at eight that had been my request; I had developed a strong love for sour. We'd looked through several cookbooks together to find just the right one, and the smell in the kitchen was overpoweringly pleasant. To be clear: the bite I ate was delicious. Warm citrus-baked batter lightness enfolded by cool deep dark swirled sugar.

But the day was darkening outside, and as I finished that first bite, as that first impression faded, I felt a subtle shift inside, an unexpected reaction. As if a sensor, so far buried deep inside me, raised its scope to scan around, alerting my mouth to something new. Because the goodness of the ingredients — the fine chocolate, the freshest lemons — seemed like a cover over something larger and darker, and the taste of what was underneath was beginning to push up from the bite. I could absolutely taste the chocolate, but in drifts and traces, in an unfurling, or an opening, it seemed that my mouth was also filling with the taste of smallness, the sensation of shrinking, of upset, tasting a distance I somehow knew was connected to my mother, tasting a crowded sense of her thinking, a spiral, like I could almost even taste the grit in her jaw that had created the headache that meant she had to take as many aspirins as were necessary, a white dotted line of them in a row on the nightstand like an ellipsis to her comment: I'm just going to lie down. . . . None of it was a bad taste, so much, but there was a kind of lack of wholeness to the flavors that made it taste hollow, like the lemon and chocolate were just surrounding a hollowness. My mother's able hands had made the cake, and her mind had known how to balance the ingredients, but she was not there, in it. It so scared me that I took a knife from a drawer and cut out a big slice, ruining the circle, because I had to check again right that second, and I put it on a pink-flowered plate and grabbed a napkin from the napkin drawer. My heart was beating fast. Eddie Oakley shrank to a pinpoint.

I was hoping I'd imagined it — maybe it was a bad lemon? or old sugar? — although I knew, even as I thought it, that what I'd tasted had nothing to do with ingredients — and I flipped on the light and took the plate in the other room to my favorite chair, the one with the orange-striped pattern, and with each bite, I thought — mmm, so good, the best ever, yum — but in each bite: absence, hunger, spiraling, hollows. This cake that my mother had made just for me, her daughter, whom she loved so much I could see her clench her fists from overflow sometimes when I came home from school, and when she would hug me hello I could feel how inadequate the hug was for how much she wanted to give.

I ate the whole piece, desperate to prove myself wrong.

When Mom got up, after six, she wandered into the kitchen and saw the slice taken out of the cake and found me slumped at the foot of the orange-striped chair. She knelt down and smoothed the hot hair off my forehead.

Rosie, she said. Sweets. You all right?

I blinked open eyes, with eyelids heavier now, like tiny lead weights had been strung, fishing-line style, onto each lash.

I ate a slice of cake, I said.

She smiled at me. I could still see the headache in her, pulsing in her left eyebrow, but the smile was real.

That's okay, she said, rubbing the underside of her eye bone. How'd it turn out?

Fine, I said, but my voice wavered.

She went and got herself a piece and sat down with me on the floor, crossing her legs. Sheet lines pressed into her cheek from the nap.

Mmm, she said, taking a small bite. Do you think it's too sweet?

I could feel the mountain swelling in my throat, an ache spreading into the lining of my neck.

What is it, baby? she asked.

I don't know.

Joe home from school yet?

Not yet.

What's wrong? Are you crying? Did something happen at school?

Did you and Dad have a fight?

Not really, she said, wiping her mouth with my napkin. Just a discussion. You don't have to worry about that.

Are you okay? I said.

Me?

You? I said, sitting up more.

She shrugged. Sure, she said. I just needed

a nap. Why?

I shook my head clear. I thought —

She raised her eyebrows, encouraging.

It tastes *empty,* I said.

The cake? She laughed a little, startled. Is it that bad? Did I miss an ingredient?

No, I said. Not like that. Like you were away? You feel okay?

I kept shaking my head. The words, stupid words, which made no sense.

I'm here, she said, brightly. I feel fine. More?

She held out a forkful, all sunshine and cocoa, but I could not possibly eat it. I swallowed and, with effort, the spit slid around the mountain in my throat.

I guess I shouldn't spoil my dinner? I said.

Only then — and only for a second — did she look at me oddly. Funny kid, she said. She patted her fingers on the napkin and stood. Well, then. Should we get started?

Dinner? I said.

Chicken, she said, checking her watch. It's late!

I followed her into the kitchen. Joseph showed up about ten minutes later, the thud of his backpack on the floor like an anvil had dropped from the ceiling. He was flushed from the walk home, gray eyes clear, dark hair dampened with sweat, and the red in his cheeks and brightness in his eyes made it seem like he would want to tell us all about his day, with high-flying anecdotes and jokes and ribbings. Instead, he washed his hands at the kitchen sink, silent. He seemed to gather air around him in a cloak.

Mom hugged him like he'd been gone for a year, and he patted her shoulder like she was a puppy, and together the three of us chopped and cleaned while she made breaded chicken breast with green beans and rice. Joseph sprayed diluted bleach on the cutting board in the sink. Oil crackled in the fry pan. I tried to push my mind back to thinking about school, but the anxiety kicked in for me about halfway through the preparation; as I watched my mother roll raw chicken in breadcrumbs, I thought: What if I taste it in the chicken too? The rice?

At six-forty-five, my father's car drove up and parked. He pushed the door open, jovial, bellowing I'm home! as he usually did. He said it to the hallway. By the end of the day, his hair, black and thick, was matted and rumpled, having taken the hit for all the work worry in his hands.

He paused at the kitchen door, but we were all too busy to run to greet him.

Look at the team go! he said.

Hi, Dad, I said, waving a knife back. He always seemed a little like a guest to me. Welcome home, I said.

Glad to be home, he said.

Mom glanced up from her fry pan and nodded.

He looked like he might want to come in and kiss her but wasn't sure if it would work, so instead he lined up his briefcase against the closet wall, vanished down the hall to change, and joined us just as we sat down with the food surrounding steaming in bowls and platters. Joseph began serving himself, and as slowly as I could, I put everything on my plate in even spoonfuls. Half a chicken breast. Seven green beans. Two helpings of rice.

It was dark outside by now. Streetlamps buzzed on with their vague blue fluorescence.

The dinner taste was a little better than the cake's but just barely. I sank down into my chair. I pulled at my mouth.

What is it? Mom asked. I don't know, I said, holding on to her sleeve. The chicken tastes weird, I said.

Mom chewed, thoughtfully. The breadcrumbs? she said. Is there too much rosemary?

Oh, it's fine, said Joseph, who ate with his

26

eyes on the dish so no one could get eye contact and actually talk to him.

As we ate, my brother told a little about the after-school astronomy program and how a cosmologist from UCLA would be visiting soon to explain universe acceleration. Right this minute, said Joseph, it's just getting faster and faster. He indicated with his fork, and a fleck of rice flew across the table. Dad told a story about his secretary's dog. Mom pulled her chicken into threads.

When we were done, she brought the iced, finished, half-sliced cake out on a yellow china plate, and made a little flourish with her hands.

And for dessert! she said.

Joseph clapped, and Dad mmmed, and because I didn't know what to do, I forced my way through another slice, wiping at the tears with my napkin. Sorry, I mumbled. Sorry. Maybe I'm sick? I watched each of their plates carefully, but Dad's piece was gone in a flash, and even Joseph, who never liked much about food in the first place and talked often about how he wished there was a Breakfast Pill, a Lunch Pill, and a Dinner Pill, said Mom should enter it in a contest or something. You're the only person I know who can build doors *and* cakes *and* organize the computer files, he said, glancing up for two seconds.

Rose thought I missed a part, Mom said.

I didn't say that, I said, clutching my plate, cake gummy and bad in my mouth.

No way, said Joe. It's complete.

Thank you, she said, blushing.

We all have different tastes, honey, she said, rubbing my hair.

It's not what I meant, I said. Mom —

Anyway, it's the last cake for a while. I'll be starting a part-time job tomorrow, Mom said. With a carpentry shop, in Silver Lake.

First I've heard of that, Dad said, wiping his mouth. What are you fixing, more doors?

I said carpenter, Mom said. Not handyman. I will be making tables and chairs.

May I be excused? I asked.

Of course, Mom said. I'll check on you in a minute.

I took a bath by myself and went to bed. I felt her come by later, as I was dozing off. Her standing, by my bed. The depth of shadow of a person felt behind closed eyelids. Sweet dreams, sweet Rose, she whispered, and I held on to those words like they were a thread of gold I could follow into blackness. Clinging to them tightly, I fell asleep.

3

My family lived in one of the many centers of Los Angeles, fifteen minutes from a variety of crisscrossing freeways, sandwiched between Santa Monica Boulevard and Melrose. Our neighborhood, bordered by Russian delis to the north and famous thrift shops to the south, was mostly residential, combining families, Eastern European immigrants, and screenwriters who lived in big apartment complexes across the way and who were usually having a hard time selling a script. They stood out on balconies as I walked home from school, smoking afternoon cigarettes, and I knew someone had gotten work when the moving vans showed up. That, or they'd worn through their savings.

Our particular block on Willoughby was quiet at night but in the morning leaf blowers whirred and neighbors revved their engines and the thoroughfares busied. I woke to the sounds of kitchen breakfast bustle. My father got up the earliest, and by seven-fifteen he was already washing his coffee cup in the kitchen sink, splashing water around and humming. He hummed tunes I'd never heard of, exuding an early-morning pep that had drained into a pure desire for television by the time I saw him at 7 p.m.

When he drove off, heading downtown to the office, he always gave one quick blast on the horn. Honk! He never said he was going to do it, or asked anything about it, but I waited, buried deep in my bed, and when his horn sounded, I got up.

Good morning. My stomach felt fine.

After breakfast, a mild and unthreatening cereal grain bar, I poured my mother a glass of water and tiptoed into her bedroom, placing it carefully on the nightstand.

Here you go, I whispered.

Thank you, she said, her eyes half closed, her hair spread in a thick fan over the pillow. The room smelled warm, of deep sleep and cocoons. She pulled me close and pressed a kiss into my cheek.

Your lunch is in the fridge, she murmured, turning over to the other side.

I tiptoed out of the room. Joseph and I

grabbed our stuff and walked single file down Willoughby to Fairfax. The sky a strong deep blue. I kicked stones as I walked, deciding the food stuff of the day before was a one-of-a-kind bad deal, and I had a good day planned ahead, one involving the study of fireflies and maybe some pastel-crayon drawing. Eddie Oakley was regaining most of his usual proportion in the indignant section of my mind. The morning was already warming up — the news had signaled an unusually hot spring week ahead, into the nineties.

At the bus stop, we stood a few feet apart. I kept my distance because I was mostly an irritation to Joseph, a kind of sister rash, but as we were waiting, he took a few steps back until he was standing right next to me. I sucked in my breath.

Look, he said, pointing up.

Across the sky, in the far distance, the thinnest sliver of white moon hovered above a row of trees.

See next to it? he said.

I squinted. What?

That tiny dot, to the right? he said.

I could catch it if I really looked: a pinprick of light, still faintly visible in the morning sky.

Jupiter, he said.

31

The big guy? I asked, and for a second, his forehead cleared.

None other, he said.

What's it doing?

Just visiting, he said. For today.

I stared at the dot until the bus arrived, praying at it like it was God, and before Joseph stepped ahead, I touched his sleeve to thank him. I made sure it was the part that didn't touch his actual arm, so he would not whip around, annoyed.

Inside the bus, he sat several rows ahead of me and I settled behind a girl singing a pop ballad into her collar. Kids around snapped bubble gum and yelled out jokes, but Joseph held himself still, like everything was pelting him. My big brother. What I could see of his profile was classic: straight nose, high cheekbone, black lashes, light-brown waves of hair. Mom once called him handsome, which had startled me, because he could not be handsome, and yet when I looked at his face I could see how each feature was nicely shaped.

I sat quietly, watching out the moth-encrusted window, tracking the Jupiter dot as we drove south. Little cars below us, zipping past on Fairfax. At a red light, I gave a nod to an older woman driving in curlers. Waved at a guy in motorcycle gear who did rocker hands back. I glanced at the back of Joseph's head, wanting to show him. He read his textbook. In my mind, I told him. He laughed, and looked.

We arrived without incident, I achieved four waves, and Joseph got off and turned down the alleyway that led to the junior high. I walked across the blacktop playground into third grade.

Math problems, reading, carpet time, oil-pastel sky drawing art project. Recess. Four square. Two points. Milk carton. History, spelling. Lunch bell.

I spent lunchtime at the porcelain base of the drinking fountain, which was half stopped up with pink gum, taking sip after sip of the warm metallic water that pushed through old pipes from plumbing built in the twenties, pouring rust and fluoride into my mouth, trying to erase my peanut-butter sandwich.

4

My mother slept in because she did not sleep well. Since she was a child, she told me once, when I brought in her morning glass of water. I would wait to feel myself fall asleep, she told me as I perched on the edge of her bed; and I would wait and wait, she said, wanting to catch it happening, like the tooth fairy. You can't catch sleep, I said, turning the glass on its cork coaster. She smiled at me, through half-lidded eyes. Smart girl, she said.

I would hear her, sometimes, as I was resettling myself in the middle of the night; at 2 a.m. it was not unusual to hear the flip of the kitchen light switch and the hum of the teakettle warming. A hint of light down the corridor casting a faint glow on my bedroom wall. The sounds were comforting — a reminder of my mother's presence, a feeling of activity and function, even though I knew come morning it would mean a tired-looking mother, her eyes unfocused, searching for rest.

Every now and then, I would crawl out of bed in the middle of the night to find her in the big armchair with the striped orange pattern, a shawl-blanket draped over her knees. I, at five, or six, would crawl into her lap, like a cat. She would pet my hair, like I was a cat. She would pet, and sip. We never spoke, and I fell asleep quickly in her arms, in the hopes that my weight, my sleepiness, would somehow seep into her. I always woke up in my own bed, so I never knew if she went back to her room or if she stayed there all night, staring at the folds of the curtains over the window.

We'd lived in this house all my life. My parents had met in Berkeley as college students, but they got married right after graduation, moved to L.A. for Dad's law school, and my mother gave birth to Joseph shortly after they'd bought and settled into the place on Willoughby. She'd had trouble picking a major in college, unsure what she liked, but she chose the house right away because it was boxy and friendly, with red roof tiles and a mass of bougainvillea pouring over the door awning, and the diagonal diamond-shaped window patterns in the front looked like they could only frame a family that was happy.

Dad studied hard, did well on his tests, shook hands with his teachers. He made sheets of checklists on pads of yellow legal paper, lists reminding him to Talk to the Librarian, Give Green Sweater to Homeless Guy on Jefferson, Buy Apples. Find a Wife hadn't been on any visible list, but he'd proposed earlier than most of his peers and something did seem to get checked off inside him once they were married. He bought gifts in line with the anniversary materials and framed their best wedding photograph for the hallway, and even though Have a Son and Have a Daughter looked better on paper than in the crying and diapering day after day, my father was pleased by the elder son/younger daughter arrangement. The world had matched what he'd dreamed up, and he settled himself inside what they'd made. He was cheerful enough when he came home from work but he didn't really know what to do with little kids so he never taught us how to ride a bike, or wear a mitt, and our changes in height remained unmarked on the door frames, so we grew tall on our own without proof. He left at the same time each morn-ing and came home at the same time each evening, and my earliest memories of my mother were of her waiting at the door as soon as it was anywhere near time, me on her hip, Joseph at her hand, watching car after car drive by. He was never late, but she watched early anyway. During the afternoons, when she was tired of kid activities, she would sometimes roll around a white plastic Wiffle Ball and tell us stories of our first few years. In particular, she told the stories of our births. For some reason, Dad refused to go into hospitals, so Mom had given birth to each of us by herself while Dad waited outside on the sidewalk, sitting on a crate, half reading a detective story.

Lucky me, she said, as she pushed the plastic wobbly ball over. I got to meet you both first.

When Dad got home, he'd bound up the walk and throw open the door, kissing her, kissing us, lining up his shoes, sifting through the mail. If anyone had been crying for any reason, he'd pull out a tissue and pat down our cheeks and say salt was for meat, not faces. Then he'd run out of greetings and glance around at the walls until he headed off to their room to change. What my father did most comfortably and best was log those long hours while my mother bathed and fed and clothed and burped, viewing the world at large as the vastest of colleges, a repeat of the trouble she'd had earlier deciding on a major. Possibilities seemed to close in on her. I love everything, she told me when I was still little enough to sit high on her hip. I don't know what I like! she said brightly, kissing me on the nose. You're so cute! she said. So cute! You! You!

I hardly knew any of my other relatives. Either they lived far away or they were dead. Three of my four grandparents had passed on to other unknowns by the time I was four, but my mother's mother was apparently as healthy as an Olympian even though she'd never exercised a day in her life. She lived north, in Washington State.

She hated travel, so she didn't visit, but one Saturday afternoon during my eighth year, a big brown box package arrived at our doorstep with GRANDMA in capital letters as the return address. A package! I said, dragging my parents to the door. Is it somebody's birthday? No, Mom said stiffly, pushing it inside with her foot.

Inside, beneath layers of foam, I found a dish towel with my name on it. For Rose, she had written, in spidery handwriting on a scrap of paper taped to the towel itself. It was frayed, the pattern faded. I grabbed it out of the box and held it to my cheek. What *is* this? Dad asked, pushing foam strips onto the floor and lifting out a chipped daisy-patterned teacup with his paper taped to it: To Paul. Her broken teacup? he said. Joseph's gift was a series of clean blue pillowcases, and my mother's name was attached to a plastic bag full of cracked tins of rouge. She's old now, Mom had said, circling a bit of rouge onto the back of her hand. Grandma lived alone, and probably at that point had lost part of her mind, but no one dared move her. She can still get to the post office, right? said Mom, shuttling the bag of rouges to the back of a kitchen drawer. Dad pulled handfuls of coins from his pockets. Whew! he said. Not a lot of love lost between you two! He dumped all his change into the teacup so that no one would ever drink out of it.

I loved my dish towel. This one was two-toned, and had, on one side, stitchings of fat purple roses on a lavender background, and on the other side, fat lavender roses on a purple background. Which side to use? An optical-illusion namesake with which I could dry our dishes. It was soft and worn and smelled like no-nonsense laundry detergent.

Because she did not visit in person, Grandma called once a month, on Sunday afternoons, and my mother would gather us around, put the phone in the center of the kitchen table and press speaker. She was gruff, Grandma, but funny. She liked to tell about her geology rock parties, where she had invited people over to the house to dig up and label rocks from the yard and when they walked in the door she specifically requested that no one speak.

Sometimes I even put tape on their mouths, she said. If they let me. It was bliss. You understand, Joseph, correct?

Yes, said Joe.

We did drink a lot, said Grandma, a little wistfully. That you, Rose? You there?

Hi, Grandma, I said.

You're too quiet, said Grandma. Speak up.

I rolled a vinyl place mat into a tube.

I love you, I said, through the tube.

There was a pause. Across the room, from her listening position wedged in the far corner, Mom flinched.

Love? said Grandma, through the tiny black holes.

Yes, I said.

But you don't even know me, said Grandma. How can you love me? It should be earned. You're too clingy. She's too clingy, Lane, Grandma said.

Ma, said Mom, picking at the ends of her ponytail.

I'm not clingy, I said.

She is extremely clingy, said Joseph. What rocks did you find?

How are things there, Ma? Mom asked. All's good?

No, Grandma said, all is not good. They're taking away my driver's license. Basalt, Joseph, she said. We found a whole lot of basalt. I'll send you some.

Boxes of it, the following week. Dark and glassy. We repopulated the garden. When a teacher had us draw our grand parents for an assignment on ancestry, I monopolized the black crayon, and my picture had been of a thick black box with grating, lines extending outward to indicate voice.

5

After lunch, my teacher sent me to the nurse.

We studied nature in the afternoons on Wednesdays. In third grade, the nature section was all about bugs and I had been very excited about the upcoming lesson on fireflies, but my mood had changed drastically during the lunch hour, and as soon as we were back in the classroom, I put my head on my desk. I didn't intend to do it; it was like someone had attached a magnet to my forehead, and then tucked another inside my notebook. That was where my head had to go.

My teacher stopped halfway through her lesson.

Close your eyes, class, she called out, and imagine you're a firefly, flying and blinking in the darkness of the night.

Then she walked to my desk and knelt by my side and asked if I was okay. I told her I thought I was sick, and my friend Eliza, imagining next to me, popped open one eye and explained how I'd spent the entire lunch hour at the drinking fountain.

She was very, very thirsty, Eliza whispered.

Is it the heat? asked our teacher.

I don't think so, I said.

I stood at her desk as she signed a pass with my name on it. While my classmates extended arms to make wings, I walked down empty halls, past old trophies and paintings of houses, up to the open door of the infirmary, where I stood, gripping the hall pass, waiting. I had never visited the nurse before. I was rarely sick. I never faked.

Inside, sitting at a scuffed pine desk, a woman in a yellow gingham blouse was sorting through stacks of orange and pink files. When I held up my pass, she beckoned me inside.

Hang on a sec, she said, scribbling something on a piece of paper.

I had seen this nurse before at school assemblies, usually standing with whoever had a broken bone. She was the chaperone of the broken bones. She didn't wear white, but she had soft-looking arms, one wrist encircled by a watchband of overlapping burgundy silk. After adding comments to two files, she looked over at me, sitting in

43

the one free chair. Another sick kid, in a long line of sick kids.

So what's the problem, hon? she said, picking up a thermometer and shaking it out.

I held my elbows, thinking.

Do you feel hot?

No, I said.

Is your nose stuffy?

I sniffed. The room smelled faintly of cherry medicine. I looked back at her soft elbows, her dark-red ribbon watchband. I used those arms as the first point of trust.

Food tastes bad, I said then.

This was not entirely true — I'd eaten a pretty good apple in my lunch. The recess milk carton was fine. But almost everything else — the cake, the chicken dinner, the homemade brownie, the craving in the peanut-butter sandwich — had left me with varying degrees of the same scary feeling.

What kind of bad? the nurse said, glancing over my body. Do you think you're overweight?

No, I said. Hollow, I said.

She attached a fresh piece of paper to a clipboard. You think you're hollow?

Not me, I said, scrambling. The food. Like there's a hole in the food.

Food has a hole in it, she wrote slowly, on

the paper. I watched as she added a question mark at the end. Arc, line, space, dot.

The air in the room thinned. She took my temperature. I closed my eyes and imagined I was a firefly, flying and blinking in the darkness of the night. Normal, she said, after a minute, reading the side. So — you're sure you don't think you're fat?

No, I said.

They're getting younger and younger, she said, as if reminding me.

But I'm eating, I said.

She wrote that on her clipboard too. *Says she's eating.* Good, she said. Here.

She handed over a little paper cup of water. The water was supposedly from a mountain spring, but it had resided in plastic for many weeks and so it was like drinking liquid Lucite with a whisper of a mountain somewhere inside it.

There, honey, she said.

I nodded. I still wanted, very much, to be agreeable.

Now, wasn't that good? she said, wiping down the thermometer with an alcohol-dipped tissue.

Water is important, I said, gripping the cup. We have to drink it or we die.

Just like food, she said.

I like food, I said, louder.

45

Three meals a day?

Yes.

And do you ever make yourself throw up?

No.

Or are you taking any pills to make yourself go to the bathroom? she asked, eyebrows raised.

I shook my head. The vent whirred, and the air conditioner kicked up a notch. I could feel the tears beginning to collect in my throat again, but I pushed them apart, away from each other. Tears are only a threat in groups.

Well, she sighed. Then just give it a couple of days, she said. She put her clipboard to the side.

That's it?

That's it, she said, smiling.

No medicine?

Nah, she said. You seem fine.

But what *is* it? I asked.

She fixed her watch on her wrist, lifted her shoulders. I don't know, she said. Maybe an allergy?

To food?

Or, she said, maybe an active imagination?

I picked up the hall pass. The rest of the day stretched long before me.

Just get some rest and I'll send for you again in a couple days, said the nurse, tossing out my paper cup. Drink fluids, she said. Take it easy. Your family okay?

My family? I said. Yes, why?

Just checking, she said, settling back down in her chair. She pulled a canary-yellow knit cardigan over her shoulders. Sometimes these things go around, she said.

6

I spent the rest of the school day on the flat hard green carpet of the classroom library reading picture books about animals getting into fixes. A splinteringly dry afternoon. Eddie and Eliza came over with curious eyes to see if I wanted to play four square or dodgeball after school, but I told them I wasn't feeling well. You don't want to get this, I said, coughing a little in their faces. I dragged my feet to the bus. At the stop, Joseph looked wrung out from the day too and took his usual spot right up against the window, but this time he sat with a friend, a guy with high arched eyebrows and rangy arms and legs. They hunched over a textbook and talked and pointed the whole ride home.

It was Wednesday, and George always came over on Wednesdays after school. He was Joseph's best and only friend. George Malcolm: half white, half black, with messy tousled hair, rumpled and tugged between kind of curly and extremely curly. Once, a year or so before, he'd been at our house and he'd pulled out a lock of his hair and used it to teach me about eddies and helixes. It's a circular current into a central station, he'd explained, giving me one to hold. I pulled on the spring. Nature is full of the same shapes, he said, taking me to the bathroom sink and spinning on the tap and pointing out the way the water swirled down the drain. Taking me to the bookshelf and flipping open a book on weather and showing me a cyclone. Then a spiral galaxy. Pulling me back to the bathroom sink, to my glass jar of collected seashells, and pointing out the same curl in a miniature conch. See? he said, holding the seashell up to his hair. Yes! I clapped. His eyes were warm with teaching pleasure. It's galactic hair, he said, smiling.

At school, George was legendary already. He was so natural at physics that one afternoon the eighth-grade science teacher had asked him to do a preview of the basics of relativity, really fast, for the class. George had stood up and done such a fine job, using a paperweight and a yardstick and the standard-issue school clock, that the teacher had pulled a twenty-dollar bill from his wallet. I'd like to be the first person to pay you for your clarity of mind, the teacher had said. George used the cash to order pizza for the class. Double pepperoni, he told me later, when I'd asked.

That afternoon, we all got off the bus at Fairfax and Melrose and I followed the two of them home, wilted, trailed by the greasy salty smell of pastrami burritos at Oki Dog, and when George turned around to show something about the direction of an airplane, he saw me tripping along behind and waved.

Hey, Rose! he said. How's it going?

Hi, I said. Hot, I said.

Joseph kept walking in his faded blue T-shirt, his back to me.

You've been walking behind us all this time? George asked.

I nodded. He kept walking backwards, as if he was waiting for something, so I raised my hand.

George laughed. Yes? he said. Miss Edel-stein?

Have you ever been to the school nurse?

No, he said.

Don't bother, I said.

Okay, he said. He looked a little bored.

He started turning back, so I waved my hand again.

Wait, I said. Sorry. I have a real question, I said. A science question.

Now my brother glanced around. Irritated.

Hey, he said. We're busy. We don't want to talk about fireflies.

What if, I said, food tastes funny?

Have you tried those cafeteria burritos? asked George, still walking backwards, tapping his pencil on his head like it was a drum. I had one of those today, he said. Now that was hilarious.

Don't you have flute? Joseph asked, throwing his words back.

On Mondays, I said. Most food.

Or Eliza? said Joe.

Ballet, I said.

What do you mean? George asked.

What should I do?

I don't get it, said George.

I think there's something wrong with me, I said, voice cracking.

George squinted, confused. Both he and Joe were weird-looking in junior high; their features kept growing at different speeds and falling out of proportion and at that point George's eyebrows were so high and peaked on his forehead that he always looked either skeptical or surprised.

We reached the door to the house and Jo-

51

seph dug around in his backpack to find his keychain. He was in charge of Wednesday afternoons and he had a new keychain he'd bought with his allowance — a solid silver circle with a clever latch that sank into the stream of the circle invisibly. He found it, let us in, and then attached the circle to his belt loop, like a plumber.

He turned down the hall to head straight to his room, but George lingered in the entryway.

You play flute? he said.

Just a little, I said.

Hey, George, Joseph said, heaving his textbook from his backpack and flipping it open. Race you on twelve. A speedboat full of villains is leaving a twenty-foot-high pier at a steady fifteen mph. A car full of cops is about to drive off the pier to catch the villains. How fast should the car be going to land on the boat, if the car leaves the pier when the boat is thirty-five feet away?

But George crossed his arms, the way he did sometimes when he was in and out of Joseph's room, pacing. They'd copy extra physics questions from the library and settle in for the afternoon — Joseph at his desk, George pacing. They'd prop open the side door for fresh air and flick twigs and hammer through the extra credit that the teacher put up for them, that even the teacher didn't really know.

He fixed his eyes on me. Brown and sharp.

What's so wrong with you? he said.

I flushed. I went through what I'd told the nurse. George stayed in the hallway to listen but Joseph ducked inside his room, tossing the textbook on his bed and sitting down at his desk, where he lifted a piece of graph paper and a compass from his folder. As I talked, he placed the steel point of the compass on the graph paper, strapped in the pencil and started to draw, with his careful hands, a beautiful arc. Every action so assured, like he knew exactly what mystery of the universe he was about to puncture.

So is it like Swiss cheese? George asked when I was done.

No, I said. It's one big hole. The nurse said I had an active imagination.

Joseph crumpled up his perfect arc and pulled out a fresh piece of graph paper.

Don't crumple, Joe, said George.

I fucked it up, said Joseph, tossing it into the trash.

I have that plan for my bedroom, remember? George said. All mistakes wallpaper, he said, turning back to me. Anyway, he said, let's test you. We have to have a snack anyway.

Now? said Joseph, stretching the compass again and placing the point at the intersecting corner of two blue graph squares.

Just for a few minutes, said George. You free? he said, looking at me.

I'm free, I said.

He clapped his hands. First item on the agenda: discover what is going on with Rose, he said.

Joseph opened his mouth to protest.

Second item, George said, get to work!

I bowed, a little. What a lift, whenever he said my name. It was like getting my number called out in a raffle.

Joseph nearly crumpled his page again, then stopped his fist and handed it over. George held it up to the light, admiring the curves as if it were a painting. North wall, he said, nodding. Perfect.

That afternoon involved four sandwiches, soda, chips, buttered toast, chocolate milk. I ate my way through the refrigerator. Mom was still away at her new job, at the woodworking studio near Micheltorena, off Sunset into the hills, and my brother and George poured sugar and jam over toast and talked about their favorite TV series with the robots while I bit and chewed and reported to George. He'd found a yellow legal pad by the phone which he held on his lap, with a list of foods in the left column and then all my responses on the right. Half hollow, I said, about my mom's leftover tuna casserole. Awful! I said, swallowing a mouthful of my father's butterscotch pudding from a mix, left in a bowl. Dad's, so distracted and ziggy I could hardly locate a taste at all. The sensor did not seem to be restricted to my mother's food, and there was so much to sort through, a torrent of information, but with George there, sitting in the fading warmth of the filtered afternoon springtime sun spilling through the kitchen windows, making me buttered toast which I ate happily, light and good with his concentration and gentle focus, I could begin to think about the layers. The bread distributor, the bread factory, the wheat, the farmer. The butter, which had a dreary tang to it. When I checked the package, I read that it came from a big farm in Wisconsin. The cream held a thinness, a kind of metallic bumper aftertaste. The milk — weary. All of those parts distant, crowded, like the far-off sound of an airplane, or a car parking, all hovering in the background, foregrounded by the state of the maker of the food.

So every food has a feeling, George said

when I tried to explain to him about the acidic resentment in the grape jelly.

I guess, I said. A lot of feelings, I said.

He drew a few boxes on the yellow legal pad. Is it your feeling? he said.

I shook my head. I don't know, I said.

How do you feel? he asked.

Tired.

Does it taste tired?

Some of it, I said.

Joseph, who was sitting with his textbook at the table, had made himself a piece of toast with butter and jam and sprinkles of sugar. When he wasn't looking I reached over to his plate and tore off a section. I must've made a face right away, because George glanced over, quick. What? he asked, writing Joseph's Toast in the left column in big letters. Oh, I said, dizzy, mouth full. Tell us, said George, pencil ready. I couldn't look at Joseph. I couldn't even eat it very well. The bread felt thickly chewy, like it was hard to chew. A blankness and graininess, something folding in on itself. A sea anemone? I mumbled. Joseph looked up from folding his iced-tea label into a neat square. His eyes traced the door frame. I'm fine! he said, laughing. I feel fine.

I spit the bread into a napkin.

Joseph took his plate to the sink.

We done yet? he said. I promised Patterson we'd crack the racing code.

All right, said George, standing. He stretched up, and his T-shirt lifted slightly to show a band of skin. Then he smiled at me. Good job, kid, he said.

After they both left the kitchen, I put the milk and the jam back in the fridge and took out a knife and scraped my tongue lightly with its notched edge to get the taste of Joseph's toast away. When that didn't work, I grabbed a package of swirled sugar cookies from the pantry; the cookies, made by no one, had only the distant regulated hum of flour and butter and chocolate and factories. I ate six. The heat softened outside, and I washed the dishes, cool water running over my hands, returning a shine to the knives and the forks.

When I was done, I took a board game out of the hall closet and set it up right outside Joseph's room so I could be as close as possible without actually violating the *Keep Out* sign. Holding on to the muted sound of George's voice through the wood of the door.

How you doing out there? he called out every now and then.

Okay, I said, moving a yellow pawn forward four spaces.

She's nuts, called Joseph, typing. Or it's her bad mood, he said. You've heard of it. It's called moods.

My stomach clenched. Maybe, I said, quietly, into the piles of fake money I'd been winning in the board game I was playing against myself.

We'll test her in a better way on the weekend, said George. Outside the house. Hey, Joe, read eight out loud again.

The weekend? said Joe. It was impossible to miss the tremor in his voice.

Just for part of Saturday, said George, okay, Rose? A little more information? Saturday at noon?

Sure, I said, paying myself a million dollars from the stockpile.

7

One time, a year or so earlier, I had surprised my father with a flair for drawing accurate soccer balls, each hexagon nestled neatly next to its oppositely colored neighboring pentagon. He, a huge soccer fan, had been pleased. He held each one up and hooted as we sat down to watch the game together. Now, *this* is what I call art! he said, taping it above the TV. But I soon began the less approved-of habit of adding big eyes with long eyelashes and a smiling red mouth inside the white spaces on the ball. Rose — oh, no? said Dad, scratching his chin. I can't help it, I told him, handing over the fifth smiler. They looked too plain, I said.

I stopped watching sports with him after that, but it was the one time I could remember showing off any particular special skill at all. Feeling so pleased at getting all six sides even with their five-sided neighbors. Making dashes to indicate stitching. I was not, usually, a standout participant, good or bad. I read at an average age. I did fine in school but no one took either parent of mine aside to whisper about my potential — I seemed to be satisfyingly living up to mine.

My brother was the family whiz. At six years old, he was building models of star clusters out of Legos that he'd pockmarked with a dental instrument he'd purchased from our dentist with his allowance. He used big words too early, saying things like, I must masticate now, as he took a bite of cereal, and adults laughed at him, loving his big gray eyes and so serious look, and then they tried to hug him, which he refused. Me no touch, he said, bending his arms back and forth like a robot.

Joseph is brilliant, adults often said as they shuttled out of the house, shaking their heads at the precise drawing he'd made on sketch paper of planets yet to be discovered, complete with atmosphere thicknesses and moons. Our mother lowered her eyes, pleased. I was often admired for being friendly.

You meet people so easily! Mom said, when I smiled at the man who changed the car oil, who smiled back.

Certainly I had very little competition,

since Joseph smiled at no one, and Dad just flashed his teeth, and Mom's smiles were so full of feeling that people leaned back a little when she greeted them. It was hard to know just how much was being offered.

8

At around five-thirty, after George and I had thoroughly plundered the refrigerator, Mom came home from her first day at the carpentry studio. Her cheeks were red, as if she'd been jogging. It was wonderful! she said, grasping my hand. She looked for Joseph but he was reading in his room. George had gone home. We'll just do a quick tour of the neighborhood trees, Mom said in a confiding voice, tugging me out the front of the house. So this is a fir, she said, pointing at a dark evergreen growing in the middle of someone's yard. Softwood, she said. This one: sycamore, she said, tapping on the bark of the next. She frowned. I don't think they build furniture from sycamore, she said, but I'm not sure why not.

I peeled a gray jigsaw-shaped piece of bark right off the trunk. I recognized her enthusiasm as phase one of a new interest. Phase two was usually three or four months later, when she hit the wall after her natural first ability rush faded and she had to struggle along with the regularly skilled people. Phase three was a lot of head shaking and talking about why that particular skill — sociology, ceramics, computers, French — wasn't for her after all. Phase four was the uneasy long waiting period, which I knew by the series of 2 a.m. wake-ups where I stumbled down the hallway into her lap.

Too peely, I said, folding the bark in two.

I leaned on her arm a little as we walked down the shady side of Martel. Waving at some neighbors out on their lawn with a hose. By five-thirty, the heat was light, pleasurable, and the air seemed to glisten and hone around us. She asked if I was feeling better and I said a little, pushing the upcoming dinner out of my head and trying to concentrate on what she was saying next, something about worrying she could not keep up with the others at the studio. Which made no sense. My mother had trouble choosing and sticking but she was initially good at everything, particularly anything involving her hands; the bed she made was so perfect that for years I slept on top of the sheets because I did not want to wreck her amazing exactness by putting a body inside it.

I think you'll be good, I said.

She tucked a stray hair behind my ear. Thank you, she said. Such a sweet supporter you are. Much nicer than your father.

She did seem lighter, in a newly good mood, as we toured the trees up and down Gardner and Vista and then steered ourselves back inside.

Leftovers at dinner was a whole repeat of the previous night's upset, just softened by the one day of time and the kindness from George. I kept the nurse's advice in mind, looking to see if it was going around, but no one else seemed bothered by any of it. Dad asked about the studio, and Mom told us her first assignment would be to cut a board.

A board! he said, clinking his glass to hers. How about that.

She frowned at him. Don't be mean, she said.

Did I say anything? he said, widening his eyes. I can't build anything. I can only rebuild stools that are already built, he said.

He winked at her. She cleared her glass.

You know that story, Rose? he said.

A hundred times, I said.

Joseph picked up the pepper pillar and shook it over his food in a rain of black specks. Like our mother, he too had long beautiful hands, like a pianist's, fingers able to sharpen and focus like eyes.

Too bland? Mom asked.

Joseph shook his head. Just experimenting, he said.

Today, Dad announced, patting his place mat, I saw a man walking a monkey. True story.

Where? I said.

Pershing Square, he said.

Why?

He shrugged. I have no idea, he said, wiping his mouth. That was my day. Next.

Joseph put down the pepper. Fine, he said.

Half good, half awful, I said.

Half awful! said Dad, waiting.

My head, I said, is off.

Looks on to me, Dad said. Very on.

Oh, Rosie, no! Mom said. She sprinkled some pepper onto her dish too and then leaned over to hug my forehead into her side. You have a beautiful head, she said. A fine beautiful girl in there.

Food is full of *feelings,* I said, pushing away my plate.

Feelings? Dad said. For a second, he peered at me, close.

I couldn't eat my sandwich, I said, voice wobbling. I can't eat the cake.

Oh, like that, Dad said, leaning back.

Sure. I was a picky eater too. Spent a whole year once just eating French fries.

Did they taste like people? I said.

People? he said, wrinkling his nose. No. Potato.

You look well, Mom said. She tried a careful bite of her chicken. Better with pepper, she said, nodding. Much better, yes.

Joseph folded his arms. It was just an experiment, he said.

I'm going out with George and Joseph on Saturday, I said.

Only because it's your birthday, said Joseph.

Her birthday, Mom echoed. Nine years old. Can you believe it?

She stood and went to the recipe page and wrote on it in big capital letters: ADD PEPPER!

There! she said.

I stacked my plate on Dad's. He stacked our plates on Joseph's.

Don't you see? I said to Dad.

See what?

I pointed at Mom.

Lane, he said. Yes. I see a beautiful woman.

I kept my eyes fixed on him.

What? he said again.

Her, I said.

Me? Mom said.

What is it, Lane? Dad asked. Is something going on?

Nothing, Mom said, shaking her head, capping her pen. She laughed. I don't know what she's talking about. Rose?

She said she wants support, I said.

Oh no, no, said Mom, blushing. I was just teasing, earlier. I feel very supported, by all of you.

Can I go? asked Joseph.

She's making a board, Dad said, bringing the stacks of plates to the sink. What else is there to say about that? She'll make a perfect board. Any dessert?

I didn't move. Mom kept smoothing her hair behind her ears. Smooth, smooth. Joseph stood, at his spot.

Can I go? he said again.

What do you want to do on Saturday, Rose? Mom asked. We could dress up and walk around in the park together. There are a couple more pieces of lemon cake, Paul, she said. Over there.

I have an important plan with George, I said.

Joseph squeezed out of his end of the table. After Saturday, nothing, he said to me. Got it?

George? Mom said. Joe's George?

I'd know if she needed support! said Dad,

at the sink.

Joseph left the room. My parents turned to me, with bright, light faces. We stood in front of empty place mats.

Do we say grace? I said.

Grace is what people say before the meal, said Mom. She moved to the piles in the sink. It's to give thanks for the food we are about to eat, she said.

I closed my eyes.

For the food that is gone, I whispered. Grace.

Due to his role as moneymaker, my father was excused from doing the dishes, and Joseph was so overly meticulous with dish-doing that it was easier when he was off in his room, so it was my mother and me in front of the soapy sink: her washing, me drying. I zipped through the silverware using my new worn rose dish towel from Grandma. Mom seemed in good spirits, squeezing my shoulder, asking me a series of fast questions about school, but the aftertaste of the spiraled craving chicken was still in my mouth and I was having trouble trusting her cheer, a split of information I could hardly hold in my head. I circled the dish towel over wet plates, stacking each one in the cabinet. Dug the dish

68

towel into the mouths of mugs. Strung it through the metal ring on the drawer when I was done.

Afterwards, I heaved my book bag onto my shoulder and headed down the hall towards my room. I kept my walking slow, like my brain was a full glass of water I needed to carefully balance down the corridor.

To my surprise, the door to Joseph's room was propped half open. This was as rare and good as a written invitation since he'd recently installed a lock on his door, bought from the same hardware store with his allowance. He kept the new key also on that elegant silver circle keychain.

There was still a wisp of daylight outside, but his window shades were pulled, and he had clicked on the desk lamp instead. He was lying on his bed, feet crossed, reading *Discover* next to a clump of silvery radio innards.

Hi, I said. He looked up, over his magazine. His eyes did not reach out to say hello but instead formed a loose wall between us.

Sorry for hogging George, I said.

He blinked at me.

You don't have to get me anything for my birthday, I said. Saturday can be my birthday present. You feeling better? I asked.

What do you mean?

Just earlier, with the toast?

He returned to his magazine.

Jesus, he said. You think everyone is in bad shape. I was fine all day, he said, into the pages. I just didn't want to spend my afternoon watching my little sister eat snacks, okay?

He turned another page, reading.

I waited there, in his doorway, for a while. I poked at the *O* in the *Keep Out* sign on his door.

He raised his eyebrows: Anything else?

That's all, I said.

Good night, he said.

I turned to go and was almost out the door when something blurred in my peripheral vision near where he lay on the bed. As if for half a second the comforter pattern grew brighter or the whites whiter. Then I turned back to look and everything was the same, perfectly still, him reading away.

Are you okay? I said, shaking my head clear.

He glanced up again. Didn't we just go through this?

Just —

His eyes wide, looking. Half interested.

Did the colors change? I said. Is George coming by?

Now? he said. No. It's nighttime.
Did you just move, or something?
Me?
Yeah, like did you move from the bed?
He laughed, short and brusque.
I've been here, the whole time, he said.
Sorry, I said. Never mind. Good night.

9

Mom loved my brother more. Not that she didn't love me — I felt the wash of her love every day, pouring over me, but it was a different kind, siphoned from a different, and tamer, body of water. I was her darling daughter; Joseph was her it.

He was not the expected choice for favorite. Dad, who claimed no favorites, sometimes looked at Joseph as if he'd dropped from a tree, and very few people reached out naturally to Joe except for George. He'd always been remote — I had a vague memory, from when I was two, of finding Joseph sitting in his room in the dark, so that even my baby toddler brain associated him with caves — but sometime in his third-grade year Mom started taking him out of school. He was bored in class, outrageously so, and the teacher had taken to giving him her purse to sort through and organize while the rest of the class did beginning addition.

Mom would pick him up and he'd have made some kind of chain-link out of Tic Tacs, threading each one with a needle he'd dug from the classroom sewing kit. Look, Mom, he said, holding up the mint-green linked cord. Bacteria, he said. The teacher flinched, embarrassed. He is so smart, she whispered, as if he had hurt her with it.

One afternoon, Mom showed up with me on her hip, told the office Joseph had a doctor's appointment, and took him out, right in the middle of the gym lesson on how to throw a ball. So he never learned to throw a ball. The office did not question the doctor's appointment, and neither did the other students, because Joseph was skinny and pale and hunched and looked like he needed a lot of medical care. Mom walked us to the car and strapped me into my car seat.

What doctor are we going to? Joseph asked. Am I sick?

Not a bit, she said, driving out of the school parking lot and turning up the radio. Trumpets blared. You are perfect and perfectly healthy, she said. We're going to the market.

What was he supposed to do, string mints all day? she asked me later, when remembering that year.

I was with them for all of it, but more like an echo than a participant.

That afternoon, the three of us went to the dress store, the farmers' market, the dry cleaner. We drove the full length of Wilshire Boulevard, from the ocean to the heart of downtown, winding our way back home on 6th through the palaces of Hancock Park. Beneath tall graceful pines, planted in 1932 by the bigwigs of the movie industry. We stopped by the market to pick up ravioli and spinach for dinner. My mother was in between jobs that year, and she did not like to drive alone. Sometimes the two of them talked about how trees grew, or why we needed rain; sometimes they just sat silently while I threw cracker bits around the back seat. Mom loved to listen to Joseph — she nodded with encouragement at every single word he said. Occasionally, we'd pull over to the curb and she'd ask him advice on her life, and even at eight, he'd answer her questions in a slow, low monologue. She would hold tightly on to the band of her seatbelt and fix her eyes onto his, listening.

All this happened for many months, and no one mentioned anything to Dad, and all was fine until one afternoon when Joseph was at school, staying in during recess because he did not like to play dodgeball.

The teacher was cleaning the blackboard with a damp cloth. Joseph was crouching on the floor of the classroom, analyzing the color gradation of the carpet fibers, when the teacher asked him, with great concern, if he was feeling any better. Joseph said he was feeling fine.

But the doctors must be giving you a lot of medicine? the teacher said. She was kind of a dumb teacher. I met her later and she cried a little when she met me, like I was going to torture her again with the Edelstein brilliance. When I told her that I wasn't a genius, she visibly relaxed.

No, said Joseph.

But so what do they do, these doctors? the teacher asked, as she cleared the remaining bits of chalk off the board. Joseph was out of the classroom for most of the day, sometimes three times a week at that point. He didn't answer. He squatted at the foot of her desk now, investigating the grain of the desk wood.

Joseph?

We go to the market, he said then.

You go to the market with the doctors?

Me and Mom, said Joseph.

Before the doctors? asked the teacher, slowing her hand.

It's what the doctor ordered, said Joseph,

looking up for a brief moment to catch her narrowing eye.

I knew the whole story backwards and forwards, because I heard it told and retold over the phone, to friends, to my father, to anyone, as my mother got investigated. She talked about it for years. A couple of social workers came by and asked her questions in the living room for two hours. The home-schooling contingency in the neighborhood dropped off a stack of handmade pamphlets. When Dad found out what was happening, he brought a notepad to the dinner table to try to understand, asking the same questions over and over while Joseph and I dug through our food. But explain again, he said, lowering his brow. *Why* were you taking him out? Because he is bored out of his mind, said Mom, waving her fork in the air. Let him discover the world on his own! Dad scribbled jagged lines on the pad. But you didn't go to a *museum,* he said. You went to the dry cleaner. Mom gritted her teeth. He liked it, she said. Didn't you learn something, honey? Joseph sat up straighter. They use liquid solvent but no water, he recited.

Mom had to be talked to by the president of student affairs and the school principal, and she was on mom probation permanently. A few years later, when she wanted

76

to take me out of school for a real doctor's appointment to deal with a stubborn flu, I had to wait in the main office, staring at the dark fishtank with the rows of tiny blue fish zigging and zagging, while the secretary called Dr. Horner to confirm my appointment.

Cough, Rose, Mom had said when we walked into the main office together. I let out a ripping bronchial spasm.

See? Mom said to the secretary. Can we go?

The secretary gave me a look of concern. I'm sorry, he said, wincing. School policy, he said. He was on hold at Dr. Horner's for fifteen minutes, and we almost missed the slot. In the doctor's waiting room, Mom flipped through the magazines like the pages needed to be slapped.

Those months of errands seemed benign: kid and Mom, going to stores together. It was even sweet, in a way. The social workers left the house that day holding slices of Mom's freshly baked banana bread, calling thank you as they got into their car. As soon as Joseph was back in a regular school routine, Dad forgot all about it. But the one true result of all those absences was that Joseph, who was already unfriendly, made even fewer attachments in the classroom. He'd had a couple friends in earlier years — no one to bring home, but his conversation was peppered with repeated names — Marco, Marco, Marco, Steve, Marco, Steve, Steve. After that third-grade year, it changed to Them and They. They went out to recess. I don't like them. They all played chess. They have fruit punch in their lunches; can I? Can I stay home? Not like any of this was a problem for Mom — she thought Joseph was perfect, even though he was often in a bad mood, rarely made eye contact, and ignored everyone. She called Joseph the desert, one summer afternoon when we were all walking along the Santa Monica Pier, because, she explained, he was an ecosystem that simply needed less input. Sunshine'll do it for Joe, she said, beaming upon him. Joseph walked two feet to the side, absorbed in the game booths that lined the south side of the pier.

He is economical with his resources, Mom told me, since Joseph wasn't listening.

And what am I? I asked, as we walked down the rickety wooden pathway that led to the end of the dock, where the fishermen stood all day with their old-style fishing poles.

You? she said, looking out over the water.

Mmm. Rain forest, she said.

Rain forest, what does that mean? I asked.

You are lush, she said.

I need rain?

Lots of rain.

Is that good? I asked.

Not good or bad, she said. Is a rain forest good or bad?

What are you?

She raised her shoulders. I change around, she said. Like the Big Island in Hawaii.

You get to be Hawaii?

The Big Island. It has seven different climates. You can be Hawaii too, if you want.

Are you a rain forest?

I don't think so, she said.

A desert?

Sometimes, she said.

A volcano?

On occasion, she said, laughing.

I went to walk by myself at the railing. The ocean looked specific and granular in the high heat. When we reached the very end of the pier, I stood by a short old Japanese fisherman who told me he had been there reeling up the mackerel since six-thirty in the morning. What time did you get up? he asked me. Seven, I said. I was already here, he said, looking at his watch. A full bucket of fish nestled at his feet, in a cooler. It was three-thirty. I'm still here, he said.

Now I'm here too, I said.

The two of us, here, he said.

Did you see the sunrise?

Over the mountain, he said.

Pretty?

He nodded. Orange, he said. Pink.

I want to be the ocean instead of the rain forest, I said on the drive home.

Sure, said Mom, whose mind was long gone into somewhere else.

Joseph would reach out to me occasionally, the same way the desert blooms a flower every now and then. You get so used to the subtleties of beige and brown, and then a sunshine-yellow poppy bursts from the arm of a prickly pear. How I loved those flower moments, like when he pointed out the moon and Jupiter, but they were rare, and never to be expected.

So, because of all this, it was no small surprise one fall afternoon when I spied Joseph, walking from the bus stop, arriving home from seventh grade with another person at his side. A person his own age. I was drawing lightning bolts with colored chalk on the sidewalk because the school nature lesson that day had been about weather: thundershowers, tornadoes, hurricanes. All so exotic to the blue skies of Los Angeles. I was busily getting the edges right on the first bolt when I looked up and saw them walking around the corner, and at first I thought I was blurring my vision. I colored the bolt bright orange. Looked up again: still two. My second thought was that it was a trick. Maybe Joseph had been assigned this other kid. Maybe the guy was a jerk, playing a joke on my brother.

What are you doing here? I asked, as soon as they reached the front lawn. I think I was seven. Joseph, like usual, didn't answer. Desert wind. Snakes and scorpions.

Hi, said George. I'm George. He bent down and shook my hand. He had a good handshake for a seventh-grader.

Lightning! he said, looking down.

But why are you here? I asked again, following them inside.

Joseph headed to his bedroom. George turned back, and said they were there to do homework.

Is he teaching you? I asked George.

No, said George.

But why are *you* here with my brother? I asked.

Science homework, said George. Science stuff.

I noted his eyebrows. His pants, which were the normal pants a boy his age wore.

You like science too? I asked.

Sure do, said George, disappearing into Joseph's room.

I spent the rest of the afternoon going back and forth from the chalk drawings to Joseph's door. I couldn't exactly hear what they were doing but it sounded like they were talking about schoolwork. I drew a whole line of lightning bolts very fast, and then took the blue chalk and made slashes of rain everywhere, in the dry and cloudless air.

It was during George's fourth or fifth visit that the blow hit me. I was sitting outside Joseph's door once again, trying to listen; I still assumed that Joseph must be tutoring George, because I could not understand why the guy kept showing up, two or even three times a week. I pretended I was happily building a train track out of Legos that, due to zoning laws, absolutely had to go over the carpet right in front of Joseph's door.

What's the reason for that? a voice asked. My brother's voice.

It's wind resistance, said George.

I waited for Joseph to explain something to George.

Why'd you solve it that way? Joseph asked.

It's quicker like this, said George, scratching on a pad.

Wait, do that again, said Joseph.

Which part?

That.

The toy train bumped along a track of red and blue. I sat and listened for a half-hour, and not once did Joseph explain something to his guest.

Had I been at school with him, I would not have been so surprised. The fast pace that had stunned everyone when he was my age couldn't be maintained, and by the time he was in seventh grade, he was in advanced math, yes, but there were at least three in the class ahead of him. For once, he had to glance at his homework to keep up. He had shifted from genius to very smart, and although very smart is very good, to a prodigious kid it's a plummet.

Train, bumping back to the station.

For me, it had ramifications beyond his brain. I had assumed, since birth, that Joseph was so weird because he was so smart. But here was George, even smarter, and he knew my name. When he came over, he made a point of saying hi. When he left, he waved.

I got caught, that day. I was lying on my

back on the hall carpet, spinning the train wheels, when George opened up the door to make a phone call.

Hey, Rose, he said.

Sorry, I said. I'm making a train.

Where's it headed? he asked.

I mean a train track, I said. What?

The train?

Oh, I said. Ventura?

Go *away,* Joseph growled, from the depths of his bedroom.

I moved my train closer to the kitchen and listened to George's call. He was checking on his sister, who was retarded. He said, into the phone: I need a new drawing of an elephant, okay? My old elephant needs a buddy.

Mom was also in the kitchen, rinsing a colander of broccoli under the faucet.

I looked at her when he was off and back.

Nice boy, she said.

Not a desert, I said.

What do you mean? She put the broccoli aside, to drip into the sink.

You said Joseph was the desert?

She ran her hands under the tap. Nah, not the desert, she said, as if that conversation had never happened. Joseph, she said, is like a geode — plain on the outside, gorgeous on the inside.

I watched her dry her hands. My mother's lithe, able fingers. I felt such a clash inside, even then, when she praised Joseph. Jealous, that he got to be a geode — a geode! — but also relieved, that he soaked up most of her super-attention, which on occasion made me feel like I was drowning in light. The same light he took and folded into rock walls to hide in the beveled sharp edges of topaz crystal and schorl.

He has facets and prisms, she said. He is an intricate geological surprise.

I stayed at the counter. I still held the Lego train in my hands.

And what's Dad? I said.

Oh, your father, she said, leaning her hip against the counter. Your father is a big strong stubborn gray boulder. She laughed.

And me? I asked, grasping, for the last time.

You? Baby, you're —

I stood still. Waiting.

You're —

She smiled at me, as she folded the blue-and-white-checked dish towel. You're seaglass, she said. The pretty green kind. Everybody loves you, and wants to take you home.

It took a while to pick up all the pieces of my train track and put them away in my

85

own bedroom. It was a compliment, I kept
thinking to myself, as I stacked the parts;
it's supposed to make you feel good, I
thought.

10

Saturday dawned, sunny and hot. Officially nine. I was ready to go the minute I woke up. George wasn't due until noon, but I bounded around the house, opening the front door and peeking down the sidewalk as early as ten in the morning, making a pathway of fallen leaves, and when George turned the corner onto our block I ran back inside to open the door for him as if I was surprised. Hi! He said hello and sang me a quick happy birthday and then went right into Joseph's room. After ten minutes of convincing, Joseph exited wearing a baseball cap that read *The Best Part About Baseball Is the Cap,* and George asked me how I felt about walking all together over to a bakery on Beverly which specialized in homemade cookies that cost a whopping three dollars apiece. Good, I said, bobbing my head. I feel good about that.

The heat wave was lighter, breezier, on

this warm white-skied Saturday afternoon, my father out playing tennis, Mom at the studio learning tools, as the three of us headed off together, crossing Melrose, walking south past the jacaranda-bordered fourplex apartment buildings that lined up in friendly rows down Spaulding.

When I crossed the street, according to my mother, I still had to hold someone's hand. At ten, I would be able to cross streets unhanded. I'd held on to Joseph's many times before, for many years, but holding his was like holding a plant, and the disappointment of fingers that didn't grasp back was so acute that at some point I'd opted to take his forearm instead. For the first few street crossings, that's what I did, but on the corner at Oakwood, on an impulse, I grabbed George's hand. Right away: fingers, holding back. The sun. More clustery vines of bougainvillea draping over windows in bulges of dark pink. His warm palm. An orange tabby lounging on the sidewalk. People in torn black T-shirts sitting and smoking on steps. The city, opening up.

We hit the sidewalk, and dropped hands. How I wished, right then, that the whole world was a street.

As the two of them walked ahead, Joseph using a ficus leaf to swoop the air and demonstrate something about torque, I watched their backs and their gesturing arms. In my pleasure at being included I completely forgot about the reason for the trip, but the minute we reached the corner and turned onto Beverly, the silky wafting scent of butter and sugar brought it all back, and a smell that usually made people drool tripped dread right up in my stomach.

Yum, said George.

Joseph rolled his eyes. He seemed to be smell-proof, somehow. He took a seat outside the bakery, on a low rock wall surrounding some limp azaleas, and pulled out his usual stack of graph paper.

I'll be out here, he said. Doing actual work.

He started sorting through the graph paper pages. George held the door open for me, and we filed inside, together.

If I rarely spent time with just Joseph, I had certainly never been alone with George. I had no idea what to do. It was like being asked to dance, or really asked anything. The store was empty, and I stood in the middle of the room, twisting, reading as much as I could sound out of the enthusiastic signs that covered the walls, assuring us that every cookie was baked on the pre–mises, which George and I had agreed earlier was a key factor in today's test.

It's better to be away from your home, he said, coming up to me. We may be able to tell different things, if you don't know the people.

Okay, I said.

Take subject out of environment and re-test, he said, making quote fingers with his hands.

At the bins, I picked out a chocolate chip and an oatmeal. George got the same and looked at me close, under those arched eyebrows. Good, he said. You ready?

I guess, I said.

I sat myself down at a red-and-beige table.

Take your time, said George.

I bit into the chocolate chip. Slowed myself down.

By then, almost a week in, I could sort through the assault of layers a little more quickly. The chocolate chips were from a factory, so they had that same slight metallic, absent taste to them, and the butter had been pulled from cows in pens, so the richness was not as full. The eggs were tinged with a hint of far away and plastic. All of those parts hummed in the distance, and then the baker, who'd mixed the batter and formed the dough, was angry. A tight anger, in the cookie itself.

Angry? I said to George, who was up browsing the rows — white-chocolate chunk, no-sugar shortbread — chewing his own.

It's an angry cookie? he said.

I nodded, tentative. He took another bite of his, and I could see him paying close attention, trying to taste what I did. His eyes focused in the near distance.

Man, he said, after a minute, shaking his head. Nothing.

He went to ring the bell on the counter. After a minute, a clerk wandered in from the back, a young man with short black-dyed hair and a proud arched nose, wearing a dusty red uniform.

Yeah, he said. What.

Did you bake these? asked George.

The young man, probably in his early twenties, looked down at the half still in George's hand.

What type?

Chocolate chip, George said.

He sniffed. He looked at the clock. Yeah, he said.

George put his elbows on the counter and crossed his feet, in his khaki pants of a million pockets. I was in love with him, pretty much, by that point. I did not care that my brother had been shooting me evil-eye laser looks of hate all week. Soon, I knew, they'd get distracted by something else — by the broken sprinkler, or by the weather pattern changes, or by traffic system routes along La Brea, but for the moment I was Project Number One, and the young man in the red cookie uniform responded to George, as most people did, because George wanted something from him, wanted his unique specificity right then, with that beam of friendly focus that was so hard to resist.

We're doing a school project, said George, leaning closer. Can I ask you a few questions?

I guess, said the guy.

What was your mood when you made this?

No mood, said the guy. I just make the cookies. In the bowl, stir, bake, done.

Do you like making them?

Nah, said the guy. I fucking hate this job.

George shifted his position at the counter. He turned around for a second to look at me directly. Sugary dust slid down my throat.

Why? George asked.

Would you want to sell cookies first thing after college? said the guy.

Probably not, said George.

I don't even *like* cookies, said the guy.

I bit into the oatmeal. Same levels — now

the oats, well dried, but not so well watered, then the raisins, half tasteless, made from parched grapes, picked by thirsty workers, then the baker, rushed. The whole cookie was so rushed, like I had to eat it fast or it would, somehow, eat me.

Oatmeal in a hurry, I said to George, a little louder.

Chocolate chip, angry, he said, turning around. What's that, about oatmeal?

Rushed, I said.

He turned back. You make the oatmeal?

Nah, said the guy. That's Janet.

Who's Janet?

She works here in the mornings, the guy said. She talks a lot about traffic. He glanced over at me. She's always running late, he said.

I could feel my face reddening. George smiled. Thank you, he said, to the guy.

George returned to me, and pulled my hair into two ponytails with his hands.

Some-one is sm-art, he sang.

I wanted to grab on to him, tie myself to his sleeve.

But I don't want it, I said, to no one.

So what's the project? the guy asked, casually neatening the stacks of coupons on the front counter.

I was sitting in a red chair, which had been

pinned to the floor with several plastic nails. The tips of my feet just touching the floor. The table, a thick shellac over a pattern of beige dots that seemed to be trying to suggest spontaneity. I couldn't eat any more of either cookie, so I left them crumbling on the table.

I guess you could call it a test of location, said George, reaching over to finish my leftovers. Like, where do we locate the feeling inside the cookie, he said, chewing.

The guy scrunched up his forehead, and a lock of black hair fell over his eyes.

Or, am I bonkers, I said, from my chair.

And? said the guy.

Truth was, it was hard to see George eat those cookie halves without hesitation. Without tasting even a speck of the hurry in Janet's oatmeal, which was so rushed it was like eating the calendar of an executive, or without catching a glimpse of the punching bag tucked beside every chocolate chip. I was so jealous, already, of everyone else's mouth. But I loved George in part because he believed me; because if I stood in a cold, plain white room and yelled FIRE, he would walk over and ask me why. It was the same thing that would make him into a very good scientist.

No, I said. Maybe not.

Wait, hang on. The guy ducked into the back, and came out with a sandwich in his hand, wrapped tightly in plastic.

Does it work with sandwiches? he asked.

I didn't move. He handed it over. George was watching with a kind of neutral curiosity, and I wasn't sure what I was supposed to do, so I just unwrapped it and took a bite. It was a homemade ham-and-cheese-and-mustard sandwich, on white bread, with a thin piece of lettuce in the middle. Not bad, in the food part. Good ham, flat mustard from a functional factory. Ordinary bread. Tired lettuce-pickers. But in the sandwich as a whole, I tasted a kind of yelling, almost. Like the sandwich itself was yelling at me, yelling love me, love me, really loud. The guy at the counter watched me closely.

Oh, I said.

My girlfriend made it, he said.

Your girlfriend makes your sandwiches? asked George.

She likes doing it, said the guy.

I didn't know what to say. I put the sandwich down.

What? said the guy.

The sandwich wants you to love it, I said.

The guy started laughing. My voice, though, was dull. George reached over and took a bite. Is that ham? he said.

The sandwich? asked the guy.

Was yelling at me, I said, closing my eyes. It was yelling at me to love it.

George took another bite, and then re-wound the plastic tightly around the bread. Does that sound like her?

Nah, said the guy, laughing a little still.

I mean, do you love her? George asked.

The guy shrugged. Depends on what you mean by love, he said.

I laid my head on the table. The yelling was loud, and it was too much information to sort through, and it was way too much for nine years old. George handed the rest of the sandwich back over the counter.

That's it, he said. No more tests for Rose. He reached over and took my hand and squeezed it. We weren't even in traffic.

Thanks for your help, said George, standing, pulling me up. You've been great. Tell Janet to slow down.

Whoosh, said the guy, shaking his head. Sheesh. Thanks? he said, with a voice that sounded like he wanted us to stay.

We threw out our napkins and pushed back through the door, me still holding tightly to George's hand. I was so relieved to hear the traffic outside, to see the bubbles of closed car windows, people I couldn't access in their cars going about their day.

Outside, Joseph was still sitting on the rock wall that protected those few scraggly pink azalea plants, making a petaled arrangement of curves on paper.

Well, she's for real, said George, stepping up close. He raised my hand, like I'd won something. Your little sis. She's like a magic food psychic or something, he said.

Joseph looked up. He didn't move his face at all. Instead, he handed over three pages of graph paper with perfect shapes on them. Screw-ups for your wall, he said. Cool, said George, taking a minute to look at each one.

So, George said, turning to me as we started to walk. Seems like it's mostly the feelings people don't know about, huh?

Seemed like that to me too but I didn't like the idea at all.

The guy was *so* angry! he said, laughing, telling Joseph about the clerk.

Joseph listened as George went through the story, and I took George's hand every time to cross the street and he held mine back with fingers warm and firm. Sometimes he forgot to drop my hand at the sidewalk and I would hold on as long as he let me, until he needed his arm to make a gesture about the gothic beauty of black rose cacti or the jaunty angle of someone's chimney. I knew just how that sandwich felt.

With my hand in his, I looked at all the apartment buildings with rushes of love, peering in the wide streetside windows that revealed living rooms painted in dark burgundies and matte reds. I'm a food psychic, I told myself, even though the thought of it made me want to crawl under the buildings and never come out.

I savored that walk, and rightly so, because as soon as we got home the cord snapped. Or Joseph cut it. The second we walked in, he ran to his room and brought out a rare hardback illustrated book on fractals he'd checked out of the library, which was catnip to the eighth-grade science mind, and the two of them spent the rest of the daylight and into the evening staring at a leaf.

11

In the lengthening days of spring, Dad upped his tennis and went to work on a case about redistribution rights and my mother continued her carpentry, returning home smelling warmly of sawdust and resin. She brought home a teak board and a box sanded to the smoothness of satin. A pine slingback dining-room chair, with straight square legs and a complex pattern in the backside stained a golden brown. We circled it, in admiration. She fanned her fingers and complained of the splinters, so she and Joe went on a special trip to a beauty supply shop, where he picked out the finest pair of tweezers on the shelf. They still enjoyed running errands together. That Sunday evening, after dinner, Joseph sat close to Mom on the sofa, and with care, he dipped the tweezers in a shallow bowl of warm water and patiently used his long fingers, his shared dexterity, to clear her hands.

Once he removed a splinter, he wiped it on a paper towel, re-dipped the tweezers, and dug around for the next. It took an hour, and quickly became a regular routine, every Sunday evening.

You could be a brain surgeon, Joe, Mom murmured, watching.

Sometimes I wondered if, on Saturdays, she dragged her hands over raw wood to preserve this special time with him.

I struggled by, for the rest of the school year. I filled in my spelling workbook. I took the bus. At recess, I was first in line for the dodgeball group, and several times the teacher had to pull me out for throwing the ball too hard. Eddie called me a cheater. Eliza looked at me from the sidelines with too much sympathy; I threw the ball at her. I broke a kid's glasses because I threw too close to his face.

I didn't know who else to talk to, or tell, so, on my own, I ate packaged snack food, learning the subtle differences in tightness and flatness from the various factories across the country, and I ate pre-prepared food from the grocery store that had been made by happy clerks, and uptight clerks, and frustrated clerks, and sometimes I felt scared to open up the refrigerator. Baked goods were the most potent, having been built for the longest time from the smallest of parts, so I did best with a combination of the highly processed — gummy fish, peanut-butter crackers, potato chips — made by no one, plus occasional fast-food burgers, compiled by machines and made, often, by no one, and fruits and vegetables that hadn't been cooked. At school, I ate my apple and carrots and then used my allowance to buy food out of the snack machines and made it through the day that way.

I asked my father if we could go out to eat more often, to give Mom a break from the cooking. But I love cooking! Mom said, brushing at the air. Is there something so bad about my cooking? No, no, I said; it's for school? I pulled on my father's cuff. Please? Dad disliked the outlandish portion sizes in restaurants, but he pushed his lips together, thinking, and mentioned a new Italian place he thought might be good, on Beverly. We went on a Saturday. The chef was a little surly in his minestrone, but also agreeable, easygoing, easy to eat. It's a tradition? I sang, hopefully, in the car.

Do I need a pound of meat at a sitting? Dad said, driving through yellow lights. Do I really?

Mom rubbed his neck. You're a growing

101

man, she said.

But I'm not! Dad said, hitting the wheel. I'm not growing at all anymore! Only horizontally!

The school nurse sent for me as a followup. I'd dropped four pounds. She recommended ice cream. Ice cream was generally okay. I gained it back.

But so what do I *do?* I asked George, a couple months after the cookie store visit, when Joseph had left his room to make a bowl of popcorn. George was lying on the floor, on his back, and had somehow acquired one of those red-point laser beams, and was pointing it up to the corners of the ceiling.

Hey, he said. Check this out.

I stepped a foot inside, and watched the red light mark a dot at each ceiling convergence.

Light rays, he said.

Pretty, I said.

But what do I do about it? I asked again, after a minute.

About what?

About my food problem?

He put the red dot right on my forehead. Now you look Indian, he said.

George?

It's not a problem, he said, moving the

dot away. It's fantastic.

I hate it, I said, tugging at the sides of my mouth.

Or maybe you'll grow into it, he said, shooting the red dot through the keyhole in the door.

He smiled at me, and it was genuine, but it was also a smile from further away. Our boats on the river had drifted apart. There was a loyalty call he'd had to make, and I could hear the popcorn popping in the kitchen, and the alluring smell of melting butter in a pot. Joseph muttering away, as he prepared it. That popcorn, a puffy salty collapsing death. I would not eat a piece of it.

Maybe, I said.

I think, George said, you should become a superhero. He put the dot on my mouth. Open up, he said.

Laser, down my throat.

There, he said, bouncing the dot around. Supermouth.

Almost six months after the incident with the cake, on a Saturday morning in August, I awoke to the smell of fruit and leaven to discover that Mom was rummaging around in the kitchen, cooking up a summer pie from scratch. Joseph had left early to launch

103

a battery-operated rocket with George in the park, and Dad's car had honked at its usual exit time even though it was the weekend. Things had been tense around the house. Dad, brusque. Mom, wound up. When Dad was home, she'd tell him stories in a really fast voice and he seemed barely able to listen, eyes floating around the room.

When I shuffled into the kitchen in my pajamas that morning, she greeted me as if I was her long-lost best friend. Rose! she said when I walked up to the door. Good morning! How are you? How'd you sleep? She grabbed me in for a hug and held me tight. Her hair, freshly washed, smelled like a field of new lavender. So! she said, clapping her hands. Honey. What do you think about pie for breakfast?

The fact that she was up at all likely meant that she'd never gone back to sleep after her 2 a.m. wake-up, and that she'd started baking out of boredom at around five. Mixing bowls and spoons and sprinklings of flour covered the counter.

Or cereal? I said.

I'm trying out the newest recipe in the paper, she said. Peach-and-dingo pie. Ready, kiddo? Will you taste it with me?

Dingo? I said. Isn't that a kangaroo?

Lingo? she said. Lingoberry? Something

like that.

She pulled me to the kitchen table, beaming. It was unlike her, to be so imprecise. The morning had warnings written all over it.

My mother had been baking more often in general, but she took plates of desserts to the carpentry studio, where her boss, thank God, had a sweet tooth. He just loved the cheesecake, she'd tell me, shining. He ate all of my oatmeal cookies. Some charmed combination of the woodwork, and the studio people, and the splinter excising time with her son kept her going back to Silver Lake even when she hit her usual limits, and every night, tucked into bed, I would send out a thank-you prayer to the carpentry boss for taking in what I could not. But this morning I was the only one, and it was the weekend, and carpentry rested, and the whole kitchen smelled of hometown America, of Atlanta's orchards and Oregon's berry bushes, of England's pie legacy, packed with the Puritans over the *Mayflower.*

You try, as a child. There was the same old dread, and there was the same old hope, and due to the hope, I ate the piece of pie she sliced on the small white plate, with a silver fork, beneath the dual lightbulbs in the ceiling fixture. In my daisy pajamas and ripped bunny socks. The taste so bad I could hardly keep it in my mouth.

What do you think? asked Mom, squinting as she tasted, leaning back in her chair, just as she had before.

We began with cake; we end with pie.

I leaned over, too. I could not, for this last time, hide any of it. I leaned right out of my chair and slumped down on the tile floor of the kitchen. I got on the floor because I had to go low. The chair was too tall. The light fixture, glaring.

Rose? she said. Baby? Are you okay?

No, I said, low.

Are you choking? she asked.

No, I said. But I closed my eyes. A gripping in my throat. The graininess of the pie dough, of the peach syrup: packed, every bite, with that same old horrible craving.

Was it her? Was it me?

It was mid-morning, and outside, I could hear the neighborhood kids on their bikes, wheels splashing through puddles from early-morning lawn waterings. It had been an unusually mild August so far, and the light outside was open and clear. In the dewy air after the spray of the sprinklers, I liked to wander down the sidewalk and scoop up any flapping worms with a folded leaf and stick them back in the dirt. I was, in general, an easygoing kid like that, a rescuer of worms. But this morning, while kids biked and swished outside, I grabbed a paper towel and dragged it hard down my tongue.

I started tearing at my mouth. Get it out! I roared.

What is it, baby? Mom asked, struggling out of her chair.

My mouth, I said, suddenly crying. The tears steaming hot, down my face. Everything flooding. I tried to pull at it — my mouth — with my fingers. Take it out! I said. *Please.* Mommy. Take it off my face.

The floor tile was cool, and I was so glad it was there, the floor, always there, and I put a cheek down, right on the tile, and let the coolness calm me.

Mom knelt by my side, her cheeks flushed with worry. Rose, she said. Baby. I don't understand. What do you mean?

I threw the paper towel away. Pulled off another. Wiped down my tongue. Pulled off another. I had been avoiding my mother's baked goods, but I had eaten her cooked dinners now for months and months, which she made for us every evening with labor and love. Trying not to show everything on my face. Eating a potato chip after every bite. I'd been spending my lunchtimes tasting bites from my friends' lunches, navigating the cafeteria, finally finding a good piece of doughy pizza made in the school kitchen by a sad lady with a hairnet who worked far on the left. She was sad, true, but the sadness was so real and so known in it that I found the tomato sauce and the melted cheese highly edible, even good. I would try to time it just right in the cafeteria every lunchtime to get her food, because sometimes she took her lunch break right at ours; I would shove to be first in line to catch her before she left, rushing ahead, and my teacher had taken me aside to ask what was going on. There's a lady, at the cafeteria? I said, staring at her bright-blue earring stud. You still have to stay with the class, Rose, she said, pulling me to her gaze. That same sad lady returned from her break ten minutes before the bell rang, so I took to nibbling on an apple or anything packaged until she returned and then running to her window and getting whatever she put her hands on, so that before lunch was over I could eat a feeling that was recognized. I ate fast food whenever I could, which was not unlike holding Joseph's forearm to cross the street instead of bearing the disappointment of his hand. I was working to find, in every new setting, something filling, and my whole daily world had become consumed by it. And, day in and day out, I had been faking enjoying eating at home, through the weekly gaps and silences between my parents, through my mother's bright and sleepless eyes, and for whatever reason, for that one time, I could not possibly pretend I liked her pie.

The pie, sitting on the counter, with two big brown slices cut out of it.

What is it? Rose? It's the pie?

You feel so *bad,* I said, to the floor tile.

What do you mean? she said, touching my shoulder. Are you talking to the floor? You mean me again, Rose?

You're so sad in there, I said, and alone, and hungry, and sad —

In where? she said.

In the pie, I said.

In the pie? she said, flinching. What do you mean, baby?

Not baby, I said. No more baby.

Rose? she said, eyebrows caving in. The sheets of tears came down over me again. Blurring. I clawed at my mouth. What are you doing? she said, grabbing my hands. Honey?

I pulled away from her. I tasted it, I said,

pitching.

But, Rose, she said, tasted what —

I TASTED YOU, I said. GET OUT MY MOUTH.

She drove me to the emergency room. I cried on the whole drive over, and I cried all through the waiting time, in the plastic chairs. Eventually, the doctor came in, and gave me a shot, and put me in a bed. She's inconsolable, I heard my mother say, her voice high with concern, as I drifted off.

12

The doctors didn't know how to diagnose me, but I did have a delusion, they said, about my mouth. I stayed six hours in the wing off the emergency room of Cedars-Sinai Medical Center that day, taking tests, answering questions, peeing into a cup.

We arrived at around ten-thirty in the morning, and after I calmed down, and the shot wore off, and after a few hours of basic medical work-ups, a tall male doctor with half-moon spectacles came into the room where I was recovering. I rested in bed, silently. Embarrassed by the scene I'd made.

My mother sat in a side chair, nervously cleaning out her purse. The room around us was painted in layers of beige — a dark beige trim, an ivory wall, and a tastefully framed watercolor of some straw in a vase.

He sat down on the edge of my bed, and asked me a list of questions. How I felt. If I slept. What I ate.

Your bedtime is eight-thirty? he asked, writing it down.

Yes.

And you wake up at?

Seven.

And do you wake up in the middle of the night?

Sometimes.

He scribbled something on the chart. Why?

Just some days, I said. I wake up at two.

Mom wrinkled her nose, as if something smelled funny.

Just when she's up, I said, pointing.

The doctor turned to Mom. Ah, he said, sympathetically. Insomnia?

Oh no, Mom said. Just a little restlessness.

Oh sure, the doctor said. Restlessness, I know that. You from here?

Bay Area, Mom smiled.

Bay Area! the doctor said. Such a nice place. I'm from Sacramento.

Oh, really? Did — Mom said.

Excuse me, I said.

They both turned to me.

Am I done? I said.

The doctor opened his mouth to say more but then turned back to his chart. He asked me a few more questions about throwing up, just like the school nurse had, jotting it all down in his boxy doctor-handwriting. Then he left. Mom went out to talk to him. I lay against the pillow and aged many years in that hour on my own. After a while, he and Mom re-entered the room with another doctor and stood at the foot of my hospital bed. Used tissue and sticky candy and worn business cards filled the trash, the dregs of her handbag.

They all stared at me from their heights of adulthood.

Thank you for your help, I said, sitting up straight. I feel better.

They'd served me a hospital bowl of noodle soup, which tasted of resentment, fine and full. I ate it all, making sure they could see. I ate each of the salt crackers, tucked in their ridge-edged plastic wrapping, factory-made in East Hanover, New Jersey.

I'm very sorry, I said. Did I have a fever?

You know you can't remove your mouth, the tall doctor said.

I know, I said. It's part of my body.

The other doc scratched her head. But —

I don't know why I said that, I said. I was feeling sick.

My mother, standing to the side, leaned in. Is she — she whispered to the taller doctor.

Both doctors tilted their heads. She seems to be okay. Give her time, they said. Perhaps it's an isolated incident.

I finished my soup. Changed back into my clothes while they gave my mother papers to sign. An old man in a wheelchair rolled past our doorway. Out in the hall, the fluorescently lit corridors lent a dull glow to the white linoleum floor, making it hard to tell the time of day, but I caught a glimpse of a far window, floor-to-ceiling, lit yellow with the blaze of a fading afternoon.

As my mother finished the paperwork, the doctor handed me a cherry lollipop, popped out from a factory in Louisiana where, once flavored, the hot sugar cooled on a metal table of small circles and then got stamped onto a white cardboard rod. Not a single hint of a person in it. Thank you, I said. I ate it down to the stick.

In the parking lot, I opened the car door carefully and settled into my seat.

Thank you for taking me, I said.

Of course, Mom said, backing out.

Were the tests okay?

They were okay, she said.

She threaded her fingers through the steering wheel, driving as if she wanted to pull the wheel into her chest.

The traffic was thick on 3rd Street. Some

114

sort of walk-a-thon was happening. The stores, with dresses in windows, with blown-glass vases, packed with browsing people.

I scared you, I said, in a small voice.

She sighed. She reached over, and stroked my hair with her hand. You did scare me, she said.

I'm sorry.

Oh, Rose.

I won't do it again, I said.

She rolled down her window and stuck her elbow out, her fingers on the side of the car, drumming.

You said — Oh, never mind. Let's just get you home.

What?

You said I was feeling bad, that I'm so unhappy, that I'm hardly there, she said.

I did? I said, although I remembered the whole conversation like it had been re-corded. From the open window, fresh air sifted through the car. It was almost four o'clock by now, and the sunlight was gold and streamy.

I'm fine, she said. I just want you to know, baby girl. I don't want you to be worrying so much about me.

She said it, and she looked over, and her eyes were big and limpid, a dark-blue color like late-day ocean water. But in the look was still that same yearning. Please worry about me, I saw in there. Her voice not matching her eyes. I knew if I ate anything of hers again, it would likely tell me the same message: Help me, I am not happy, *help me* — like a message in a bottle sent in each meal to the eater, and I got it. I got the message.

And now my job was to pretend I did not get the message.

Okay, I said.

She turned on the radio. We listened together to a program with quiz questions, about words that had multiple meanings. I couldn't concentrate very well, and I just watched the houses and stores slip by on Fairfax, fwip, fwip, momentarily in view, then gone.

It can feel so lonely, to see strangers out in the day, shopping, on a day that is not a good one. On this one: the day I returned from the emergency room after having a fit about wanting to remove my mouth. Not an easy day to look at people in their vivid clothes, in their shining hair, pointing and smiling at colorful woven sweaters.

I wanted to erase them all. But I also wanted to be them all, and I could not erase them and want to be them at the same time.

At home, Joseph was nicer to me than

116

usual and we played a silent game of Parcheesi for an hour in the slanted box of remaining sunlight on the carpet. Dad came by and brought me a pillow. Mom went to take a nap. Joseph won. I went to bed early. I woke up the same.

■ ■ ■ ■

PART TWO:
JOSEPH

■ ■ ■ ■

13

My parents met at a garage sale, held by my dad's college roommate. All three were in their senior year of college at Berkeley, and Dad's roommate, Carl, was an unusually fastidious type for someone in his early twenties. He oiled door hinges, for fun. Dad, a natural slob, said he would sometimes open up the freezer just to look at the frozen food stacked in such nice piles, corn bags nested on top of pizza slabs.

He was good for me, Dad said.

Carl also organized a biannual garage sale, to purge the house hold of crap. Mom liked garage sales, because she had very little money and was, she said, a fan of the found object. Most interesting to her was furniture, even then, and she had at that point acquired several velvet-topped footstools that she used in her apartment as guest seats. Her roommate at the time, tawny-maned Sharlene, was passionate about cooking, and they often had big dinner parties of cuisines from around the world, Moroccan feasts and Italian banquets, the table decorated with purple-glassed votive candles and old cracking out-of-date maps, because neither could afford to travel. Her roommate took weeks planning the menu, and Mom's job was to supply the seating. She'd been spending her Saturdays scouting around San Francisco and Oakland and Berkeley for more footstools, at the Ashby Flea Market and at every open garage, and on that particular morning, sunshine freshening up the gardens, she had stopped to browse through the tidy piles at this little house in the foothills when the tall handsome man in the lounge chair asked if she needed any help.

You don't happen to have any velvet footstools? She scanned the lawn, eyes grazing over shoes and kitchenware.

Footstools, he said, as if thinking about it. All velvet?

Just the top, she said.

He shook his head. I'm sorry, he said.

Or all velvet?

He shook his head again. Not even close, he said.

She tipped her chin, and smiled at him. In those days, she let her hair loose, down to her waist, and whenever I met old friends of hers, they would describe my mother as having resembled a mermaid with legs. With a sheerness to her skin that people wanted to shield.

Dad liked a task.

What kind of velvet footstool? he asked, rising from his chair.

Doesn't matter, she said. About so high? She held her hand at knee level. With a velvet top? Any color?

Across the lawn, Carl was attaching price labels to a few more books. Nope, he called out. But how about a whisk, for fifty cents?

Mom dipped her head. There were posters pinned to telephone poles around the neighborhood for other sales. Thanks anyway, she said.

Or a toaster oven? Carl said, making sparky sale motions with his hands.

Mom laughed. Nice try, she said. But I'm a woman on a mission.

Dad asked if he could accompany her, and she shrugged, in the way that most men at the time used as a doorway or lever. A shrug was as good as a yes, sometimes, particularly for a delicate beauty such as this. He ran inside and grabbed the local paper, which had listings of sales in the back placed by the truly motivated garage-sale givers, and together, they did a walking tour of the neighborhoods, past Shattuck and over to Elm, and Oak, where the house lawns waxed and waned in shades of green and yellow and beige. At each stop, Mom strolled around the piles, and Dad would make an excuse and duck inside, asking the house owner if he could please use their phone. It's important, he said, urgently. I would be very grateful, he said. He was charming, and tall, and offered to haul any heavy items outside, and the owners all said yes, and at house after house, he called up Carl with instructions. Please, he whispered. I need you to send someone to the fabric store to pick up some velvet. He cupped his hand over the receiver mouthpiece. In a fierce hiss, he promised Carl that he, Dad, would start cleaning the living room of his textbooks and shoes, yes, if only he, Carl, would rip off the wool top of the one footstool they had. It's *my* stool, Dad said, pacing, trying to stand far enough away from the front door and the garage sale itself so that she, opening and closing the drawers of an old oak nightstand, would not hear.

I will, all year, clear the rooms of my stuff, Dad told Carl.

Carl's girlfriend, who liked pranks, dashed to the closest fabric store, bought and trod on the cheapest mauve velvet, and cut it into a square. Dad kept Mom busy with the tour of the sales for as long as he could, and then they went to lunch at a little café on Durant, where they talked about college and the abyss post-college and he bit his tongue and did not ask for anything else. After splitting a double-chocolate brownie with whipped cream, she sighed. Her eyes shining. I should get back, she said. Of course, he said. Let's go. He picked up her bag, which held a few new books and records in it. Maybe we can double-check my place on the way, he offered, as lightly as he could. Who knows, he said, sometimes people trade items instead of money.

Since it's right by your car anyway, he said.

He let her walk ahead, down the sidewalk, and Carl and his girlfriend were tired, lounging in chairs, counting the money and deciding if they should lower prices for the remaining scattering of goods, when Mom saw it. She ran ahead, and clapped her hands with delight at the squat low wooden footstool covered with a kind of worn pink velvet that curled under the base of the seat and was stapled neatly to the inside. She saw it over on the side, by the stack of mildewed books and mismatched silverware.

Can you believe this? she said. Paul? Look!

She held it up in her arms, running her fingers over the plush.

Dad rushed over. You're kidding! he said to Carl. Someone traded this?

For the toaster oven, Carl said, pointedly. So now we need a new toaster oven.

Dad nodded. I'd like to buy us a new toaster oven, he said.

Sounds like a plan, said Carl, closing his eyes. I thought you might be interested, he said, to Mom.

The color was high on her cheeks. I am very interested, she said.

She sat on the stool and crossed her legs and said she liked the feel of it, liked it very much. It's pink as a rose, she said, and Carl's girlfriend beamed. The label read seven dollars, and Mom dug in her purse and paid for it, which Dad let her do, and she lugged it to her car, which he helped her with, and they made a date for the following night. It was as natural a plan as if they'd been seeing each other for months. Date Her, on his most current checklist with a nicely filled-in box. At their wedding, Carl, the best man, told the full story, holding up his flute of champagne, a story Dad had not told Mom ever. The guests roared. Light hit the gold of the champagne in a spear. Mom, in the photos, was wearing a dress that seemed sheerer than it actually was, so in every photo she looked like a ghost, a ghost that at any moment you might catch nude. It was a work of art, the dress, because it danced right in between the very tangible and the very intangible, and her skin and the dress were hard to distinguish. In the toast photo of her standing with Dad, who was all tangibility, black suit and firm shoulders, her eyes burn.

I'd started asking her questions about the wedding one afternoon when I was eleven, trying to understand how two such different people had gotten married at all, and she pulled the photo album off the shelf and opened it on our knees, between us. For a while she kept it on that page with the photo of Carl holding up his champagne, his mouth half open as he spoke his toast. She traced the fringes on his wingtip shoes and told me the story, and as she did, I felt the two parallel strands in her telling: awe, that a man had done so much for her in a couple hours, and how competent a man he was, to make that happen, and even how he had become neater, as a result of his promise to Carl, something she thanked Carl for whenever she saw him, explaining how every day Dad would place his briefcase in the hall closet and take off his shoes and hang his jacket — all of that, plus a kind of slippery unease, that it had not been fate after all. I thought, she told me, that the signs were pointing to him. But it turned out he'd *made* the signs! she said, poking at the photo with the tip of her finger.

Were you upset? I asked.

It was our wedding day! she said.

She turned the page. We looked at people dancing: people I knew, all younger.

But had you trusted the signs? I asked.

She shook her head, but not as in no. As in shaking her head free of the thought. She turned more pages, dusky-black paper with delicate photo corners holding the pictures in place, and she pointed out relatives I hadn't met, or Dad's dad, who'd died before I was born, holding a napkin to his face like a cowboy. The day grew darker outside, and the whitish sheer dress provided us light on the pages. I looked at the people, and grunted in response as if I'd moved on, but I was still caught back in pages before. My mother looked for signs all the time. A person would be curt to her at the supermarket and she would view it as a sign that she should be nicer to strangers. Joseph would give her an unexpected smile and she'd retrace all her actions to see why she deserved it. Once, we arrived home to a snail at the doorstep and she said it was a sign to slow down, and she took a walk around the block at a funereal pace, saying there was something in there for her if she just took her time. She came back just as vivid-faced as ever. Thank you, little snail, she buzzed, lifting it up and placing it in the cool shadows of a jasmine bush. She was always looking for unexpected guidance, and at that garage sale the world had spit up just exactly what she'd asked for, and what could be a better omen than that? So it must've been a real blow, on her wedding day, to find out that the larger hand in action was the hand she was then holding.

We turned the last few pages of the album. Grandma, in a daisy-patterned sack dress. Mom's sister Cindy, wearing jeans. Some of Dad's red-cheeked uncles.

You're in here, Mom said.

No, I said.

You are, Mom said. You and Joe. In the air. The beginning of you, she said. She kissed the top of my head.

On the last page, as if to underline her comment, the kiss: Dad and Mom, pressed close together, layers of that ghostly dress blowing around him. We looked at it for a while.

Do you still have that footstool? I asked.

We crept into the garage, flicking on the light. In the coldness of the room, with its old stone floor and whistling window, Mom and I rummaged through piles, setting aside crates and boxes. After a half-hour or so, wedged behind a rake and a series of brooms, I found it: a moth-eaten sun-bleached peach velvet seat, stretched over a shiny brown wicker crisscross-patterned stool. Look! I said, brushing my hand over the top. Mom, knee-deep in a pile of baby toys, eyed it the way you eye a person you haven't seen in a long time when the last exchange was complicated. I can build you a better one, she said, dubiously. I patted the seat. This one, I said. The velvet was soft. I sidestepped the piles and took it for my room. Furniture.

14

There are heightened years. One was nine. Another twelve. A third, seventeen. My brother used graph paper to make shapes out of sequences; I saw those years as a trio, but not one I wanted to map out on those small graph-paper squares. I didn't know how I would label that graph, what the x and y axes might be called. Instead, they cluster together in my mind, like a code to a padlock that might hang on a locker. It's a confounding mechanism, but with all three numbers in place, lined up just right on the notched mark, something in the arch clicks, and releases.

In the movies, an affair is often indicated by spying at motel rooms, or lipstick marks dashed on a white collar. I was twelve when I sat down to a family dinner of roast beef and potatoes, on a cool February evening, and got such a wallop of guilt and romance in my first mouthful that I knew, instantly, that she'd met someone else. Thick waves of it, in the meat and the homemade sour cream and the green slashes of carefully chopped chives. Oh! I said. I drank down a full glass of water. Ah! my father said, letting out an end-of-day sigh. Roast beef, he murmured, patting his belt. My favorite. I got up to find some factory catsup to help me out, while Joseph turned pages of his book and Mom poured herself a glass of wine. Like it? she said. I glanced over at her. It fit, too: she'd been looking better lately, dressing up more, a little happier, wearing patterned headbands with her ponytail, bracelets on both arms. And things, in general, were in a new flux: Joseph had applied to colleges and was hoping to move out of the house and into the dorm room at Caltech he wanted to share with George. Mom talked often about how much she would miss him, but he didn't really respond, and whenever a box arrived for any kind of package delivery, regular or Grandma's, Joseph would empty it and then squirrel it away and begin to put things in it. He was half packed already, months in advance. If he could've eaten dinner in his room, he would've, but our father insisted we sit together at the table.

I read a study, Dad said, flaring his napkin into his lap. Families that eat dinner together are happier families, he said.

I think those families also talk to each other, I said.

Mom, behind us, spooning up a vegetable, laughed.

It was true: our dinners, always at the table, framed by floral-print kitchen curtains and the rising steam off casserole dishes, were almost always silent in those days unless Mom felt like filling us in on the latest news and gossip in carpentry. Dad didn't talk much about work: I leave work at work! was his mantra. Of course, right after dinner he'd put his dish in the sink and go into their bedroom to make calls, and he'd work, often, until ten or eleven unless I knocked lightly on his door to deliver the name of an upcoming TV drama like a fisherman's lure for a reluctant tuna. Even as young as ten, if I whispered the name of the show with enough pull, I could get him to put aside his stack of papers and wander in to watch. If I was quiet enough, he wouldn't send me to bed. We colluded in this way: as long as I didn't announce that I was a kid, he wouldn't rise up as a parent, and for an hour, we could both have a little respite from our roles.

He only liked the medical dramas. The law shows made him crabby.

At dinner, as part of his adolescence, Joseph had taken a liking to reading and eating, so he generally brought a book to the table which he would spread in his lap and peer at between bites. Often a textbook, sometimes a thriller. Both parents had given up trying to stop him, because when, previously, they had wrenched a book out of his hands, he had stared into space so disconcertingly it made the rest of us feel like putting a bag over his head. Sometimes, if he didn't have a book, to occupy Joseph's eyes I would plant a cereal-box side panel in front of him, and his eyes would slide over and attach to the words, as if they could not do anything but roam and float in the air until words and numbers anchored them back to our world. By the time he was seventeen, he must've memorized the vitamin balances in various raisin-and-oat cereals, and if I'd asked him what percentage of niacin one might find in a single serving of Cheerios, I would not have been surprised if he'd been able to spout the numbers as precisely as his own height and weight.

On this night, he was hunched over, reading the Caltech general information pamphlet about campus for probably the twentieth time. He didn't read the course catalogue but seemed far more interested in the dorms. Mom refilled her glass of wine. She caught me watching her, and winked.

I didn't talk at the table because I was busy surviving the meal. After the incident in the ER, I no longer wanted to advertise my experience to anyone. You try, you seem totally nuts, you go underground. There's a kind of show a kid can do, for a parent — a show of pain, to try to announce something, and in my crying, in the desperate, blabbering, awful mouth-clawing, I had hoped to get something across. Had it come across, any of it? Nope.

I had been friendly when I was eight; by twelve, fidgety and preoccupied. I kept up my schoolwork and threw a ball when I could. My mouth — always so active, alert — could now generally identify forty of fifty states in the produce or meat I ate. I had taken to tracking those more distant elements on my plate, and each night, at dinner, a U.S. map would float up in my mind as I chewed and I'd use it to follow the nuances in the parsley sprig, the orange wedge, and the baked potato to Florida, California, and Kansas, respectively. I could sometimes trace eggs to the county. All the while, listening to my mother talk about carpentry, or spanking the bottle of catsup. It was a good game for me, because even though it did command some of my attention, it also distracted me from the much louder and more difficult influence of the mood of the foodmaker, which ran the gamut. I could be half aware of the conversation, cutting up the meat, and the rest of the time I was driving truck routes through the highways of America, truck beds full of yellow onions. When I went to the supermarket with my mother I double-checked all my answers, and by the time I was twelve, I could distinguish an orange slice from California from an orange slice from Florida in under five seconds because California's was rounder-tasting, due to the desert ground and the clear tangy water of far-flung irrigation. This all kept me very busy. I had little to add to the conversation.

But my mother would talk. Once she sat down, she would take a couple sips of wine to warm up, and the rest of us would lean in as she filled the space. We were grateful, for the distraction of her. We could float in and out of her speeches, her hand light on the curved neck of the wine bottle. She told us everything about the carpentry co-op, which had managed to hold and even extend her interest; her skills had advanced fast in four years, and she talked about cabinetry, and cutting rabbets, and of the various pitfalls and triumphs involved in ripping a board with a table saw. Of the textural differences between cedar and spruce. Of the mortise, the dowel rack, the transom. She told us about all of the other carpenters, and her opinions of each one, and it was in this way, while I was desperately exploring the distant subtleties of the roast beef, trying to figure out if it was from central California or southern Oregon, that I stumbled across the source of her affair.

Bobbie, Mom said, does *not* do her share of clean-up.

Amber, she muttered, is a fine craftsman but no visionary.

Larry! she said, voice lifting in a curl, put up the new group assignment:

Desks, she murmured, as if she were talking about roses.

I'd been half listening, sawing off a new piece of the roast beef, still warm and savory and swirling with feeling, beef from Oregon, I'd decided, raised by organic farmers, when the curl-up in her voice matched what was in my mouth. Larry, spoke the roast beef. Larry. I chewed and chewed.

Who's Larry? I asked, taking a sip of water.

Joseph turned a page of his pamphlet. Dad made neat cuts into his potato.

Larry? Mom said, fixing round eyes on me.

Larry, I said. Is he a regular?

He's co-op president, she said, shifting in her chair, and no one who had any listening skills could've mistaken the glimpse of pride in her voice.

Ah, I said. President. I spit a bit of gristle into my napkin.

How's the beef?

Fine, I said. Oregon?

I think so, she said. Did you see the wrapper?

No, I said.

We all voted for president, she said, pushing a row of bracelets up her arm. She said it the way a young girl with a crush tries to slip details into a conversation, to prolong the topic without too much emphasis or spotlight. No wonder she'd stayed. Joseph drank a long sip of juice. Dad mopped up his plate with the soft interior of a dinner roll. By then, I'd plowed through enough of the meat to get by, so I got up and went to the pantry where I found a half-eaten cylinder of stale Pringles.

May I? I asked, placing a curved wafer on my tongue.

138

Mom sank back in her chair. Teenagers, she sighed.

After a few minutes, Dad cleared his plate and excused himself. Joseph returned to his room, where he was working on some homework about electromagnetics. Mom ran a sponge over the counters. After I'd bussed the rest of the table, I wrapped up the remaining roast beef in plastic and put it in the refrigerator for some adultery sandwiches the next day.

I just have to run some errands, Mom said, as the dishwasher began its chugging wash cycle. She said it to the air, as a throwaway: Dad and Joseph had long ago left, but I was just done cleaning, standing in the doorway, and the words fell to me. Something small and fragile punctured, inside my throat. Where? I said. Just to get some materials for my desk project, she said, kissing my cheek. Can I come? I asked. Sorry, Rosebud, she said. You have homework. See you in a couple hours! as she sailed out the door.

15

We still got regular packages of household items from Grandma, slowly mailing her life away in Washington State. They came more frequently now, almost every other week, and in the last one she'd sent me a half-used bar of soap. I didn't want to use it up, so I put it in a drawer.

She'd started good — those two-tone towels, old-fashioned glass paperweights, even a toy bear — but she seemed to grow more bitter over time, and the items deteriorated until we were opening boxes containing a baggie of batteries, the silver backings of a pair of earrings, a half-checked-off laminated grocery list which made my father twitch. The latest box was in the living room, nudged against the red brick fireplace. A couple years back, I'd asked my mother why Grandma didn't ever visit in person. Mom bent her head, thinking, zipping the scissors along the narrow center line of the brown box tape.

Grandma doesn't like to travel, she said.

Then why don't we go see her? I asked, popping open the flaps.

Grandma doesn't like guests, Mom said.

I made some kind of questioning peep, and Mom ran a finger lightly over the raw end of the scissor blade.

Your grandmother, she sighed, was raised with seven siblings. So, when she moved into her own household, she wanted quiet.

What do you mean? I asked.

She put down the scissors and scooted closer. Picked up my hand. Look at your pretty nails, she said.

Were you quiet? I said.

She laid my hand on top of hers.

I tried to be, she said. She used to call me garbage truck when I asked for too many things.

She put her cheek down to rest on our matched hands and closed her eyes. She was wearing a new eye shadow, pale pink on her brow bone, and she looked like a flower resting there. How much I wanted to protect her, her frail eyelids, streaked with glimmer. I put a hand lightly on her hair.

That's mean, I said.

Her lids fluttered. After a few seconds, she sat up and folded the box flaps back fully. She didn't look inside. All yours, baby, she said. I mean Rose, sorry. Take whatever you'd like.

That evening of her errands, I settled down with the new box. In this load, we had a diminished pad of pale-green Post-its, a book on the history of Oregon with a broken binding, and a bag of crackers. I ate a couple. Stale. Kentucky. I filched the Post-its for my room, and put the rest in the garage next to the bulk of Grandma's other mailings, wedging it all onto a shelf next to a jar of jam coated in mold that my mother did not want to refrigerate. The brown box was in good shape, so I lugged it over to the hall outside Joseph's door. New box, I said, rapping on his door. Within minutes, when I walked by again, it had been absorbed into his room.

I still felt upset about the roast beef, so I put in a call to Eliza Greenhouse, my old lunchtime friend with the razor-straight bangs, to ask about the history homework. While it rang, I ripped fringes into the pad of paper by the phone, and when she picked up, someone was screaming in the background. Sorry, she said, laughing. My little sister is having a tickle fight with my dad, she said.

Are you serious? I said.

Stop it! she called past the phone, slapping at someone.

We talked about school for a little while and I tore the fringes into scraps, and after we hung up, my own house felt especially vast. The foundation ticked and settled. All things cleaned and put away. I stood over the trash can and dribbled the torn paper bits out of my fists. That took four minutes. I thought about calling George just to say hi, but I wasn't sure what a person might say after that, so I left the phone and went into the TV room. My father was sitting on the sofa, reading a newspaper article, his feet wiggling away on the ottoman. He wiggled those feet so often it was like we had a pet in the room.

What are you watching? I asked.

Nothing, he said. He pulled a red leather ledger off a bookshelf, in arm's reach, and opened it to rows and columns of numbers.

That one soccer-ball drawing spree had been the most eager I had ever seen my father about fatherhood. I'd glimpsed a little me in his eyes then, inhabiting the pupil, sitting next to him in Brazil at the World Cup finals, drinking a beer. But when I'd drawn the faces on the soccer balls, like a TV blinking off, the little me in his eyes had blacked out.

But, Rose, he'd said, holding up the latest eyelashed soccer drawing, why?

Beer is gross, I said, leaving the room.

Still, regardless of his general lack of ability in the paternal realm, my father was a very decent man. He worked for middle-money law so he did not have to screw the little guy, and he studied the books hard because he wanted to do his part correctly and well. He made a good salary but he did not flaunt it. He'd been raised in Chicago proper by a Lithuanian Jewish mother who had grown up in poverty, telling stories, often, of extending a chicken to its fullest capacity, so as soon as a restaurant served his dish, he would promptly cut it in half and ask for a to-go container. Portions are too big anyway, he'd grumble, patting his waistline. He'd only give away his food if the corners were cleanly cut, as he believed a homeless person would just feel worse eating food with ragged bitemarks at the edges — as if, he said, they are dogs, or bacteria. Dignity, he said, lifting his half-lasagna into its box, is no detail.

When we left the restaurant, he would hand the whole package, including plastic knife and fork, to a woman or man wearing an army blanket outside, at a corner on

Wilshire, or La Brea. Here, he'd say. Just please don't bless me. I watched this happen, over and over. He wanted my mother to wear nice dresses and to buy the jewelry she wanted to buy so he could take it off her. He wanted to dress and undress her. The best way I can describe it is just that my father was a fairly focused man, a smart one with a core of simplicity who had ended up with three highly complicated people sharing the household with him: a wife who seemed raw with loneliness, a son whose gaze was so unsettling people had to shove cereal boxes at him to get a break, and a daughter who couldn't even eat a regular school lunch without having to take a fifteen-minute walk to recover. Who were these people? I felt for my dad, sometimes, when we'd be watching the TV dramas together, and I could see how he might long for the simple life in the commercials, and how he, more than any of us, had had a shot at that life.

The one unexpected side of him — beyond his choice of our mother, who really did not seem like a likely match at all — was his incredible distaste for hospitals. Beyond distaste: he loathed them. When driving through a part of town with a hospital, he would take a longer route, us-

145

ing meandering ineffective side streets to avoid even passing by.

The story went that when Joe and I were born Dad couldn't even enter the lobby. Mom had struggled out of the car and checked into Cedars-Sinai, a lovely hospital, a hospital with money, about twenty or thirty blocks from our house. After Dad parked he located the maternity ward, called up, found the number of her room, and asked the harried nurse for the exact location of Mom's window. When the nurse wouldn't tell him, he called back repeatedly, every minute, until she yelled it into the phone: South Side! Eighth Floor! Third Window From Left! Now Stop Fucking Calling! after which he promptly dialed up a local florist to send the nurse a gorgeous bouquet of tulips and roses, one that arrived long before Joseph did.

The same determination and competence that had led him to conjure up a made-to-order footstool meant he was settled right outside the perfect window for hours, staring up, but the limitations this time were far less appealing. During the hours of labor, Mom pushing and pushing, her best friend, Sharlene, cheering her on, Dad waited outside on the sidewalk. There he stayed, for the eight hours needed for Joe, and the six for me, pacing. He chatted with pedestrians. He did jumping jacks. Apparently, for my birth, he brought a crate, and sat on it for long hours reading a mystery until the parking cop told him to move.

Mom told the story, even though Dad would get embarrassed. She told the story fairly often. For Joseph's birth, she said, she was in there all day long; when she was done, she shuffled to the window in her torn hospital gown and held the screaming little baby up. Dad was just a small figure on the sidewalk but he saw her right away, and when he glimpsed the blue-blanketed blob, he jumped up and down. He waved and hooted. My son, my son! he called to all the cars driving by. Mom dripped blood onto the floor. Dad lit up a cigar, passed out extras to pedestrians.

16

After I talked to Eliza, after my mother had left to go on her errands, I parked myself on the other side of the sofa, in the TV room. My father held that red leather ledger in his lap, and he was inputting numbers into new columns. The TV muted across the room. For a while, I just sat and watched him.

Yes? he said, after a few minutes. May I help you?

No, I said.

He had a striking forehead, my father: long with a slight slope at the hairline that lent him an air of officiality. His hair — thick, black, streaked with gray — gripped closely to the top of the forehead, making a clear and assured arch. He looked like the head of a corporation.

Just the previous night, George had been over for dinner and had started asking my father questions about his time in high school. That my father had ever been to high school was funny, and that he was willing to talk about it? Shocking. Somehow, with George there, asking, lightly, the tight box of Dadness was open for looking. I was the lead in my high-school play, Dad said, sipping his water. I dropped my fork on the floor. What? Oh sure, Dad said. Everyone did it, he said. A musical? George asked. Of course, Dad said. Even Mom laughed. Dad filled his mouth with yam. What musical? I asked, and we all waited while he went through the process of chewing, and swallowing, and dabbing with his napkin, ending in the new word *Brigadoon*.

Who was he? That night, the romance in the roast beef had so excluded him, even as he ate it, every last bite of it, and maybe for that reason, he just seemed a little more approachable than usual. I leaned closer, from my end of the couch.

Yes? he said, from his seat. Rose?

Hi, I said.

He put down his pencil.

Don't you have homework?

Yes.

He raised an eyebrow. And why don't you go do that?

Can I bring it in here?

He coughed, a little, into his hand. If

149

you're quiet, he said.

I ran and grabbed my notebook and textbook. While he worked on the details of his schedule and budget, I did California history on my side of the couch, dutifully answering the questions at the back of the chapter before I'd read the chapter. It was so easy to locate the sentence referenced in the question, and I plugged in the appropriate lines like a good little lab rat, looking up occasionally to see the muted actors arguing on-screen, their eyes emphatic. We worked in silence together. With him sitting there, lightly writing those numbers with his slim mechanical pencil, I seemed to get my work done about twice as fast as usual.

Dad? I said, looking up, after writing in the five reasons that the gold rush built up the Californian economy.

Yes?

Where'd Mom go?

On errands.

When will she be back?

Soon, he said. I imagine by ten, at the latest.

Dad? I said.

He raised his eyebrows again. Yes, Rose?

Never mind, I said. Nothing.

He continued his work. I finished up my assignment and went ahead to the next chapter, since our teacher did not believe in homework variety and gave us the identical task for each week. The clock ticked along.

After another while, I looked up again. Across from me, in the red ledger, my father had written many neat new numerical rows. It seemed he was getting more work done too.

Can I ask you a question? I said.

He kept his eyes on the page, deep at the base of the latest column. Then laid down the pencil.

Knock yourself out, he said.

The couch creaked as he resettled himself. It was an open doorway. I could hardly remember the last time I'd sat across from my father without anyone else nearby. I really had no idea what to ask, so I just blurted out the first thing that came into my head.

Did you ever know something? I said.

Excuse me?

I took a breath. Sorry, I said. I mean, did you ever know something you weren't supposed to know? I asked.

He tilted his head. What do you mean?

Like — did you ever walk down a hall and accidentally overhear a secret?

He thought about it, for a minute. No, he said. Why?

What if you did?

I'd keep the secret, he said.

I shifted around in my seat. Okay, I said. Okay. Or, just do you have any special skills?

He chuckled a little. No, he said.

I didn't mean that you don't, I mean —

No, really, he said. He turned to me fully, and his face was friendly. I hit the mean all through law school, he said. I scored exactly in the fiftieth percentile on the LSAT. Five oh. He nodded at himself, pleased.

I closed my textbook.

But you were in *Briga* — I said.

Doon, he said. I was a perfectly average singer, he said. Even the teacher said so.

You hate hospitals, I said.

So?

I don't know, I said, pulling at the corner of my textbook. Why do you hate them?

That's not a special skill, he said.

No, I said, waiting.

He re-shaped the pillow at his back. Show previews skimmed across the screen, advertising our favorite high-intensity medical program, which was coming up soon.

I just don't like sick people, he said.

Is it because you feel something?

What?

Like you feel their sickness, or something?

He scratched his nose. He looked at me a

little funny. No, he said. I just don't like them. How do you know about that anyway?

Was he kidding? The TV switched to commercials, of dancing kids on tree-lined streets.

Mom tells our birth stories all the time, I said. How come you can watch it on TV?

He waved his hand at the screen. Oh, that's different, he said. That's fun.

It's in a hospital, I said.

It's a set, he said.

I think it's set in a real hospital, I said.

Doesn't matter, he said. No smell.

But what if *you* get sick? I said.

I never get sick, he said.

He picked up the remote. Twirled and twisted it, on the sofa. The questions were drumming in me, piling on each other, and I dug deeper into my end of the sofa and tried to remember how George did it, at the dinner table. Softly, as if the answer was not dire. As if the question was a seed placed a few feet in front of a curious bird.

You never get sick? I said, after a pause.

Dad glanced back over. Wiggled his feet.

I just have healthy genes, he said, lifting his shoulders. Always have. All that good Lithuanian chicken.

We stared ahead, together. I picked at the corner of my textbook where the lamination

153

had broken open, revealing the soft layers of brown cardboard.

Would you visit if I have to go to the hospital sometime? I said.

He flapped a hand at me. You're a healthy kid, he said.

But just in case, I said. If it's serious?

Hasn't been, he said.

But if it was?

He looked over at the clock, blinking greenly at the base of the TV. In two minutes our show would come on.

I, he said.

His eyes on the clock.

Might, he said.

His hand rested in the fold of the red ledger. Colors scattered across the screen.

There was nothing much else to say, so we watched the series of car commercials flying by. According to the ads, the first car made you manly, the second made you rich, the last one made you funny.

I pointed out a zippy yellow hatchback driven by a clown. I didn't really like it so much one way or another, but I just needed something to do. Dad peered at the picture. Then he turned to a blank page in his ledger, jotted down the name of the car, and wrote my name, with a precise little arrow pointing to it.

You're not so far from sixteen, he said.

He pressed the mute button, and the room filled with sound. Horns, voice-overs, snatches of songs. It was like we were exchanging codes, on how to be a father and a daughter, like we'd read about it in a manual, translated from another language, and were doing our best with what we could understand. Thanks, Dad, I said. The commercials ended, and the show began with a couple of nurses bustling through an ER. A man had a seizure on the tile. Someone yelled through the intercom. I got pulled into the story, and so at first I didn't hear when he said my name at the break.

For you, Rose? he was saying. For your birth?

When I turned, his face was closer than usual, and I could see the slight strain in the lines above his eyebrows. The quiet urgency in whatever he wanted to tell me.

Yes? I said.

His hand hovered in the air.

For you, he said, I brought binoculars.

Mom came home right as the TV show ended. Ten p.m., on the dot. We heard the car in the driveway, and then the key in the lock, and she breezed into the room with a shine to her cheeks I couldn't look at. I looked at my father instead, to see if he saw any of it, but he was half caught in the images flashing by of another car, a fourth car, one that made you perceptive, a car he probably should buy, and he saluted my mother from his spot on the couch and asked how the errands had gone.

Great, she said. Fine. Rose, you're still up? How was the show?

What errands did you run?

All sorts, she said, brushing a wisp of hair out of her eyes.

Where are the bags? I said.

Oh, she said, waving her hand. In the car, she said.

She winked at me again.

Time for bed, I said, before she could.

Come sit, said my father to my mother, patting a couch cushion.

I left the room.

17

That night, as I burrowed into the sheets, my mother still tucking in sheets better than anyone, I closed my eyes and went through my usual routine, which involved thanking God, or the mysterious bounty of the world, for the vending machine at school, for the sad lady with the hairnet who still worked at the cafeteria, for the existence of George, and for whoever ate my mother's cookies at the co-op. It was my usual routine, so it took a second for the change to sink in, and then I shook awake, pressed into my pillow: Larry, rising, *Larry,* the likely man who saved me from eating her cookies, the man I'd been praying a thank you to for the last almost four years as Mom brought tray after tray of baked goods to the studio. Joseph! I said, knocking on the wall we shared. I said it loud. I knocked again, rapping my hand hard on the wall. To wake him up, from whatever deep state of study he was in. I kept knocking.

After ten minutes, he strode into the room in his pajamas. What, he said.

He was tall, like Dad, but skinny, unlike Dad. He did not care about soccer. His eyes were caverns. And I could see how he was leaving, how he was halfway out the door. Still, as he stood there, arms crossed, hair flat, grim, tense, I remember it as a wash of relief, that he was still there, tangible, able to come in, annoyed, to be in my room. It was an antidote to the feeling that nobody was home.

18

My brother had taken to disappearing. Not in the way of a more usual adolescent boy, who is nowhere to be found and then arrives home drunk, with grass-stained knees and sweat-pressed hair, at two in the morning. No. It would be the middle of the afternoon, airy and calm, and Joseph would be home and then not home. I would hear him packing up those college boxes in his room, shuffling, rustling, and then I'd hear nothing.

He was scheduled to babysit me on Sunday night, just a few days after the roast beef dinner, while our parents attended a law office party downtown. It was my father's annual post-holiday work party, this year located at the Bonaventure, a pole-shaped silver hotel Joseph had always admired for its outside elevator, one that rode up and down the building like a zipper. He appreciated the vacuum closure inside the booth; I liked the rotating bar at the top. My mother enjoyed parties but my father dismissed them as an unpleasant job necessity, and the two of them would dress up and drive off and hold cocktails and chat while Joseph got twenty bucks for half watching antsy me.

To be babysat by my brother was basically to share the house for the course of an evening. Usually we weren't even in the same room. At twelve, I was too old for a babysitter by a lot of people's standards anyway, but it was a good way to avoid acknowledging that a lot of seventeen-year-old boys would push to go out, and my brother did not: either push, or go out. He went once with George to a rock concert and came home in a taxi after an hour, alone. Too much, he said, when Mom asked.

I asked my mother if I could do something else that night, go to a friend's house or something, but she said she liked paying Joseph to watch me. Please? she said, touching my hair. It makes him feel like a big brother, she said. But he doesn't *watch* me, I said, kicking at the wall. She took out her wallet from her purse. How about I pay you too? she said, slipping me a twenty-dollar bill.

■ ■ ■ ■

That Sunday, I spent the afternoon watching TV. I rolled up my twenty-dollar bill and tucked it inside a jewelry-box drawer. I played twenty-five games of solitaire, and I lost twenty-four of the times, until I got so sick of the deck I took it outside and made the entire suit of diamonds into a streamlined fleet of mini paper-plastic airplanes. I put the final touches on my current-events modern world presentation, and then stared into space for a while, outside on the grass, surrounded by thirteen snub-nosed diamond-planes, crashed. I felt over-stuffed with information. Over the course of several packed days, I'd tasted my mother's affair and had the conversation with my father about skills. I was not feeling very good about any of it — I felt a little closer to my father, yes, but if I was dying in the hospital, he would probably wave a flag from the parking lot. I felt relieved that my mother had another person to give her cookies to, but that person tore up the family structure and my father had no clue. And who could I tell? I loved my brother, but relying on him was like closing a hand around air. I soaked up my time with George, still, but

161

he was stepping ahead into a future that did not include me.

Sometimes, at school, across the dirt quad that separated the junior high from the high school, I'd see George with an arm slung casually around a girl, talking into her hair as if it was the most normal thing on earth to do. Not only were his eyebrows growing into proportion with his face, but he seemed to be progressing internally at a regular rate as well. Eliza, too — when I went over to her house after school, we flipped through fashion magazines and tested lip glosses. There, we were becoming teenagers; at my house, I pulled a shoebox of dolls and stuffed animals and Grandma's objects out from under my bed. Beheaded cherubs, old overly bent Barbies, broken jewelry. Eliza went along with it, agreeably, but she made me swear I would never breathe a word to anyone at school. If you tell about this, she said once, her eyes wide, brushing down the long plastic hair of a Barbie, I will *bury* you, she said. I'd nodded, mildly. It seemed reasonable to me. We were, after all, almost thirteen. With naked dolls in hand, or even the occasional doll-baby, it sometimes felt like we were pedophiles.

My mother had bought a new dress for the

work party, and she modeled it for me as my father got ready, the lavender pleated skirt skimming the air. Very pretty, I'd told her, in the mirror. Dad will love it, I said.

You okay with tonight? she said, standing in my doorway.

Sure, I said. I got paid.

Oh, and please don't tell about that, she said, lowering her voice. Usually the babysit-*tee* doesn't get any money.

I looked up at her. You're kidding, I said.

No, she said, with total sincerity. It's a unique setup.

I returned my gaze to the floor of my bedroom, sorting through some of Grandma's latest: a polished brown rock, a red rhinestone bracelet with a bent clasp.

And the hotel number is on the fridge, Mom said. She swished the folds of her skirt. She seemed both fidgety and calm at the same time. The guilt in the roast beef had been like a vector pointing in one direction just barely overpowered by the vector of longing going the opposite way. I hated it; the whole thing was like reading her diary against my will. Many kids, it seemed, would find out that their parents were flawed, messed-up people later in life, and I didn't appreciate getting to know it all so strong and early.

That afternoon, the house smelled of roasted pine nuts, because she'd spent the day in the kitchen, making homemade trail mix. I made my own pretzels! she'd announced at 4 p.m., turning off the oven, whipping her hair into a fresh ponytail. I had to taste them — she had presented a few tiny warm pretzels on a plate to me with such a look of triumph and hope — and it turned out to be the food that best represented her: in every pretzel the screaming desire to make the perfect pretzel, so that the pretzel itself seemed tied up in the tightest of knots, the food form, for once, matching the content. Now, that's a pretzel all right, I'd said, chewing.

In my room, she glanced around the space, filling time, until her eyes came to rest near my bed.

Oh! Now, look at that!

Their velvet-and-wicker marriage stool served as my nightstand, pushed right up next to the bed. I'd had it for a while, but it must've slipped my mother's watch. One book fit nicely on its soft top, and I could wedge homework papers into the interwoven pattern of the base.

I like it, I said.

She walked over, pushed at the cushion. God, it's so old, she said. We should re-upholster it; I could do it at the studio, in a day. Can we? You could pick your favorite color and material —

I like it how it is, I said.

Hey, Paul, she called. Come look at this!

In the other room, Dad shut some drawers. He strode over to my doorway, with two ties around his head.

Blue? he said. Or red?

Look, she said, pointing.

At what?

Red, I said.

In the doorway, he nodded at me, almost shyly. We'd been a little friendlier with each other since the TV watching. He was decked out in a blue blazer, gold buttons winking. Her lavender dress, his red tie. It was like they had traded in their used-up models for a glamorous in-love pair.

Very nice, I said, as he pulled the blue tie off his collar and draped it on a bookshelf.

Mom pointed at the stool. Look, she said. Our daughter, the family historian.

Dad, preoccupied with straightening the red correctly, skimmed the room, but when his eye caught the stool, his face cleared. He stepped in, closer. Knelt on the floor and ran a hand over the eaten velvet.

Ah, he said. He looked over at me, still sitting and sorting on the floor. Where'd you find this?

In the garage, I said. A while back.

The moths love it, said Mom.

Dad leaned in, to smell the cushion. The peach color, now a pale beige from age. He felt the structure of the wicker base, which was still in good shape.

Mom wants to re-upholster it, I said.

Oh no! he said. He shook his finger at the air. Never! he said. Hey, he said, to me; you asked about special skills? He rose, to stand. This was my special skill, he said. Making this happen.

Mom crossed her arms in the door frame. The holes in it! she said. What special skills?

He went and put an arm around her. It's our original anniversary, he said, kissing her cheek. Rose, you know the whole story?

I laughed. Mom laughed. She did not put an arm around him. The calm look I'd seen in her just minutes earlier had stiffened, her eye hollows deepening. Neither of them seemed to understand how things had gotten so strained — at the start of their courtship, Dad had thought Mom's lostness was a sign of her spontaneity and he let her lead the way on weekends, taking the BART around and getting off at unexpected places to buy discarded records at street fairs. Mom had thought Dad's steadiness meant he could handle and help anything, and she loved to watch him mailing his bills, studying, making his lists. All of which he still did.

At my door, my father kept his arm tight around her, but he suddenly seemed stuck there, like a person who stumbles in public and apologizes to the air.

You take good care of that, he told me, sternly, pointing at the stool.

Somebody has to, I said.

For a second, his shoulders tensed, in his blue blazer. I waved goodbye, to get them out of my room. Go to your party, I said. Have fun.

Mom fled first, in a circle of purple. Bye! she called, to Joseph's room. Out we go! said Dad, too loud, as they passed, sparklingly, through the front door.

The car drove off. The house settled itself around its new number of inhabitants. Outside, the day was ending, sky a middle blue. I flipped on the light and kept myself busy for an hour, zipping the doll gals around in boats made of slippers, marrying and divorcing the stuffed animals. I had stolen Grandma's chipped teacup from the kitchen cabinet, and I used it as a friendly companion to the stuffed flamingo, who had

167

an unusual love of tea. The polished brown rock was best friends with the beheaded Barbie. The blue tie a river to swim upon. After a while, even I grew bored, and embarrassed. I felt half five years old and half forty. It was too dark to throw tennis balls around the neighborhood, the only activity I knew that seemed to fit my age. In the kitchen, I dawdled around, eating a piece of factory bread coated with factory margarine, opening and closing some drawers. Thought about calling Eliza but remembered she was out. I found my way to Joseph's door. I knocked. No answer. I knocked again.

Usually on Sunday nights, Eliza went to the movies with her parents. She got to pick. She said they also all enjoyed sharing a large popcorn, with salt and butter flavoring. The popcorn would reside in Eliza's lap, and both parents would dip in as they flanked her, as if she were the sole precious book between their sturdy bookends.

No answer at the door. I knocked again.

I made a gagging sound. I let out a half-strangled cough. Emergency! I said. Choking!

Nothing.

The air felt much too quiet in the hallway, bordered by the walls covered in framed family portraits. Cars puttered by outside, heading south to park near Melrose. Nightgown elastic cut into my arms. I was restless, and tired, and the tension of the week had built up in me and I felt my usual pool of politeness draining away. What was the point? My mother had a second life, my father revered the long-ago past, soon George would eat at the dorm instead of our house, and my usual obedience felt up. Done. For once, I ignored the *Keep Out* sign written in seventeen different languages, and the black-inked skull and crossbones which usually gave me nightmares, and I put a hand right on the doorknob and turned.

It was probably eight o'clock. The sun, down. The house was dark, because our father, along with cutting his restaurant meals in half, also believed strongly in only lighting the room one was inside. Something to do with bills. I, in contrast, enjoyed sitting in a fully lit house when they were away, and I was minutes from running through the rooms and switching everything on. Light is good company, when alone; I took my comfort where I found it, and the warmest yellow bulb in the living-room lamp had become a kind of radiant babysitter all its own. But that night I wanted to locate my assigned guardian, and I hadn't given up yet, and against my usual instincts, I pushed in. The door creaked open. Cr-rrk. Had he rusted up the hinges deliberately? No lock in place, and no light on inside — only a crossbeam through his back door, from our neighbor's backyard lamp-pole, angling downward to the floor like a shaft of moonlight. It was a cave, in the house, a basement that had risen. I stepped inside. My heart picked up a beat. No movement, no stirring. Piles of books on the floor. A to-go container of romaine lettuce on his desk. He wasn't in the room, but it felt, faintly, like he was in it. I peeked in the closet. His shirts! His shoes! Bare hangers; umbrellas. Joe? I said, trembling. Are you here? All silence. Empty but not empty. Was someone watching me? The walls? Joe? I whispered.

It was so eerie a feeling that I ran out of the room and ran around the house, flipping on lights, calling his name, opening closet doors, calling, turning on every switch I could find — over the oven, TV on, flashlights on, closet lightbulb pulled, starting to get actually scared, calling — and when I roared back to the now wildly yellow-lit hall outside our rooms, there he was, tall, leaning, looking like someone had socked him in the face. I'm here, he said, thinly. You don't have to shout. But where WERE you? I asked, still too loud. Sssh, he said. Nowhere. Just busy. But *where?* I said, jumping a little, in place, and the glare of the hall lights revealed the bags under his eyes and the lines in his cheeks, a face too lived in for someone who had not yet lived all that long.

I was in your room, he said.

I squinted at him. What? I said. He hated my room, all its girl things. Really? Are you okay? Why?

He took a long moment to scratch the side of his nose.

I needed a pink Pegasus pen, he said.

It took me a minute to hear him. A blankness, while we stared at each other. The words disintegrating around us. Pin. Nk. Peg-a. Sus. Pen. Then he made some kind of sneezing snort sound, and we both started to laugh. I held my stomach. He sat on the floor, and laughed and laughed. My stomach cramped. I pulled at the carpet, to stop. I was laughing through mouth and nose at the same time. I can't breathe! I said once, and then we both dropped into laughing again. His: low and almost silent and throaty. I hugged my body to the wall, to calm down, and when he let out a raggedy sigh, I exploded for another ten minutes.

Stop! I said, wheezing, pressed into the wall.

When we finally stopped, spent, coughing, Joseph lifted him self slowly up off the floor. As if each joint and bone was more weighted than usual. With deliberate steps, he walked through the rooms and turned off every light, one by one. I listened from the hallway as he clicked the switch on each flashlight. As he pulled the metal chain in the hall closet to ink out the bare bulb. Across the house, blocks of light darkened, like a miniature city going to sleep in neighborhoods.

Something inexplicable had exhausted us both, so by 9 p.m. we were in our beds, asleep.

19

I didn't hear my parents come home. Monday morning broke in with my father's usual honk, and I stirred in my bed, and listened. Quiet from my parents' bedroom, where Mom slept in. A bird outside, calling a trill across the neighborhood.

From the kitchen, I could hear the sounds of breakfast, as performed by my brother: a crash of cereal into a bowl, a sloshy pouring of milk.

I pulled myself out of bed, and found Joseph in his usual spot at the kitchen table.

Hey, I said.

He kept chewing.

At the base of the dishwasher, Mom's high black heels tilted against each other, kicked off her feet. Her jewelry glinted in a little pile inside one of the shoes. Most likely this meant she'd stayed up after they returned, to make tea and sit in the orange-striped chair and stare out the window.

I opened the refrigerator and looked inside. The evening with Joseph replayed itself in my mind. A little chuckle bubbled up.

While serving myself an orange juice, made from Florida oranges, picked by workers plagued with financial worries, fruit piled in trucks that drove overnight across the country, I sat down at the kitchen table across from my brother and started a monologue about the previous night that ended in the retelling of the pink Pegasus pen joke.

While toasting and eating my waffle, the circle split into small indented squares formed in a factory in Illinois, each square equipped to hold the maple syrup collected and boiled by a hardworking family in Vermont who had issues with drug and alcohol addiction, I made the joke again. I made it at the sink, while we were washing our dishes. It was my job, as annoying younger sibling, to beat that joke to death. Each time, I spluttered the sentence out and held my body still, waiting for that tickle in my throat, the uncontrollable overtake.

Joseph didn't laugh once. His mouth a line, while he watched me slap the table.

It was a one-time thing, he told me, going to grab his backpack.

■ ■ ■ ■

Our respective schools extended down the same block of Wilshire, so we rode the bus together as usual, several rows apart. Outside, men stood on a billboard ledge pushing up rolls of paper to construct the shape of a woman's giant chin. Clusters of teenagers stood at a fence around Fairfax High. I'd stopped waving to passengers in cars by then — I'd grown suspicious of people and all the complications of interior lives — so I sat and watched and rode and thought, and as soon as the bus doors opened, we all rolled out the door and split apart like billiard balls.

In third-period Spanish, I settled into my seat behind Eliza. As our teacher started to hand back last week's quizzes, I moved in close, to whisper in her ear.

I had an *amaz*ing weekend with my brother, I said. We laughed so hard I nearly threw up, I said. *Vómitos.*

She turned to smile at me, distantly. She had an iridescent star sticker attached high on her cheekbone.

How was your weekend? I asked.

While our teacher roamed the aisles, Eliza's eyes moved past my face and out the

175

open doorway. The late-morning sun was turning the hedges outside the classroom a steely helicopter green. When I went over to her house, her father, on breaks from doing stock-market work at home, would sometimes bake a batch of cupcakes to clear his head. Each little chocolate muffin packet burning through with fullness.

We were thinking of a movie, Eliza said. But everyone was tired, so we stayed home and played Yahtzee instead, she said. She yawned, out the doorway. Excuse me, she said. It was fun, she said.

I drew a star on my desk, in pencil, and then crossed it out with slash marks. Mrs. Ogilby returned my quiz. B plus. I'd missed the past-perfect conjugation of "to go." Everyone in my quiz was going in the present.

Was that guy George there? Eliza asked me, sliding her quiz into her notebook pocket.

Where?

At your house? she said. With your brother?

I sat in, closer. George? You mean George Malcolm? I said. He's over all the time, I said.

She sighed. Her cheek glinted in the light. He's like my second brother, I said.

Except I could marry him.

Eliza ran a finger along the pencil moat on my desk. He seems nice, she said.

He hates Yahtzee, I said.

What?

Just he said that once, I said. He finds it despicable.

Excuse me? Rose? He said what?

Nada, I said, when the teacher glared at us both.

Going, going, going, I said.

My presentation was due in fifth-period current-events class. We were supposed to write on something in modern society that we valued that was not around in the time of our grandparents, and then read a paragraph or two aloud. I went after a girl talking about the advantages of mountain biking, and before a guy who had a whole three-part cardboard presentation on the treatment of malaria.

I cleared my throat. Ahem, I said. My paper is on Doritos, I said.

The teacher nodded. Nutrition is important, she said.

This is not about nutrition, I said.

I held up my page.

What is good about a Dorito, I said, in full voice, is that I'm not supposed to pay

177

attention to it. As soon as I do, it tastes like every other ordinary chip. But if I stop paying attention, it becomes the most delicious thing in the world.

I popped open a supersize bag — my one prop — and passed it around the room. Instructed everyone to take a chip.

Bite in! I said.

The sound of crackling. Eliza giggled in the back. Her parents did not allow her to eat Doritos. I was her drug dealer, in this way.

See? I said. What does it taste like?

A Dorito, said a smartass in the front row.

Cheese, said someone else.

Really? I said.

They concentrated on their chips. That good dust stuff, said someone else.

Exactly, I said. That good dust stuff.

What I taste, I said, reading from my page, is what I remember from my last Dorito, plus the chemicals that are kind of like that taste, and then my zoned-out mind that doesn't really care what it actually tastes like. Remembering, chemicals, zoning. It is a magical combo. All these parts form together to make a flavor sensation trick that makes me want to eat the whole bag and then maybe another bag.

Do you have another bag? asked a skateboard guy, licking his fingers.

No, I said. In conclusion, I said, a Dorito asks nothing of you, which is its great gift. It only asks that you are not there.

I bowed a little, to the class. Eliza clapped. The same skateboard guy, reeking of pot, asked if I had any Cheetos to compare. Please? he begged. If the teacher allows it, I said, maybe we can take a quick field trip as a class to the snack machine? The class was up and at the door before she could protest. We spent fifteen minutes in a huddle, pushing all our quarters into the slots, tasting every bag available, reading unknown unpronounceable ingredients aloud. Sure, sure, said the skateboard guy, chewing. When I concentrate, it's all different, he said. He closed his eyes. Eliza hugged me three times, her hands dusted with ranch-flavor powder. We returned to the room buzzing, and after class, the teacher called me over and handed me a printout of the food pyramid, telling me I did a good job but it was important that I eat protein as a growing girl. Thank you, I said, and she dipped her head, and we both nodded in admiration at her helpfulness.

20

Joseph had a test to re-take after school, so I took the bus home by myself, stopping at the small magazine-shop on Melrose at Fairfax to buy my usual bag of chips as a celebratory finale to my paper. The streets were quiet as I strolled. Fewer cars on the road in the middle of the day. A man with a leaf blower steered clumps of grass into the gutter.

I came home to another delivery from Grandma. A long slatted box containing a gray folding chair and a refrigerator-sized box inside of which was an old bookshelf and a broken stool wrapped in newspaper. They'd all arrived together, in a delivery van.

Mom was in the kitchen, starting in on a new recipe from the newspaper.

How old is she now? I said, wandering in.

Eighty-one, Mom said, waving hello with a wooden spoon.

And what is she sitting on?

She shrugged. Beats me, she said.

She flattened the newspaper, peered at the ingredients.

Today's recipe was ripped from the Metro section, something of a southern-Italian mushroom-tomato sauce, slow-cooked, with good fruity olive oil as the base. My father loved Italian food the best, and my mother made it on days when she was feeling guilty. She'd taped the recipe to the cupboard, for easy viewing. Her eyes were creased with lack of sleep, but she was wearing a new pink lipstick and there was still a clear elevation to her mood.

Want to help? she said, as I washed my hands.

She set me up with a knife and a cutting board and a pile of green peppers. My mind still clear from the chip bags. I liked this aspect of cooking, being a distant hard-to-identify participant, all so long as I didn't compile or stir anything. Way too scary, to eat a whole meal I'd made myself, but I did enjoy the prep: chopping and dicing, mincing and paring, shredding and slicing, just attacking all these objects that dominated my days even though I knew that nothing would take away the complexity for me, nothing short of not eating them. Still: it gave me such pleasure to grate cheese, like I was killing it.

While I picked seeds out of a green pepper, Mom stirred onions in the pan and told me about the party and all the funny lawyers. She asked about school, and when I told her I didn't know what class I liked the best, she nodded. I understand, she said, bobbing her head. You have trouble picking, like me. Too many choices!

I don't know if that's it, I said, sweeping seeds into the trash. To change the subject, I told her a little about Joe's disappearance. I didn't describe anything in detail — just that during the babysit, he had vanished for twenty minutes or so and I hadn't been able to find him.

Just he was kind of gone, I said. And then, all of a sudden, he was back. It was really funny, I said.

Mom pivoted around. An eagerness crept into her face. Do you think he's sneaking out the side door? she asked, dropping her voice to a whisper.

I tossed the core of a green pepper into the trash.

Nope, I said.

Or, Rose — maybe he has a girlfriend?

I almost laughed. Um, no, I said.

She laid the wooden spoon carefully on

182

the counter. Checked the recipe on the cupboard.

Peppers?

All set, I said.

She slipped the cutting board out of the counter and scraped the bumpy squares into the pan to join the golden onions and garlic. We watched the pepper parts crackle in the oil.

She put an arm around me, our simplest exchange. I leaned against her side. Rose, she said, stroking my hair. Sweet Rose-oh-Rose, she said.

She picked up the spoon, absently pushing around the parts.

Well, she said. He is secretive, but that isn't necessarily a bad thing.

Runs in the family, I said.

She smiled at me, eyes unsure.

I rinsed and replaced the cutting board and began dicing tomatoes.

I'll take the stool, I said. From Grandma.

Do you think he has a boyfriend? she asked, hopeful.

No, I said.

I would understand if so, she said, leaning against the stovetop. I could hear her brewing, beginning to form her monologue of understanding. I think that could be very nice, she said, in a small voice.

183

Sorry, Mom, I said.

How do you know? she said. You don't know!

She turned back to the pan, to the wooden spoon. Moved around the various bits.

It's missing a leg, she said, after few minutes, into the pan. What are you going to do with a two-legged stool?

I wedged it outside, near that side door, in the narrow strip of yard that bordered the house. If placed against the outdoor wall, it functioned nicely as a half-ladder. At the next babysit, when I could still hear him poking around inside his bedroom, I tiptoed outside and climbed up the stool rungs to peek inside the little window at the top of his side door. The lights inside were out and all I could catch were shadows over shadows, and darkness, and the usual bulky shapes. It seemed he was sitting at his desk, reading, in the dark. Turning pages.

I watched him for a while, from the stool rungs. My eyes adjusted to the light. He read each page slowly, and when he was ready to turn, he slid a finger up to the top right corner, lifting it as lightly as a wing. He took such care, particularly when alone.

I went to the bathroom. Wandered around. When I returned to the stool/ladder, he wasn't there.

So preoccupied was I with trying to grab back the laughing lightness with Joseph that I did not think again about where he'd actually gone. When I ran around the house again, knocking on his door, calling his name, circling, opening doors, doing the whole routine over only to finally find him standing outside his room again, with that same unusual weightiness to his eyelids and skin, I skipped right over my former rabid curiosity and returned to the script that had led up to the laughter. I knew my part perfectly. Where was he? He'd been busy? Where? I asked if he'd been in my room, and he said yes, and I said why? and he said, in a weary voice, that he'd needed a pink Pegasus pen. It was around eight-thirty. Over a week since the first disappearance. Parents out, at another dinner. The walls, cool. Joseph, tall, his side pressed against the door frame. I could feel his effort, his playing out of the lines for me. And even I, ever ready to fake the laughing, again, forever, could hear how flat it fell, and we stood, quietly, facing each other, in the planes and stretches of dim hallway. He looked old; he was only five years older, but he seemed then like an old man, a grandpa.

Are you sick? I said.

He shook his head. I'm practicing something difficult, he said. And it tires me out.

What is it?

It's hard to explain, he said.

Oh. Can I help?

No, he said.

He rested his head against the top hinge.
Closed his eyes.

Is it illegal?

No, he said. He smiled a little.

We stood there together for a while. His
breathing deep and measured, drinking the
air in slow draughts. Those antenna-like
eyelashes and fingertips. I wondered what
he knew about the family; what he didn't
know. What family he lived in. My mind
wandered around.

Hey, I said, after a couple minutes. Could
you do something for me?

It was the first of two favors I ever asked
my brother, and although this one was far
less important, it was still one of the best
moments in my whole junior high. The next
day, at school, at lunch, while Eliza sat
cross-legged and carefully unpacked her
brown bag of joy, George turned a corner
and came walking over from the high school.
His loping, long-legged friendly walk. He'd

recently been accepted early admission at Caltech, and it was a soaring lift to see him appear from behind the brick wall that separated the two schools, striding over in his jeans like he had a reason to come over. Which he did. Which was me. He waved as he drew closer. Eliza waved back. A few other middle-schoolers watched from their spots, chewing on the split ends of plastic straws. Any kind of high-school visitation was notable, but this was better than most: by high school, George had grown into himself, and any remnants of isolated nerd-dom had been softened by his easy manner, his good teeth, his comfort with girls, his shopping choices. Lanky, smart, dignifying. He had a rubber band wound around his thumb and was twanging it like a guitar string, something he did sometimes at our house when he was sorting through an idea.

He nodded at Eliza, and then beckoned me over. We'll just be a sec, he said. Of course! she said, full of cheer, a moon sticker shining on her inner wrist like tattoo practice. George and I stood by a cement pole, and he leaned closer, voice dropping to a whisper. Joe told me to come by and see you, he said. I glowed at him. All okay? he said. All is great, I said. I just wanted to show off to Eliza, I said, and you are the

187

best show-off person I know. He grunted a little, and glanced over at Eliza, who was several feet away, watching us from under her bangs, biting into her turkey sandwich. And oh. I'd tasted that turkey sandwich before. The whole thing was just a sonata of love — the lettuce leaf, the organic tomato grown on a happy farm, even the factory mayonnaise took on such delicacy of feeling it seemed like an exquisite violin solo. It was difficult, and rude, to hate my friend so much.

When do you leave for school? I said.

Usual time, he said. Late August. I'll come visit, don't you worry.

Is your mom happy?

Oh sure, he said, twanging his thumb. She's thrilled.

I could see my brother, far in the distance, perched on a flesh-colored bench, overseeing.

Joe's watching, I said.

George let out a puff of air. Funny guy, he said. So. All okay over here?

All is fine, I said.

No bullies in the hallways?

No, I said. No bullies at all.

Any boys giving you trouble?

Not so much, I said. We smiled at each other.

You wait for a good one, okay? he said.

Okay.

Food?

Same old crap, I said.

Same, he sighed. Brave girl.

Eliza was now sorting through her three kinds of homemade cookies: chocolate chip, oatmeal, sprinkle shortbread. George's eyes started to graze over my head, to move on to other topics.

Is that enough time? he said. I should get back.

Sure, I said, bowing. That's great. Thank you so much. I patted his shoulder. Maybe you could laugh?

He laughed at the suggestion, which fulfilled it.

21

When Joseph was born, my mother's closest friend, Sharlene, the one with wavy tawny hair who'd cooked the glorious French Tunisian feasts of lamb stew and eggplant-tomato tart in their Berkeley days, showed up at the maternity ward right on time wearing a lime-green T-shirt that said *Team Baby.* Dad outside. Grandma in Washington.

Sharlene received my waddly mother like a football pass, and for a while, she was the perfect helper — brightening, in command, loving, focused — but Joseph, curled up contentedly in the warmth of the uterine sac, did not feel so motivated or timely. By the fifth hour of heated helping, Sharlene, face red, T-shirt drenched to jade, dragged herself to the pay phone in the lobby and apologized extensively to her boss at a catering company. Mom hollered obscenities so loud you could hear them down the corridors. As soon as Joseph popped his head

out, screaming, alive, bluish, squirmy, Sharlene kissed my mother on the forehead, said
congratulations, great job, oh happy day,
and then hightailed out across town to stuff
mushrooms.

The doctor left to attend to another
patient. The nurse clipped the umbilical
cord and went to bury her face in tulips and
roses.

Once she was holding the baby close, my
mother slowly sat up and swung her legs
around. Her body ached. She stepped off
the bed and trundled to the window, where
she held up the blanket and watched in
silence as small Dad jumped up and down.
He lit a cigar. He danced a jig. It was like
the silent-movie version of her life. He did
this whole routine several times through
until he was too tired and squinty and then
he blew kisses goodbye and headed off to
ready the house. Mom was left, all alone,
with her son. It was a private room. And
even with the women yelling nearby, and
the clicking and beeping of machines, she
told me that something seemed to empty
out at the ward then, and everything grew
very quiet, and still, and there was a window
of time and calmness, when Mom and the
new baby had several hours together, just
staring into each other's eyes. His eyes, wob-

bly and new; hers, weary, alone, depthful.

She told me this story for the first time when she was combing out my hair after a weekly shower. I was seven, or eight. I saw in him, she said, and her voice drifted off. I saw, she said. She hung her head. We sat together on the floor of the bathroom, on the fluffy damp lavender rug, and she had shaken my hair dry with a towel and held the comb high over my head, ready to nudge it through the snarls. To copy her, I had grown out my hair as long as possible, down to the butt, and washing it was a major hour-long ordeal of shampoo, conditioner, toweling, combing, and maybe a blow-dry if I was lucky.

She was best with activities, and I cherished this time with her, warmed like baby chicks by the orange-red coils of the wall heater. If this kind of time with Mom meant hearing often about my brother, it was worth it. Plus, I had my own good story; when I was born, she said, I had laughed within minutes, even though the doctors assured her that infants did not laugh. You chuckled! she told me, beginning to pull the plastic teeth through wet hair, scoring lines into my scalp. A big belly chortle! she said.

Really?

Really, she said. She worked the comb

down, caught full drops of water in the towel as it collected at the ends, and as she did, her shoulders sank again, a graceful sinking. She glanced through the crack in the bathroom door.

With Joseph, she said.

I waited, dripping.

With Joseph, she said, he saw all the world.

Her hand paused in the middle of my hair.

As a baby? I said.

He was like a wee old prophet in the shape of a baby, she said.

She did not cry when she told this story, but her voice grew smaller, humbled. When Joseph heard it, he would usually leave the room. We fell in love in seconds, Mom continued. Literally, seconds! Boom! She smiled at him, and he would pass through the room, whatever room we were in, and go to his own, gently closing the door. I had a memory of him passing through every room in the house this way, as if all my mother did was retell his birth story, over and over and over again. In truth, she probably only told it a few times, but in my memory replay, I could picture him passing through the kitchen, the TV room, the bathroom, my bedroom, and the front lawn, Mom sitting with me for some reason — hair, homework, wedding album — him walking straight through without a response.

I knew, Mom said, that he would guide me.

Joseph's door clicked shut.

She wrapped the towel around my head, pressing down on the skull.

Do I? I asked.

Do you what, baby? she asked.

Do I guide you too?

Oh sure, she said, drying my ears. All of you do! You help me all the time, of course!

When my hair was dry and combed enough, she took her time with the three damp strands on either side, her fingers deft and accurate, doing the French style of braids that started high on the scalp. At dinner, running a hand over the bumps in my hair, I tried to catch Joseph's eyes to see what was so special in there, but he just dodged his around. What? he said, when I kept trying. What is your problem?

I'm trying to be guided by your eyes, I said.

He closed his. Long orbs of pale lids, black rims of lashes.

My eyelids are my own private cave, he murmured. That I can go to anytime I want.

He ate that whole meal with his eyes closed and somehow didn't spill a thing. Mom thought he was trying to intensify the flavor of her dinner, so she closed hers too, concentrating. Yes, she said, bringing the fork to her lips. Mmm, it's true. I can taste the thyme much better this way, she said.

Dad looked over at me and shook his head.

We can see you guys, I said, but no one seemed to hear anything either.

22

By my thirteenth birthday, I had collected over eighty dollars from being the consenting babysittee. I used most of it to buy my favorite packaged foods for snacks, or for a few cans of tennis balls that I liked to throw down the street as hard as I could (returned, on occasion, by a neighborhood dog), but with the last bit, I went to the music/video store and bought a copy of *Brigadoon* — audio and video, both. I listened to the music on my own and snuck the videotape into the TV when my father wasn't looking, on another night of my mother's errands. He looked up when the overture and credits began, in swirling violins, and at the first number, he put his ledger aside and sang out a line or two of broken lyrics. He burst out for the chorus. After a few minutes, I joined in, because I knew the words by then, too, but instead of making it all *less* exposing, the entrance of my voice had the unfortunate side effect of calling attention to what we were doing. Midway through that chorus, my father picked up the remote and clicked off the TV. I have to work, he said, returning to the red ledger. Shaking his head. Funny, he said.

On a Saturday afternoon in April, fair and light, a thin envelope arrived in our mailbox. Inside was one neatly folded piece of stationery paper from the admission offices of Caltech, stating that, although impressed by his application, unfortunately Caltech had an especially fine crop of candidates this year and would not have room for Joseph Edelstein this fall. They wished him all the best in his science endeavors of the future.

I hand-delivered the envelope into Joseph's lap, where he was sitting outside reading a book on Kepler and the arrival of new enlightenment with the orbital change of thinking. Elliptical orbits, perihelions, equal areas in equal time.

When I gave it to him, he closed the book and took the letter directly to his room, which then he did not leave for two days. Dad said to leave him be, that we should give him space. The trays of food my mother left outside the side door were eaten by birds and bugs.

Two more letters arrived in the mail. All of Joseph's envelopes were thin. He did not get into UCLA, or USC. He hadn't applied anywhere else. The competition had stiffened and his grades had been erratic: some strong A's in sciences, some C's in Spanish and English, little to no extracurricular activity, an uneven SAT. He could not write *But I'm a GENIUS* as his application essay and leave it at that. You need to show your genius, the college counselor had said, crossing her legs. How many young men had she seen going through her office with big ideas and complex skills and no way to get any of it on paper?

They're wrong! Mom said, pacing the house. She called up George, who called up Caltech. She demanded to see the college counselor. She compiled lists of visionaries who had dropped out of high school and started world-changing companies or invented vaccines. She slipped those lists under Joseph's door.

Her outrage was so large it carried with it a tinge of presentation, the way a person feigning surprise at a known surprise party will make a grander expression than one truly surprised.

Finally, we had to pick the lock with a hairpin. Inside, we found him lying on his bed, reading a textbook, jotting down notes for an assignment due. Can I still move out? he said, when Mom and I clamored around.

23

My brother's first formal disappearance —
formal meaning someone else was around
besides me — happened right before his
high-school graduation. The day of. It was a
gloomy June afternoon, skies a dirty white,
tree leaves drooping. Joseph had been both
focused and distracted since the school
rejection letters, but he had done his usual
thorough overly cozy job with my mother's
splinters on Sunday evenings, and he attended his classes until the last day. Our
parents had not gone out to any events, or
dinners, so there had been no disappearing
on any subsequent babysits, to my disappointment. No more laughing, no discussions. On this day, he was supposed to be
getting ready to go, trying on the sizing of
his cap and gown, manipulating bobby pins,
and in my role as younger sibling/
domesticated shepherd, I was supposed to
herd him into the car to get to school in

time for rehearsal. The lambs, however, were loose. I couldn't find him anywhere.

Joe's not in his room, I told my mother, who was outside, retouching her lipstick in the side mirror of the car. It's that thing I told you about, I said.

She peered up, her lips re-pinked. Maybe he's in the bathroom? she said.

I looked, I said.

It was nearly noon, time to go, sun burning behind the cloud layers, and right on time, George turned the corner at Vista and walked up. He was wearing his black graduation hat perched on his head, the ironed coat folded over his arm. He did a little jaunty bow.

I can't believe you kids are graduating! Mom said, holding her forehead. She hurried over to give him a hug.

Together, we oohed over his hat and touched the soft golden tassel with the plastic date hanging from it. The phone rang. Mom ran inside. She left the front door open, and I couldn't tell words but her voice dropped down, low, to the hushed tone of urgent intimacy I heard sometimes when she picked up in the afternoons. I turned to George.

Congratulations, I said.

Hey, Rose, he said. He re-adjusted a

bobby pin. How are you?

He looked newly older suddenly, with college admission in his pockets. Smoother at the edges.

Joe's missing, I said.

Where to?

Don't know.

So where is he? Mom asked, returning outside, her eyes a little lighter.

Somewhere other than his room, I said.

Did he just go on his own? George asked, still fiddling with his cap.

Joseph? I said, incredulous.

I guess not, said George, laughing.

My mother zipped up her purse and stepped back inside. We followed her in. Despite the awkwardness, I was glad for all of it, that they were both around while Joseph was not, that George was over, that the same thing was happening, but with witnesses. George walked through the living room, with long strides of assurance. Brownies cooled on the kitchen counter, for the party later. We called out his name like he was a lost dog.

That it was graduation day seemed notable. The very beginnings of the fork. Joseph and George still spent multiple afternoons together, and the roads named Joseph and George still appeared to be facing the same direction, but soon the angle at the base would reveal itself as large. Over the last couple of months, while George had been settling linen napkins in his lap, sipping from crystal goblets of ice water at celebratory luncheons for early-admission honors students, my mother had registered Joseph for classes at Los Angeles City College on his behalf. Sure, he'd said, when she and my father had suggested he try out school anyway. But can I still have my own place? he said, as he leafed through her piles of forms.

It's graduation day! I called, clapping my hands. Time to go!

Mom walked through the backyard, stepping carefully in her tan graduation heels, making divots in the lawn.

George stood in the front of the house, scanning the street. He traced fingers over the bark of the ficus tree whose roots made arches and bumps and broke up the sidewalk.

Jo-seph! my mother called, striding through the living room.

I joined George. Will you still be his friend? I asked.

He looked over. Startled. He reached out and pulled me in close, scrubbing my hair.

What's with you, he said. Joe and I will

always be friends, he said.

A neighborhood kid rode across the street on a bike. I rested on George's shoulder, for a second. He leaned his head on mine. He smelled of citrus soap.

Will I see you? I said.

Of course, he said. I'll come by all the time.

His cheek was warm on my forehead, but even as he spoke, it was like the opposite was forming underneath his words, like letters shaped backwards in the reflection of a pool.

My mother stuck her head out the door. Find him? she called.

Not yet, I called back.

She rustled outside, carrying Joseph's cap and gown, wrapped in plastic. In the kitchen, the phone rang again. Mom had started asking George polite questions about Caltech, so I ran in to pick it up.

Hello?

It was a man's voice. Hello? May I speak to Lane?

Who's this?

This is Larry, from the co-op, said the voice.

I picked out a pen from the pen cup, and drew a circle on a pad of paper. I didn't expect him to give his name so easily.

She can't talk, I said. We're about to go to my brother's graduation, I said.

Ah, right, he said. He had a friendly voice, easygoing, medium-pitched. Just tell her I called, he said. This is Rose, right?

I doodled a demon head on the pad. Who? Rose? Her daughter?

I gave the demon head bloodshot eyes. I could just imagine my mother telling Larry all the things in her day. Going over every detail of every piece of wood. Telling him the names of each member of her family. I hadn't been able to stop myself from thanking him every night before I went to sleep, as I watched tray after tray go to the co-op covered in cookies and pies and return the next day, empty.

I scribbled wiggly hair on the demon head. Yes, I said. This is Rose.

He made a little exhale sound, half of a laugh.

Nice to meet you, he said.

Out the kitchen window, George was answering Mom's questions. Bobbing his head. Soon to fly off into the world of dorms, and girls. It seemed brutally unfair, that he would not be coming over two or three times a week anymore. Mom walked to the car, talking, making some kind of airplane shape with her arms.

You know I know, I said, to Larry.

Know what?

I smiled a little, into the phone. Watched as my mother popped the trunk of the car and looked in there. In the trunk? Joseph? It all seemed funny, for a second, just funny and ridiculous and sad.

I just know, I said. The thing I'm not supposed to know.

He paused again. A muggy silence.

It's okay, I said. I mean, it's bad. But it's okay. Just stop calling the house. And nothing on weekends. All right?

That frozen silence, on the other end. But a heavy, listening silence. George hung up his gown and Joe's gown carefully on the inside hooks of the back seat of the car.

I think I understand, said Larry.

Mom was saying something else, animatedly, to George, by the side of the car. Her pink, wide mouth.

Thank you, I said, and hung up.

I paused over the pad of paper. Then I wrote it down, on a clean sheet: Larry called.

At a quarter past twelve, Mom honked the car horn. Soon the rehearsal would begin: all the robe-clad grads lining up to mark the ceremony in the high-school auditorium.

Our father and George's family would meet us later, at the school, for the real event.

The horn did nothing but startle the neighborhood kid who was biking, so she left the car to go check the neighbors' house. Jo-seph! she called, down the street. I stuck the note on the fridge, under a magnet. What to do? I liked seeing her happier. Life was better with her happier.

I walked through the house. Closed open closet doors, shut off lights. Finally, I went to stand in my brother's room. The whole running and looking, opening and closing, a giant ruse. Like he was anywhere else but somewhere near his room. Even though I could not find him I knew where he was not, and he was definitely not at the neighbors'. The books, the half-packed boxes, the piles of clothes. That familiar tightening tension in the room itself.

He'll be here soon, I said.

Mom was running down the sidewalk. What should we do? she called to George. It's time!

I know, I said, too quiet for her to hear. I closed my eyes. Just wait a sec, I said.

She kept running down the sidewalk, towards the end of the block. Jo-seph! I heard her calling. Jo — seph! George stood by the car, talking to the kid biking to and fro. Tossing and catching a loose pine cone.

I left my brother's room and went to my own, the land of Pegasus pens, and broken stools, and doll stuff. There, I opened the jewelry box my mother had given me for my most recent birthday. She'd made it with leftover bits of lumber, and it was a shiny even oak, with carefully set drawers, handles hewn from twigs. Each piece she made more skilled than the last.

She, who loved him more than anything, was down the street, calling. George, his closest friend in the world, stood outside scanning the sidewalk. It was an unexpected moment for me. My brother and I had never been close, and I didn't understand what was happening, but it seemed I still knew more about it than anyone else. For whatever reason, I was involved in this way. I sifted through the jewelry-box drawers, past the leftover roll of a twenty-dollar bill. Listened as carefully as I could for clues while settling colorful stones beside each other.

Nothing came from the room itself, but as I untangled a long satin ribbon, I heard two steps, out of his room, one two. When I walked into the hall, there he was, in his door frame, with that same look on his face, like he'd been washed and dried in a machine.

Jo-seph! our mother called, from down the street.

Jo-seph! George echoed.

Joseph looked over at me, calmly. We stared at each other, for a longer minute than was expected.

Ready, he said.

24

In August, they packed up, in brown boxes: George to Pasadena, Joseph to Los Feliz. On the day he headed east in his boxy U-Haul, a painted picture of rugged Alaskan mountains on the truckside, George came into my room and gave me a long hug. I'll see you soon, he said, holding me by the shoulders, looking at me in the eyes, although I wouldn't see him, not for months. Eliza was over that day, and to my distaste and her delight, he hugged her too. Take good care of Rose, he told her. I'm fine, I said, bumping inside the door frame, but Eliza nodded, solemn. Her cheeks filling at the bottom with blush. Maybe you could show us the dorms sometime, she said. I almost whacked her on the head with the yellow doll-brush hidden in my back pocket. Yes, I wanted to see the dorms, more than anything! But not with her there too.

My brother convinced my parents to rent

him an apartment off Vermont, near Prospect Avenue. About fifteen minutes away. He sat with Dad in front of the TV for a half-hour, the longest I'd ever seen them alone together, and he gave a heartfelt eyes-ahead speech about how hard he planned to study and how helpful it would be to be close to school. He had no interest in driving, and from his new doorstep he would be able to walk to Los Angeles City College, to the 7-Eleven, and to the Jons grocery store. The place was a tenplex with its name written diagonally on the front — Rexford Gardens, or Bedman Vista, or something like that. The units circled a courtyard complete with a wall of ferns and a broken mermaid fountain. Joseph's apartment was on the second level, with an outside hallway that served as a collective balcony.

To furnish the new apartment, Mom supplied him with seconds from the co-op studio. A dresser with a finicky drawer, a very small table of unclear purpose, a standard pine nightstand, a pair of spindly maple stools.

How about this? Mom said, on moving day, holding up a coat rack made by one of her colleagues; the wood was elegant, a rich striped rosewood from Brazil, but it hadn't been cut correctly with the buzz saw and something was off in the balance, so it needed to be wedged inside a corner.

Sure, said Joseph. Great.

We were loading boxes into the back of a Ford truck Mom had borrowed from friends at the lumberyard. Joseph dipped back into the house, and returned with two card-table chairs under his armpits. Grandma had sent the rest of the folding set over a series of months, in those long slatted boxes, one at a time.

How about these; can I have these? he asked, holding them up like crutches.

Mom wrinkled her nose. Those? she said. They're not very well made, she said.

Joseph took two, and then the next two, and then the folding table, and then Grandma's cracked bamboo salad bowl, and her brass desk lamp with its movable neck. Not as nice as your stuff, of course, he said, walking to the truck and loading it all inside.

The plan was that he would start with a roommate, to share his one-bedroom, but during the interviews of various contenders he sat still as a stone and said nothing. Peppy strangers came to the house and sat with me and my mother, trying to impress, but you could see their mood sink when they tried to engage Joseph and he didn't answer one of their questions. He didn't even grunt. He was worse than I'd ever seen him, radiating Get Away because what he seemed to want more than anything was to live alone. He was glad to go to LACC, he said, yes. He only wanted adequate time to work. Why do you want to live alone so much? I asked, but he pretended like he didn't hear me. Are we so awful? I said, trailing him from room to room. He'd only applied to the schools where George had also applied, and his former ravenous wish for Caltech began to seem to me less about the merits of the school itself and more about the one and only roommate he could've tolerated.

Mom, in an effort to be helpful, rented the whole apartment under her own name, and she'd wanted to pick a nice roommate to keep Joseph company, and she even tried to give a few possible people generous breaks on the rent, but when each potential eager-eyed roomie drizzled off, smiles stiffening, Joseph begged her again. He asked if he could use his savings, donated by the generous dead grandparents, to pay the extra rent, and after two more people withdrew their names, Mom talked it over with our father and relented. Fine, she said.

But you have to call every single day, she said. She stared him down until he bowed his head, yes. She worried he was devastated from the Caltech rejection, but as soon as she handed over the key, he looped his arm through hers. It's mine? he said. He danced around the house with their arms linked, singing thank you, Mom! thank you, Mom! — his elbows pointy, his voice ringing. She whooped with him, teary, laughing. Call your father, she said, wiping her cheeks, and he got on the phone, also something I'd never seen before, and called Dad at the office to leave a proper thank-you message with his secretary. When he was off, he did another little bow and promised Mom he'd still come over every Sunday night for the splinters.

He's coming into his own, she whispered to me, kissing my cheek.

So that the grandparent fund could stay untouched, she paid the rent for the full apartment from her co-op sales, augmented by my father's salary. No one made any mention of him getting a job.

On moving day, we lugged the co-op furniture and the boxes up the stairs and down the balcony corridor. Once all was unloaded, Mom and I stood around the apart-

214

ment. Opened and closed his cabinets. Admired the closet space. I flushed the toilet, for entertainment.

Looks very nice! Mom said. She slid open the living-room window to let air in. Peered out his front door. Have you met your neighbors yet?

The rows of doors down the outside hallway were all shut, curtains drawn.

We stood awkwardly in his living room, and Joseph thanked us several times, finally ushering us to the doorway. He kept swinging the door closer to closed.

We get it, I said, stepping out. Bye.

Every day, Mom told him.

Yes.

She gave him another hug, and blew her nose. After he shut the door, she rummaged in her purse and dropped a magenta-colored spare key inside the metal tray of the outside light fixture.

Just as a backup, she said, as we walked down the stairs.

George threw himself into college, and Joseph lived a hermit's life, and I went through the cycles: Eighth grade. Ninth grade. Tenth, eleventh, twelfth. I clung to Eliza, who, despite her promise to George, had found a new group of friends, girls who seemed, with their broad smiles and quick-nesses, to be like bicyclers rolling downhill. Like they lived in a miraculous Escherian land that only offered downhills.

At lunch, the group of them had started to talk about colleges. Eliza had her heart set on Berkeley, majoring in psychology. Several others were interested in political science, or pre-med. I had just applied to a couple of places, almost at random; the idea of more school just seemed confusing to me. Who could bear to pay attention all the time? I kept up my weekly flute lessons so I could play in the school orchestra, but I was content as third chair, and I often wished I'd picked trombone. You can't blast a flute. My old dodgeball rival Eddie Oakley had grown up to be a jock with nice strong arms, and on occasion, when I was feeling particu-larly agitated, I ran out to the baseball field at the end of the day and I convinced him to throw broken tennis balls with me over wire fences to roll in the streets. Take that, I said, sending them soaring.

You're an angry gal, he said, laughing at me.

I'm not angry, I said. I just have a good arm.

A couple times he and I made out outside the boys' locker room, long after the school day had ended. We pushed our faces into each other. There was something rude and bruising about it, like I was mad at him and he was mad at me and we were having a fight with our lips, but somehow it all still felt pretty good. He tasted like sports. One afternoon, just as it was getting dark, he tucked a hair behind my ear and seemed ready to say something nice; I ducked out of his arms and told him I had to go.

He pulled me in for one last kiss, which lasted for another fifteen minutes. At a pause, I tucked in my shirt.

Bye, I said. I'm going.

You're the perfect girl, he said, rubbing his chin. You expect nothing.

I scooped up one of the old tennis balls and threw it at him.

And you, I said, are the same asshole you were in third grade.

What? he said, making a mock-innocent face. It's true, right? It's good! Tomorrow, same time?

Maybe, I said, walking away.

He chuckled. Maybe, he said. Of course.

During lunchtime, while the downhill girls talked about where they would go to school, and when, and why, I sat on the outskirts of their circle, where grass met concrete, eating my lunch. I watched the science nerds over on a bench, with their books open. Like regurgitated versions of my brother and George.

Hey, how come you only eat junk food? asked one of Eliza's friends, the strawberry-blonde who was president of the tennis club. She lived entirely on celery and peanut butter. I was right at the edge of their circle, like the tail of a *Q,* and I swiveled my butt to face her directly.

Eliza looked over, listening, waiting. She had a big crush on the student-body president and wanted to ask the tennis-club girl about the latest sighting in the hall.

Because I can taste the feelings people don't know they're feeling, I told her. And it is an absolutely shit experience, I said.

I raised my eyebrows and glared.

Jeez, said the girl, turning back. I was only asking. Is Eddie Oakley your boyfriend?

No, I said.

Someone saw you guys making out by the tennis court.

Wasn't me, I said.

Rose is really good at dodgeball. And Spanish, Eliza offered. I think Eddie's okay.

No one plays dodgeball anymore, I said. And I got a B minus in Spanish.

She shrugged. You're still better than I am, she said.

What did you get?

She looked down at her fingers, nails recently painted an electric spangly pink.

She got an A, said the tennis girl.

I laughed.

Do you think he saw me in the hall? Eliza whispered.

I turned back to the quad. The science kids had left to go talk to a teacher.

For a brief stage that year, I did tell a few people about the food. How am I? I'd say when someone asked. Well, I'm a little caught up with the donut. Generally, it went one of two ways. Either the person would look at me strangely, think I was a kook, and go on to something else, like the tennis girl did. I mentioned it to Eddie as we hurled tennis balls into the street and he said huh, and then stuck his hand up my back. I figured that was the usual, but one afternoon at lunchtime a new girl showed up, freshly arrived from Montana — hazel-eyed Sherrie with all the silver jewelry. She was grateful to have a group to eat lunch with, and she'd met Eliza in English class, and as she bit into her chicken sandwich she told us all about how Los Angeles was so much better than Butte. I mean, it's huge here! she said, spreading her arms. All the movies are here! she said. Halfway through lunch, Eliza had to go talk intently with the tennis girl about something, so it was just me and Sherrie, left on the grass/cement, bored. To fill space, I held up my last crumby cafeteria chicken nugget and started to list all its various complexities. Ohio, busy factory, bad chickens, stoic breader. I just said it for something to say, but Sherrie scooted closer, her silver-filigree bracelet clunking on the ground. Wait, what? she whispered. What are you saying? she said.

Such a lift I felt that day, when she looked at me like I was the most intriguing person in the world! I explained a little more about it, tentative, and she grabbed my arm and invited me back to her house that very afternoon, where, in her parents' kitchen, she baked up a pan of brownies on the spot and handed a square over, wide-eyed. After one bite, I dropped it on the counter. Ugh, I said, muffled, grabbing a glass for water. You are massively depressed, I said. She laid her head on the counter and started to cry. It's true, she said. I could barely get out of bed, she wept. And this! — after the whole lunch discussion of how everything was so great in California, how the move was a chance to re-invent herself, how all was astounding in the new dawning day of glory. Baked goods were still the quickest like that.

So when can you come back? she asked, an hour later, her eyes round and shiny with tears. I left that day with a skip in my step: A new friend, I sang to myself. A new, true friend! A gift from the Big Sky Country! I went over to her house many more times, and each time was the same routine: an overly cheery greeting, then chocolate-chip cookies, then rice-crispie treats, down, down, down into the pit, then my response, her tears on the table, her moaning of my rightness. I didn't mind at first — I loved going over with such a sense of purpose and pacing around her kitchen expounding on my thoughts on her interior. I described every single nook and cranny of feeling I could taste. We were inseparable for months. She called me Glorious Rose, and we sat in her bathroom and played mournful electronic songs that went on for ten minutes, and while I perched on the edge of her bathtub and ate her desserts she helped me dye my hair black, then red, then black-red. But it got to the point where I'd go over to her locker and she'd shove a biscuit in my face and ask me how she was feeling, because she couldn't tell without me. She'd run after me in the halls with a slapdash sandwich she'd made in five seconds to get me to tell her if she really liked this guy or if she was just kidding herself. I don't know everything, I said, shoving sandwich bites in my mouth. You like him, I said, nodding. You really like him.

I still didn't even care until I was over at her house one afternoon and I told her about how Joseph had this disappearing trick that no one had ever figured out and she flattened her bangs over her forehead and asked who's Joseph? We were in her kitchen, baking as usual. We'd just talked at length about the intricate nuances of her crush on a stoner volleyball player.

Joseph? I said, squinting. My brother?

You have a brother? she said. Is he cute? Hey, will you taste this toast for me? Do you think I'm still depressed?

The walls seemed to sag around us. The toast wavered in the air. Hey, I said, slowly. You know, I'm kind of full. Just for today, I said. Let's do something else. Sherrie's face squinched into a purse. How about a movie? I said. But why? she said, licking the edge of the peanut-butter knife. What's interesting about a movie? I could do that with anyone! Please, she said, Glorious Rosie? Just one teeny tiny bite?

That day, I left her house early and leaned against the window glass of the bus, crying a little into the corners of the six-dollar junky cat-eye sunglasses she'd encouraged me to buy. I didn't feel like seeing anyone else. At the movie stop, I pulled the cord and welcomed the darkness of the theatre, where I sat alone and ate no popcorn and relished the soft velvet of the armrest that I shared with no one and movies are all sight and sound only and a beautiful landscape and I saw what they showed me and nothing else at all. When Sherrie called later and asked me over for the next day for lasagna, I said I had plans.

And, I thought I'd take a break from the food stuff, I said. For a little while. If you want to see a movie this weekend, or do anything else, let me know.

She called me a fickle drug dealer and slammed down the phone.

In this way, for these reasons, despite her grade coddling and gold standard normality, I was grateful for Eliza. When she overheard the tennis girl's question about food that lunchtime, she didn't say a thing, but the next day she brought out a twin to her sandwich. We had too much turkey, she said, putting the spare in its wax paper on a sunlit section of cement. It was probably the first time she understood why I might've spent an hour at the drinking fountain that

223

long-ago day in third grade. When it looked like she was just going to leave the turkey on the ground, I picked it up. Unwrapped the plastic. Ate it slowly.

If I didn't focus on how envious I was that this lightness was where she came from, those sandwiches did help me through the rest of the day.

25

It seemed to happen in springs, the revealing of things. With fresher air, and jasmine blooms, something else new. There was the spring of my food discovery. The spring of my first interactions with my father, and Joseph's disappearances, and my mother's affair, which seemed to be ongoing, since I had never tasted the teary residue of a breakup in her meals.

The fifth spring of my brother, in his own apartment, alone.

He had followed through with the daily call requirement. For years, the phone rang at five, usually while my mother was preparing dinner, and they talked about his classes and his day and her classes and her day. He seemed to be enjoying school well enough. He was studying all the time. His grades were good. Since Mom was chopping and stirring as they talked, her meals often took on a tinge of worry and also some kind of ravenous pride. My son, said her dinners, is a beam of pure focus.

He called every day, so if he was still disappearing, he did it on an effective schedule.

Only one time did Joseph fail to call at the appointed hour. When Mom called to see why not, he didn't pick up. Nor did he answer the following morning. Two days went by and still no response, so Mom drove over, worried, used the spare key, and found his apartment empty. Drove home. Paced. She called on the hour, every hour. No answer. My father, who had never found anything interesting about these disappearances, chalking them up to the private explorations of a twenty-two-year-old young man, tried to calm her down as she roamed the house. The next morning, day three, she drove over again as soon as it was light, and when she arrived at his place, she found Joseph facedown on the floor of his bedroom, limbs spread out like a starfish. His heartbeat slow. Breathing shallow. She called an ambulance and they went to the hospital right away, where they gave him numerous tests and said he was severely dehydrated and weakened but would be all right. Where were you? Mom asked, and the doctors asked, but Joseph just shook his head. Nowhere, he said, and that was the best they could get out of him.

My father did not visit, but sent his usual bunch of tulips and roses to the nurses, to ensure the best of care.

It was in mid-April, after Joseph was comfortably re-set in his apartment, fully irrigated, back to his once-a-day calls, re-registered for a spring advanced quantum-mechanics course at LACC, that my mother lifted up her fork at the dinner table and announced, her arm raised like a statue, that she would be taking a week-long trip with the co-op to Nova Scotia. It's a very unusual opportunity, she told us, to learn the basics of Japanese carpentry. We will be constructing wooden hinges that take the place of nails, she said. She poked at the mound of potatoes on her plate.

My father was eating very slowly, something he usually did when he was irritable. Streaks of gray flashed through his hair.

How's the fish? she said.

Fine, he said, pushing on his mouth with a napkin.

Rose, Mom said, turning to me, I'll only go if you'll tell me you'll keep an eye on everyone.

Sure, I said. I'll check on Joseph. Can I do the grocery shopping? Who's going?

About half the co-op, she said. We're trying to refresh our approach. You'll call every day?

Sure. Can I use your car?

With an adult, she said.

Dad slid his gaze over to me. Along with watching TV together, driving around in the car with my learner's permit was another good father/daughter activity from the manual. I was a couple years older than most learner's permit types, but I'd been slower to the car than my peers.

Okay, I said.

Thank you. Mom smiled at me, warmly. It's really a special chance, she said. I appreciate it so much. One day I'll make you a cabin, in a forest, she said, with hinges made only of wood.

I took a bite of the mashed potatoes. Northern California, a well-run potato farm. Mom's giddy excitement about the upcoming trip, paired with her usual spiral of smallness. I ate it on the side of my mouth. No need, I said, swallowing. I prefer nails, I said. And cities, I said.

My father glanced up, for a second, as if someone had called his name. He reached out an arm, as if to ruffle my hair. Since my hair was not anywhere close, his hand hovered in the air.

Rose, he said. Is so grown up! he said.

She left on a Wednesday. Her car was just sitting in the driveway, so I took it to school anyway, trolling around town after classes ended. Eddie saw me in the school parking lot and asked if he could get a ride to his friend's house. I let him climb in and we rolled around and kissed on a side street for an hour, but I was in a quieter mood that day, having run into Sherrie in the halls with her arm strung through a new girl's, and I didn't feel like doing battle. What's wrong? he said, after trying to shove his face into mine. Where's the tank? he said.

What tank?

You, he said, grinning at me. That's what I call you in my head. The tank.

I sat up. Straightened my T-shirt.

I'm no tank, I said. Someone once said I was seaglass.

Ha! he said. Seaglass. Yeah, right.

He played with the radio buttons for a while. Freckles clustered around his ear and jaw.

So what are you doing after graduation? I asked.

He turned back. Me? he said. School, I

guess. Baseball. Why? You want to keep in touch?

Nah, I said.

That's my girl, he said, nodding. He touched my hair, newly reddish from the latest dye. Drew a finger down my nose. Nice nose, he said.

I sank a little, under his hand.

Oh, stop this sad bullshit, he said, moving closer. Come on! Bring out the tank!

He put his face right up close to mine again but I just didn't have it in me. We kissed for a few minutes and then I pushed him away.

Time's up, I said.

Fine, fine, fine, he said, patting down his hair. He checked his face in the side mirror. Can you at least give me a ride to Fountain? he asked.

One click opened the car doors. Tank says you can walk, I said.

In the evenings, my father and I ate dinner quietly in front of the TV together: Wednesday night, Thursday. Frozen dinners I'd picked out at the grocery store, greatest hits by my favorite factories. One of the best ones, in Indiana, prided itself on a no touch food assembly, which meant every step was monitored by robotic arms, ones that placed the tortillas into the dish, layered them with cheese, dropped dollops of tomato sauce on top, and shoved it all into the giant oven, thus producing an utterly blank enchilada.

After Thursday's dinner, my father and I piled into the car and drove awkwardly around the blocks, him instructing me how to brake. I pretended like I hadn't been in the car in weeks and he kept reaching over and putting his hands on the wheel to angle me out of an awkward position. You're supposed to *tell* me, I said, elbowing him off.

Right, right, he said. Sorry. Turn left.

The afternoons were getting longer again, stretching. I stayed too long at a stoplight because the sunlight was so pretty, sifting through all the leaves on the sycamore trees lining Sierra Bonita, turning each a pale jade green. The jacaranda trees preparing for their burst of true lavender blue come May.

Go, said Dad.

Sorry, I said.

Two skateboarders crossed in front of us.

Is something wrong? Dad asked, as I angled up Oakwood.

With the car? I tapped the dashboard, lightly. Seems okay to me.

With you, he said. He kept his gaze forward. Page forty-three in the manual: father

231

has heart-to-heart with his daughter.

No, I said.

He drummed his fingers on the dashboard. Fast, focused. They carried the same active enthusiasm as his wiggling feet in the TV room, on the ottoman. Our bonding had not progressed much beyond watching TV together, except for these weekly lessons in driving, which were 99 percent technical.

Boys? he said.

What about them?

Any problems there?

I tugged on the steering wheel. Not really, I said.

They get better, he said, hopefully. His voice trailed off. Or do you know what you're interested in? he asked, after a pause.

No, I said. Most people don't at seventeen.

That's not true, he said. A lot of people have a little idea, he said.

Well, I said. I do not have a little idea.

I turned onto Stanley, then Rosewood. Deliberately ran a stop sign but he didn't say anything. His forehead was crushed together with effort.

I ran a second stop sign.

Oops, I said. Stop back there.

Full brake, he said, scratching his eyebrow. No rolling stop or they'll ticket you.

232

I turned onto Fairfax. Dad reached out his window to adjust the right-side mirror.

Why don't you go on up to Sunset, he said, and then make a right.

Okay, I said, accelerating.

Is school all right? Dad said, pointing at the yellow light. Slow, he said.

I hummed at the red light. The car motor, humming.

Fine, I said.

You like it?

Not really, I said.

Why not?

I don't know, I said.

I turned onto Sunset. Want a burger? Dad asked as we passed All American Burger.

No. You?

No, he said, looking at it longingly. He pointed out the window. Right on La Brea, he said.

I turned, as instructed. Rambled down, through green lights. After a few blocks, I made another turn, onto Willoughby, and drove past the Department of Water and Power building to the curb outside our house where I slid the car right into the driveway.

Nice, said Dad.

He glued his eyes on my hand as I put the

car in park, then pulled up on the parking brake.

You're nearly ready for the test, he said. One more round and I think you're set.

We sat in the car, facing the low branches of the big ficus tree. He didn't make a move to go and I didn't either and for a while we just sat there, staring at the corroded handle on the garage door, with the useless string tied to it for no reason.

Two-toned leaves brushed against the windshield. I had a flash of remembering George outside, in his cap and gown. A vision, of an earlier time.

Your brother, he said.

I waited. He shook his head.

Thanks for the lesson, I offered.

His eyes swept around the car. Outside, the motion-sensor porch light clicked on as a neighbor trotted past with her dog.

You have things to offer, he said, gruffly.

Offer who?

Just to offer, he said. The world.

He didn't move, and I felt it would be rude to move, so together we continued to stare stiffly out the windshield. A ficus twig tripped down the glass, onto the wipers.

Hey, I heard this story, I said.

He glanced over, eager. A story?

About a kid at school, I said. Want to hear?

Please, he said.

I leaned back, into the firmness of the car seat.

There's this kid, I said. In my English class? Who was failing, last year. I guess he lives in a kind of run-down neighborhood, over by Dodger Stadium, and he didn't know he needed glasses, and he saw everything blurry.

I bet he couldn't read, Dad said. His hands calmed a little with the entrance of narrative, and he reached out the side again to re-adjust the right-side mirror. You can see this?

It's fine, I said. Should I keep going?

Go, he said. Go on.

Anyway, I said, yes. He couldn't read. That was the problem. The teachers brought him into testing, and he couldn't read a word, and he never talked in English class, and he got bad grades for years, and he didn't even understand how anyone could do this magical mysterious action called reading, and finally one of the teachers said they should test his eyes, and they took him to the eye doctor.

Dad shook his head. That's the first thing they should check, he said. This crap school system, he said.

I pulled the keys from the ignition.

Well, I said. So they found out he had terrible vision, and he got glasses, and all the teachers stood around him while he tried them on.

Was he a smart kid? asked Dad.

Smart, I said. Definitely. And on went his glasses, perfect prescription, right? And he wore them and suddenly he could read, and not only that, the very act of reading suddenly seemed to him something possible, not like the rest of the world was way ahead of him in this impossible way.

A heartwarming story, Dad said, nodding. I like it. When's our show on?

Ten minutes, I said. Anyway, it's not over.

Why not? said Dad, his hand on the door handle. I like where it ended, he said. Let's end it there.

The kid goes home, right? I said. With his glasses. And his new reading book. And his mom greets him at the door. She's smiling, because the school called with the good news. But he can see she's really tired. He hasn't seen her in years, clearly: years! And she's totally exhausted, there are these dark circles under her eyes and when she smiles it looks like one of her teeth is a little brown box. They can't afford the dentist. Right? And his house? It's a wreck. One side is falling down, and there are cockroaches running across the floor and there's a big hole in the wall that he thought was a painting.

The motion-sensor light clicked off. Dad's profile, washed in darkness.

You're making this up, aren't you, he said. No, I said.

What's the guy's name?

John, I said.

John what?

John Barbaducci, I said, after a pause.

Dad coughed. Barbaducci, he said. That is the most made-up name I ever heard. Abe Lincoln, just why don't you call the guy George Washington. So, he said. Fine. Keep going. The kid hates what he sees.

So he steps on his glasses, I said.

Jesus! Dad said, hitting the dashboard. I knew something like that was coming. Now I hate this story, he said. So then he falls behind, correct?

He doesn't learn to read anymore, I said. But he gets by. He registers as half blind and gets disability.

Oh, now, that is an awful story, said Dad, shaking his head. Awful. He opened his car door.

I stepped out too. Locked the doors.

Nice work with the turn signal, said Dad. Just don't forget those side mirrors.

I thought it was a good story, I said.

It's a terrible story, he said, heading to the door. He gets disability and he's not even disabled! That's the kind of thing lawyers go nuts about. He thought the hole was a painting?

He fumbled in his pocket at the door.

Here, I said, handing over his ring of keys.

He coughed again, into his hand. I know it's bullshit, he said, opening the door, stepping in. I know you're trying to tell me something, but I have no idea what it is. Okay? I don't think like that. What are you trying to tell me?

Nothing, I said. It was just a guy at my school.

What's his name again?

John, I said. I grimaced a little, against my will.

John what?

We faced each other, in the hallway. Dad folded his arms.

John Barbelucci, I said.

With a crow, he slapped the homemade pine key-table, fixed at the entryway, made in Mom's first year of carpentry.

There! he said. He glared at me. You said Ducci, before. I'm sure of it.

Lucci, I said.

Ducci.

Do you have a tape recorder? I said.

I'm sure of it! he said. Close the door, he said.

I shut and locked the door behind us.

So can you read? he said, striding into the TV room. Is that what this is all about?

I kicked off my shoes, and Dad hung his jacket over the back of a chair.

I can read, I said.

It was eight o'clock, on the dot. Both of us zoomed to check the clock. I poured myself a glass of juice, and without a word, we took our spots on either side of the sofa and Dad clicked the TV to our favorite medical program and we rejoiced in the saving of the woman with the heart problem, whose eyes were so large and lovely.

26

Dad went to work on Friday morning without a word about our discussion, his usual honk waking me up at seven-forty. I drove myself to school, but I didn't feel like seeing anyone at lunch, so I left before noon and drove home. Took a nap on the sofa and thought about the weekend ahead. Eliza had invited me over to watch a horror movie double feature with the downhill girls. Sherrie would be there, and the last time I'd seen her at a social event she burst into tears when she saw me and ran out of the room. You're upset, I'd yelled after her, meanly. Now, maybe, she'd bring the new friend. Eliza had just kissed her big student-body crush, under the pinstriped awning by the cafeteria. She said it felt like sailing. Sailing? Several of the girls at the party had had sex, something which sounded appealing but only if it could happen with blindfolds in a time warp plus amnesia. I told Eliza I wasn't

240

sure if I could go; that I might have to go to Pasadena to visit George in the dorm instead, to help him with a school-wide prank involving graduates and umbrellas. Of course, she'd said, her face melting a little. All morning, I was in an unsettled mood, in part from the conversation with my father, mostly from everything, and I wandered into the kitchen and picked up the phone and called George's number in Pasadena for the hell of it. Maybe I could make it true after all. His machine picked up, and I left a rambly message about how I had a car if he needed anything, that I'd be glad to come to Pasadena if he needed help running any errands or anything, that I was free on Saturday, that I could do his laundry if he was busy, and I had a car if he needed help with anything at all. Halfway through, he picked up, out of breath. Hey! he said. Rose! All okay? I stumbled around the words. Told him I had a car if he needed anything. I have a car, too, he said, gently. How are you? he asked. I mumbled something about being a senior. I thought I heard a woman's voice, in the background. Everything okay, Rose? he said. I miss you, I told him, in a voice that went up too high, rolling in the upper registers, an awful wheedle. You too, he said. There was a long pause.

Anything else? he said, as kindly as he could. No, I said. Sorry to bother you. You're never a bother! he said, too quickly.

27

Within a minute, after hanging up, the phone rang again.

I picked up. Sorry, I said.

Hello? the voice said. Rose?

The wish, that George had called back, apologetic, called the number he knew so well to invite me out to spend the weekend in the dorm. Maybe he could show me the town, or be my date to Eliza's party. Instead, it was my mother's voice that rushed into my ear, running ahead fast, sharper than usual. The connection wasn't good — it sounded like she was talking from a pay phone outdoors, and great swoops of wind rushed in every few seconds. She didn't ask why I was home, but through the gaps she said something about how it was so good to hear my voice and how she was calling from the little town outside the workshop in Nova Scotia. The place had scarce technological amenities — just woodworking tools and gulls — so it was hard to catch her full sentences, but over the rushes of wind, it sounded something like she'd called Joseph seven times and he wasn't answering his phone and now the answering machine was disconnected so she needed me to write him a check.

A check?

On him, she said. Please? The line crack-led. Bedford Gardens, she said. She spelled it for me. With a *B,* she yelled into the phone.

I know where he lives, I said. Can't I just call? Can't Dad call?

Joe won't pick up, she said. His phone's out. Please.

For a second, the wind lapsed, and qui-eted. I'm worried, she said, with perfect clarity.

I'm sure he's fine, I said.

Your father doesn't take this kind of thing seriously, but I have a bad feeling, she said. We had an agreement, Rose, she said.

I pulled a pile of mail into my lap. I felt the sullenness building.

So is Larry there too? I asked.

Who?

Larry, your lover?

Excuse me? I can't hear you from the wind.

Lar-ry? Your lo-ver?

Silence, on the other end. Just the wind, talking back. Gulls, squawking.

Yes, he's here, she said, finally. Half the studio is here.

You guys having fun? I said, making an airplane out of a men's store sale card.

I didn't know you knew, she said faintly.

Oh, for years, I said.

How —

It's really hard to explain, I said. I flew the plane across the kitchen floor, where it crashed against a cabinet. So Joseph —

Does your father know?

Dad? I said. My highly observant dad? Are you kidding?

Or Joseph? she said, her voice starting to waver. Is that why he's gone?

I coughed into the receiver. No, I said. He doesn't know either. Nobody knows but me. Aren't you wondering why I'm home? I skipped school.

Her words came through in ribbons and waves. That's not why I'm away, she said. Nearly the whole co-op is here. It's a work trip, she said. We're working. I'm so sorry, Rose.

I picked at the address label on one of the bills. Electric bill. Probably big.

So when did you last talk to him? I said.

Larry?

Joseph.

Right before I left, she said. Please, honey. He always answers when I call. We'll talk about this all when I get back, I promise. Please. Did you say you skipped school?

The address label wouldn't come off so I put the ripped electric bill back in its stack by the phone. On top of all the other bills, all the papers that ran the house invisibly.

No, I said. I was kidding. It's a holiday.

Today? she said.

It's Barbelucci Day, I said.

Listen, she said. If something *is* wrong, I'll be there as fast as I can. I've called the hospitals just in case but he's not in them.

You called hospitals already?

Remember last time? If he's not home, will you check Kaiser, just in case? The one on Vermont and Sunset? You see, Rose, there's no one else. It has to be you. It's only you.

Someone called her name, from a far distance. I could hear the trees, whipped up. Another land. I'm sorry, I have to go, she said. Thank you, love. Thank you so much. We'll talk when I get back.

After she hung up, I went into the living room and sat in the striped armchair for a

while. Out the window, the breezeless stillness of a desert spring.

28

The building where Joseph lived was stucco and ugly, with boxy cypress hedges in stiff rows and that cursive name written on the front, that name so vague I could never remember it.

When I drove up, the whole complex looked emptier than it had before. Only one broken-down brown Chevy in the downstairs garage. It was late afternoon when I pulled in, the sky streaky with clouds, and on the streets, cars were arriving home, parking, work people unpacking trunks and heading into their units.

I dragged my feet up the stairs and down the balcony corridor. At the top of the stairway, in front of Joseph's apartment, someone had pushed a twin bed against the railing. With a pillow and a comforter, all set to go for sleep. By the door, I groped around in the black metal cupola that framed the solitary outdoor bulb until I found the magenta spare key — a cursive *J* on the key label in my mother's handwriting. With it, the door opened a notch, and then the chain blocked me.

Joseph? I called, into the wedge of darkness.

Nothing.

I was in a newly sour mood, after the phone calls with my mother and George. Embarrassed, about calling George. Upset, that I'd told my mother what I knew. Now that I'd told her, we'd have to have a talk. Plus, it just made me irritable to have to check on my older brother. Joseph's front door wouldn't push open, and so I snuck a grumbling hand through the open wedge and tried to unlatch the chain. I couldn't actually reach the latch, but the screws felt loose on the door-frame side, so instead of unlatching the chain I changed arms, curled my fingers, did a twist or two, and was able to dismantle the entire apparatus itself. After a minute, the whole thing fell apart and the door gaped open.

The living room was dark. Empty.

I hadn't been inside his actual apartment much. When I saw Joseph, it was because he came to us, because my mother drove out, picked him up, and brought him home. On occasion, he and George came over for dinner together, but the contrast of George's lively updates on Caltech set against Joseph's reluctant mutters was too much for even my mother, and she did not extend the invitation often.

Inside, it smelled faintly of noodles. Nothing much in the way of furniture except that card table with some science books piled on it, and a chair with a ripped seat and our grandmother's last name written on the back in cursive. *Morehead,* liltingly. All the curtains were closed except in the kitchen, where a small window sent a few late-afternoon rays onto the tiled floor, a yellow pattern of sun stripes over crisscrossing tile stripes. I left the front door open.

I'm in, I said.

No answer.

I stepped into the hallway. No pictures. The bathroom unlit. The bedroom at the end.

I'm coming in, I said, down the hallway. Joseph? Hellooooo. It's me, Mom's good old checker, I said.

Quiet. Empty. I clicked on the overhead hall light, but it only cast a burnt yellow tinge over the dimness.

No sounds coming from his room. Pure silence. I'd been through it all before. Outside, a few cars ambled up the street.

Only the faint hum and rattle of distant plumbing, somewhere deep inside the building.

Joseph did not invite people over, or have parties, so as far as I knew, other than Mom, I was the first person other than himself to set foot in his apartment in weeks. This was significant because at the end of the hall was the door to his bedroom, and on it he'd hung the old sign from his childhood, *Keep Out,* written years and years ago in thick black pen, now faded to gray. I'd long ago memorized the blocky shape of the *O,* the slightly too large *T.* It was such a familiar sight that it took a minute, here, to question. Why was it here? He must've lifted it off his old door during some visit home, and put it up again even though he lived alone. But so who was the sign for now? That badly drawn skull and crossbones.

I said his name at the door, and when no one answered, I pushed it open.

Inside his room, the light was off. I flicked it on. Joseph was sitting in the middle of the room, at a card-table desk, in a chair, at his laptop computer. Dressed. Awake. He looked sickly, and thin, but he always looked a little sickly and thin to me.

Hey, I said, startled. What's going on? You're here? Are you okay?

I'm fine, he said, quietly.

The bedroom in his apartment was small: wall-to-wall beige carpet, mirrored sliding closets, and no bed anymore, just one plain dresser, a couple of folding chairs, the desk, and a nightstand. One window, closed. In a corner, the carpet matted down in a long rectangle.

That's your bed out there?

The floor is better for my back, he said.

You're sleeping on the floor? What are you talking about?

He stared at me, his eyes flick-framed by those dark romantic lashes, the gaze too wide and unblinking.

What are you doing? I said.

Work, he said.

It was confusing, how he'd been so easy to find. In his jeans and T-shirt and shoes. No big deal. Plus, everything looked regular. On top of the dresser drawer leaned an old plaque from a string-galaxy drawing competition he'd won in junior high school, and another one of Mom's oak jewelry boxes that she'd made in her more advanced years of woodworking. A few sprinkled pennies and nickels, a loose dollar bill, worn to cloth.

He looked at me expectantly, but there was another card-table chair open in the middle of the room, also with Morehead written liltingly on the back, and something about the ease of everything was bugging me, something about actually finding him sitting there seemed worse than my usual time spent with nothingness, so I walked over to the free chair and sat down.

Why couldn't you just let me in? I broke your chain lock.

I was busy, he said. *Am.*

I scanned the room. In his closet, two worn plaid shirts hung above several pairs of hiking boots. A few rubber bands and pencils and a pen rolled on his nightstand, a brown-stained spruce model that stood boxily beside the absence of a bed. I got up again and clicked off the glare of the overhead light. Outside the window the sun had gone down, and the long end of day spread itself in swaths over the apartment buildings, where cars continued driving into their slots.

Doing what?

Work, he said again.

No, I said.

I'm *busy,* Rose, he said, clipped. Can you go?

I slid open the window, and watched a red Honda Civic back into a spot. A woman got out, shaking her hair. She didn't pay attention when she opened her car door, and another car nearly lopped off her leg.

I'll explain later, he said. It's a complicated experiment.

I bet, I said. Why aren't you answering the phone? I drove all the way over. How come you're so easy to find?

—.

Are you eating?

—.

Drinking any water?

I need to concentrate, he said, his voice dwindling away.

I kept my post at the window, watching the cars.

Outside, the white air deepened into blue. The dimming famous romantic southern-California dusk. I had done my job, so I expected myself to leave. I could call Mom to confirm his aliveness, bring him a ham sandwich and a glass of water, and drive back, continuing the debate in my head about whether or not to go to Eliza's party.

Except it was so familiar, the feeling in the room. The air held a tinge of the same heaviness I'd seen on Joseph's face many times during those babysitting moments, when he'd reappeared, exhausted-looking, tufty-haired, and, standing there at the window, I felt a little like a detective must feel when about to turn a corner on a case.

As if, if I stood still enough, very very still, as still as I possibly could, then I might see something I had not seen before.

It shifted my bad mood a little, to note this. The irritation was becoming just a staticky front underneath of which was forming an arrow of anticipation, beginning to point. I kept my post at the window until the apartment buildings across the street were obscured by darkness. The modest joy of seeing windows click on, the simple pleasure of rectangles of yellow light exposing the dark twists of tree boughs.

A few more cars crept up the street, headlights on. I returned to the chair in the middle of the room, and sat down.

At his desk, Joseph visibly stiffened.

I'll e-mail Mom, he said, how's that? Right now.

I shook my head.

Sorry, I said. I guess I just feel like staying for a little while more.

How long is a little while? he said, almost shrill.

I don't know.

He didn't turn. We sat in a row, him in front of me, facing the wall, like passengers on a stationary train. His laptop was on screen saver, swirling fish in a bubbling tank, so I couldn't see if he was really working on anything or not. On the rest of the desk/table, nothing. A couple pencils. Faint markings, in pencil, sketched out on the wall under the window. Just scribbles here and there about whatever, half an equation, or some numbers in a row.

His fingers dug into the table's rim.

Sorry, I said again.

What was also strange to me was how he didn't get back to work. Hadn't while I'd stood at the window. Still didn't now. In earlier days, when I just wanted to be in the same room as him, he would try his best to ignore me and then would bring the pad of paper or book in a huff into the next room, maybe swearing at me, or locking the door. But here he stayed put. On an impulse, I reached over and slapped down on a key, to wake the computer up, and he started — what! — and the screen cleared and it was just a news page, just the front page of the *New York Times,* talking about the economy and foreign policy. No open files, as far as I could tell.

That's your work? I said. You're reading the news?

And?

Darkness soaked into the room.

There was nothing upsetting, that I could see. It wasn't like there was anything about sex in the air — no hastily covered blanket, or lurking shame or edge of pleasure. And it wasn't emotional — it wasn't like I'd just stumbled in on Joseph rocking himself in a corner in tears or stabbing himself or like I'd found his diary in a drawer and read it aloud over the high-school intercom. No bomb ingredients or drug baggies, no samurai sword or gun or syringe. Whatever was happening was different than all of that, was more private, more closed off: all that came through was that he just wanted to be as alone as possible, aloner than alone, alonest, and my presence in the room was as invasive as if I'd strapped electrodes to his skull and was reading the pulses of his mind.

I'd just like to stay for a little while longer, I said, as quietly as I could.

You're such a fucking pain! he said. You've always been the worst pain in my fucking ass! and he slammed the laptop lid down, but he did not get out of that chair.

In any other instance, in those countless other examples, he would've stalked out, would've gone to the corner farthest from me, maybe off in the kitchen, or on the balcony, but he did not, which was notable, so I started to pay attention to the chair. Just to look closer at it. It was the same chair as mine, the third in that series of four card-table Morehead chairs, sent by Grandma, his personal choice of furnishings for the apartment.

He was sitting in the chair, the way a normal person sits in a chair, but when I looked very closely, it seemed like the chair leg vanished right into his shoe. That the chair legs went inside both legs of his pants, and when I looked even closer, I could see that he had actually cut holes of the correct size in his pants to place the chair legs through the pant legs, and then, ostensibly, the leg of the chair, a light rat-colored aluminum metal with a rubber bulb at the foot, went down to share space with his own foot, inside his shoe.

What's the chair doing in your pant leg? I asked. I said it lightly, just trying to be friendly about it.

He said nothing. No more outbursts. He re-opened and clicked up his laptop and read the news. Just observing. Just looking at what was there. I peered closer to see where the chair foot entered his shoe, but the shoe was covered by the hem of his pants, and something, somehow basic, was off. A slightly sick feeling picked up in my throat then, a dizzy feeling, a feeling like I was not going to like this, that whatever I was about to come across wasn't good. That

I should leave, return to the evening, go knock on the door of the red-car woman across the way, ask for food, any kind, to hug her, to go find a man nearby, to call Eddie out of the blue and ask him to take off my clothes, please. Now. Go. The chair leg went wrong, somehow. How? Was he inserting furniture into his body?

Are you in pain? I asked.

I'm okay, he said. He turned around to look at me, with eyes big and gray, and his voice softened, turning almost gentle.

Just go, he said. Rosie.

The room stretched longer, between us. A ringing bell. Maybe once, in our entire childhood, had he called me Rosie. He never even called me Rose. His face, those gray eyes, so big and, for a moment, all kindness. My throat tightened. I did not understand why. I did not understand what was going on.

I went to sit on the floor, at his feet. It was easy, to go kneel at his feet, and he wanted to kick me off, I could tell, but there were chair legs near his legs, so he could not kick me. And he could've grabbed me with his hand, pushed me away, but he didn't, and that gentleness was still in him: Rosie, he'd said, and I reached down, and when I lifted up the pant leg, there was no cut. I don't even know how to describe it, what I saw. There was no blood at all, and how good it would've been, to see blood — to see it pouring out of his leg, and the surgery he would've needed, the painkillers, the beige rug soaking through.

All I could grasp was just that he had not inserted the chair leg into his own, but that somehow it was mostly just a chair leg there, dressed in a sock, going into his shoe. No flesh leg visible at all, or only some kind of faint shimmer of leg that I could hardly see clearly. Had he cut off his legs? No. Again: no blood there, none. Instead, there was only that shimmer of human leg around the leg of the chair, a soft fading halo of humanness around the sturdy metal of the chair, a shifting of textures that somehow made sense. It looked like a natural assertion of chair over him, like the chair was dispelling him, or absorbing him, as natural as if that was the way it was with everyone. And then the chair leg, with its rubber foot, went inside his shoe, which no longer seemed to hold a human foot at all.

I sat there. I did not say anything. I held on to his knee, the knobby bone of his fleshy knee.

In the silence, something big and word-less. Those Morehead chairs, scattered throughout his apartment. How I'd show up, one day, and all the other furniture would be out on the balcony with the bed, and only four Morehead chairs would be in his apartment. Plus some pens and shoes.

I love them, he'd told my mom, as each one came in the mail. They're great, so functional.

How rarely we heard him use the word *love.* Or, for that matter, *great.* He was sitting on the floor of the living room, in high school, cross-legged in front of the red brick fireplace, folding and unfolding the latest. I didn't really care about the chairs, good or bad, but Joseph loved them, seemed to truly value chairs that could fold so easily into a line. The mailman had started to hate us.

God, she loves them too, said Mom. I can't stand them — no style. Cheapo.

She stood above Joseph with her hands on her hips. There's a table, too, she said, and, sure enough, it arrived the following week.

Joseph called Grandma, that night of the fourth chair.

Thank you, he told her, sincerely.

I stood in the hall. He listened to something for a while.

You too, he said.

When he hung up, I was over at his side in a second. I could not give him a moment alone. What'd she say?

She's not making much sense, he said, brushing at the air. She said something about playing cards, he said. Mah-jongg?

Well, they're card-table chairs, said Mom.

Can I have them, in my room?

Sure? Mom said, tightening her lips. She eyed a chair, the knobby aluminum screw at its joint, the plastic brown-swirled cushion.

He pulled splinters from her hand, weekly. Even in college, even during finals week. On the couch, with tweezers, for hours.

In his room, he was back to the laptop, clicking. Reading the news, as if I wasn't there. Frozen focus ahead. The moment of tenderness was over, the gateway had closed, and with the same certainty I'd felt just a few minutes before, about how much I'd had to stay and pay attention, something had flipped, like a pancake, easy, and now I had to go get the telephone and call George for help. Something big was happening with my brother, and I could hardly comprehend what I was seeing. I would have to leave the room for a second, but it had to be slow, this was not something that could happen quickly, and we had been to the hospital before and we could always go again and the doctors could take him back and maybe they would know what to do. It was twenty seconds, it was ten, to stride out of the room, to find the phone in its cradle and pick it up. And I didn't have a choice then, either; I had to have someone else see this, had to, because Joseph would never confirm it for me, no one would, and I would call George first, it could only be George, only George, who'd believed me years ago when I told him the cookie was angry or the string cheese was tired, only George could be trusted to see what was in front of him. I walked out of the bedroom, strode into the living room, hunted around, found the phone, grabbed it, clicked it to on, and brought it back to Joseph's room.

Ten seconds, eight. The window was still open, the room dark. Only an empty chair, at a table, supporting a laptop, with the front page of the *New York Times,* news bright and colorful.

Before I went out of my mind with sadness and bewilderment, and George found me at the market down the street, crying; before I called my mother in Canada and said he was gone again, had left, he had been here and seemed okay and then he was gone; before I called my father and wept incoherence to his secretary; before that, all I knew to do was to mark that one. That was my only lucid thought, and a thought I have felt as proud of as anything I've ever done in my life. Was just the impulse to take the one pen I could find in the room, the one on his nightstand, a black ballpoint, and to go to the back of that card-table chair, the one at the desk, one of four, the one in front of the laptop, and to draw a thin wobbly line under Morehead. She always signed her name the same. This one, I said, as I drew the line. Him.

■ ■ ■ ■

PART THREE:
NIGHTFALL

■ ■ ■ ■

29

My mother kept good photo albums of the family, up to date. With stickers and captions and exclamation points. In one, she showed me a group picture of us in northern California, visiting distant cousins on a seashore near Sausalito. I peered closely at the people, noting my mother in her pale-green linen dress, my father looking especially tall and tan. Who's that? I said, pointing to a brown-haired girl with a ponytail in a red T-shirt that reminded me of one of my T-shirts.

That's you, she said.

What? I said. No, I said.

She laughed at me. It's you, she said. I think you had a new haircut.

Maybe it was the angle? Or the light, or the fact that I was surrounded by people I never saw again, or the newness of the landscape, but for a few seconds before she told me, I did see myself as a stranger — an average light-brown-haired girl who looked pleasant enough, wearing a familiar red T-shirt I knew from my own closet. Once I knew it was me, the face clicked back into the formation I recognized from all the mirrors of my life. Of course, I said, laughing, as if I had known all along.

30

The way it happened with Joseph was such that I was able to tell most of the story exactly as it had happened to me, and everybody focused on facts. I had seen him, yes. At his computer. He had spoken to me, he had called me Rosie. He'd seemed preoccupied, irritable, and then deeply, sweetly kind. He had no weapons nearby, he did not seem to be on drugs, and he'd told me, many times, that he was working. He had not greeted me at the door. I had broken in. My mother had been worried. She had sent me. She had called from Canada. Nova Scotia. He had been dressed. He had looked thin, but not emaciated. Not so different than his usual self. His refrigerator was empty of food except for butter, grape jelly, and a bread so old it crumbled into dust on contact. The bedroom window had been open, and the running theory of both my parents was that he had somehow jumped out of the window from the second floor, and maybe he had even packed himself a duffel bag, for some reason stashing it in the bushes, and that now he was on a journey. He needs time to search for himself, my mother said, through her tears, when she arrived the next day, in her Canadian wool sweater, bizarre for the warm April Los Angeles afternoon. Did he seem suicidal? the policemen asked, in their navy blue, with their pads of paper, when we filed a report the following Monday. I looked at my mother and said no. And I meant no. Alone, I said, a few times, instead.

That night, after I drew the line on the chair, I could not stop shaking. I left his bedroom and sat in the stairwell, in the outdoor corridor of Bedford Gardens, shaking. I crawled into his bed. No one entered or left the building. Time passed in blank sheets.

Shadows of banana leaf plants gathered around the mermaid fountain. Car lights, turning corners, cast shafts of light through the building. His damp, old pillow.

I was still holding the phone close to my cheek, like a blanket. It held no dial tone, as my mother had predicted. The strongest pull was just to fall asleep there, in the bed, for a long time, as if it had been put there on the balcony for that exact purpose — to catch me upon leaving, the mattress my endpoint — but I had calls to make, people to inform. The closest pay phone I'd seen was on the busy street, Vermont, just a couple of blocks away.

After a while, I unfolded myself from the bed, left the phone receiver on the comforter, and descended the stairs. The air was cool, and it was dark out, the deeper, thicker dark of nightfall. My brain felt emptied, as if a wind had blown it clear. The way water from a hose pushes dirt off the sidewalk. Not in a good or a bad way, just cleared.

Friday night bloomed in full form on the city streets, and Los Feliz was busying up for a weekend evening, restaurant umbrellas opened, table candles lit by electric wands. People sat outside in pairs, hands holding flaxen-colored glasses of wine. Forks and knives clinking on clean white plates. Outside the Jons grocery store, I could see a pay phone in a small glass booth, wedged into a far corner of the parking lot. I walked over, steadily. Alert. Pried open the folding door. Inside, the booth contained a half-bench and an old worn phone book lodged

271

inside a black plastic cover. I took the seat. A tired-looking mother and son exited the store, balancing brown bags. Across the street, at the nearby triangular taco stand with the orange neon sign, two teenage girls picked at their hair, waiting in line, their wrists dressed with rows of gold bracelets. Cars drove up and down Vermont. They were all landscapes to look at, no different than a painting.

I faced the phone. Dug in my pocket for change. The silver square buttons on the pay phone itself were my sole lifeline to people. In them, a reminder that someone, once, had dug in a mine to find iron, had spent sweat, and hours, to bring up to land the supplies demanded by the phone-making company that then made an alloy and melted it into squares embossed with tiny numbers that coded a sequence that attached to electrical wiring that would pulse through poles and rubber-coated lines to ring in the household of the only person in the world I could bear to talk to.

Okay.

I faced the little squares. ABC. DEF. GHI.

George was probably out now, at some Friday Caltech event. In his car. Flooded with girls. Rising quickly, into places I could no longer reach. I knew his number by heart, and I fed the change into the slot, punching in the correct sequence. Then I sat very still, on the bench, while the wires linked and connected. The phone rang several times.

Hello?

I gripped the receiver. For a second, when he answered, I just pressed the plastic hard against my ear. I was so overcome with thankfulness that (a) he existed, and (b) he was nearby, and (c) he actually picked up.

Hi, I said. It's Rose. Edelstein, I added.

Rose, he said. I know your voice. Come on. I'm really glad you called. Listen —

George, I said. It's not about today.

I handled it awkwardly, he said. I just; I mean —

George, I said, louder.

He must've heard the jangle in my voice, because he stopped.

What? he said. What is it? Is Joe okay?

I stared through the window of the next-door liquor store, past the low shelves of candy bars to the clerk standing behind the counter. He had wavy black hair, and was resting on the expensive glowing bottles at his back, reading a *Forbes*.

Can you come out? I said. I'm at the Jons.

Where?

On Vermont, I said.

Is he okay?

I didn't answer. My throat had filled.

I don't know, I said, after a minute. I'll call my dad too. I'm at the Jons, I said again, watching as the clerk rubbed his eye and turned a page of his magazine, folding and tucking it behind the others.

Did he disappear again? George asked.

Yes, I said, low.

The grocery store door slid open and a couple in their twenties exited, in biker gear, his arm looped around her waist. She was stirring her straw around the bottom of a slushie.

George made a hmm sound, into the phone. Then he said not to worry, we'd been through this before, it would be all right, and that he'd be over right away.

Half an hour, okay? he said.

What's wrong? I heard a woman's voice ask him, from the background corners of his room.

I'll be here, I said, dimly. In the phone booth, I said. Like Superman.

Then I called my mother and left a message on the workshop machine telling her to come home, and I called my father and spoke with his secretary. Is he there? I asked. It's about my brother. Tell him to call his daughter, I said.

He's almost done for the day, she said. Are you home?

No, I said. I'm at the grocery store. I peered at the pay phone's number, written in faint pen by someone's hand on a thin strip of rectangular paper, attached under glass to the chrome body of the phone. It was a dinosaur, this phone. Everything about it, including the fragile shaky pen markings of a human hand, seemed destined for extinction.

Just tell him to come to Bedford Gardens, I said. He'll understand.

Then I hung up, and swiveled my body to face the parking lot, waiting.

To see someone you love, in a bad setting, is one of the great barometers of gratitude. Pasadena is twenty minutes east of Los Feliz, more with traffic, more on Fridays, and the parking lot of the Jons filled and emptied about five more times before George arrived, each car spilling out stranger after stranger with a need for groceries. A willowy woman with long gray hair. A compact man in a three-piece blue suit. A shaggy guy with tons of piercings. All wrong. With every unfamiliarly shaped person that drove up, my jitteriness increased. I wanted, desperately, to match up my memory with the parking lot's contents, and every new combination of nose, eyes, and mouth that stepped out was an affront to that hunger. If I'd even seen a neighbor, or my old flute teacher, or the lady who sold us bread at the bakery, I would've run out of the booth and hugged them. It's me, Rose, *Rose*, I would say. Rose.

I sat very still, in my glass booth. Hands folded in my lap. A mildew smell drifted over from the yellowing pages of the phone book. When, finally, George drove up in an old gray VW Bug, his hair matted, glasses on, stubble on his cheeks, wearing old jeans and sandals and a T-shirt, at first I just watched him park, putting on the parking brake, opening the door, and I let the relief wash over me, because I knew how he was supposed to look and there he was, real, looking exactly like that.

Hey, I said, standing, waving from the phone booth. He walked over with a stride of seriousness. We hugged. This, the gift of the steelworkers and the wire operators who had installed the poles that crossed the city. He smelled of fresh-cut apples, and sureness, and my head rested into the nook of his neck. After a minute, he pulled back, hands grasping my shoulders, and asked me what happened. I didn't know how to answer, so I just said that my dad was on the way and Joseph had vanished — that I'd seen him and he seemed off and I'd gone for the phone to make a call and ten seconds later, when I'd returned, he was gone. George nodded, listening. We left his car parked in the lot and exited the store area to walk over to the apartment building. When the light at Vermont turned green, we stepped into the street and George grabbed my hand and the ghosts of our younger selves crossed with us.

31

By the time we arrived at the front entrance of Bedford Gardens, my father was angling his car into a narrow parallel spot on the street. His office wasn't far, and it was past the worst traffic time now, so he'd just taken Sunset west as soon as his secretary passed along the message. Once the car was set evenly between bumpers, he unfolded himself out of it, in his usual lawyer suit, navy blue with faint gray stripes, and that black-and-gray hair, as imposing as ever. He wiped his forehead down as if to pat his thinking into place, nodded a hello to George and then came up and hugged me tightly, closer than usual, his hands broad paddles on my back.

It'll be okay, he said, when he saw my face.

Gone, I said, stupidly.

He peered up the stairs, into Bedford Gardens. From street level, all the lights in the building seemed to be out.

He's not there, I said.

How about this, said Dad, patting for his wallet. Let's grab some food first. And you can tell us what you know. We've been through this before. Beth said you sounded awful on the phone, he said. He looked at me closely, eyebrows low. You don't look great, he said. Did he hurt himself? he asked.

No, I said. No blood.

Drugs?

No drugs, I said.

But my voice was so quiet and faltering that I walked shoulder to shoulder between the two of them, up the blocks, as if they were bodyguards protecting me from the elements of street and store. I was still wearing the same T-shirt and jeans I had worn to school, and I had no sweater, so, halfway up the walk, my father took off his suit jacket and handed it over without a word.

We passed diners, and book buyers, and smokers, and moviegoers.

At the doorway of a French café near Franklin, we turned as a trio and entered. It was a small place with an uninviting stone façade, but inside, the room was warmly lit, with deep-red walls and a dangling gilded dimmed chandelier and menus so tall I

279

could hide my head behind them. At the back counter, several people wound around stools sipping from half-glasses of wine for the weekend wine-tasting, as advertised on the large chalkboard over the bar. The three of us settled into a booth.

Sit, Dad said. He got up and spoke to a waiter, who brought us each a glass of water. Dad pushed his over to me. Drink, he said. George waited, hands folded, across the booth. It was as if the two of them had decided telepathically not to ask me anything until we were settled. Dad returned to the waiter and whispered more. He strode back and forth between the two sides of the room with ease. I admired that stride; it was like he folded space in two with it. I rarely saw him so focused on a task like this: this father of the checklists and the special skill, the one who had made the stool, so many years ago.

He's good, George said, watching, nodding. He was pulling at the skin on his thumb. I dug in my pocket, found a ponytail holder, handed it over.

George reddened. Thanks, he said. In seconds, he had it wound around his thumb and was pulling on the elastic.

Did you call Mom? Dad said, returning to his spot.

I sipped the cool water. The waiter returned with an egg-brown mug of hot water and a basket of tea options.

Drink that too, said Dad. You're shivering.

I left her a message, I said, pulling out a peppermint tea bag. It's late there, so she probably won't get it till morning.

It's good you were there, Dad said, accepting his own coffee mug, wrapping his hands around it.

She told me to go, I said.

Your mom did? George asked.

She called this afternoon and asked me to check on Joseph, I said. She was worried.

Dad exhaled loudly. Closed his eyes. She's right about half the time, he said, shaking his head. It's confusing.

And there, in our corner, while the waiter stepped over with his pad of paper, he laughed a little.

After we ordered, I told them both the story in detail, except for what I'd seen with the chair legs. I did not explain any of that, as it did not feel to me in any way explainable. My father listened intently, still warming his hands on the thick porcelain of his coffee mug.

So it's the usual, he said. He stared into his drink, thinking. Right?

I guess, I said.

Then why are you so shaken up? Dad asked.

Good question, said George, twanging his thumb.

I rolled the tea bag envelope into a tube. Steam rose in flourishes from my mug.

I don't know, I said, unconvincingly.

George raised his eyebrows. Traced the table's wood grain with his fingers. He seemed to be feeling the missing words, the gap, and he looked at me keenly, as if to make a bookmark for later.

A steak frites arrived for George. A jambon sandwich for my father. I was waiting on an onion soup.

Start, I said.

My father tilted his head, like it didn't all fit together. His baguette sandwich was wrapped in white butcher paper and halved on the bias. He pushed it aside.

Let's just go over it again, he said, shaking a raw-sugar packet into his coffee. You called George when?

After, I said.

And the window was open? Dad asked.

When I left the room, the window was open, I said.

And when you returned?

It was still open.

And did you call George then?

Shortly after, I went to the store and called George, I said. Joseph's phone doesn't work, I said.

I think it was around seven-fifteen, George said, eating a French fry. Fry? he said.

Dad took one, distractedly.

I'm just trying to understand, Dad said. He emptied three more sugar packets into his coffee. Stirring. He only ate that much sugar when he was really trying to focus; once, during the research phase of a difficult case, he'd gone through fourteen bars of chocolate in one weekend.

So what did you do *right then?* he asked. He leaned forward, intent. In addition to the medical dramas, he also enjoyed a lot of cop shows.

Right when?

Right when you walked back into the room. He was gone then?

Yes.

Did you go to the window? Dad asked.

From the booth, I looked through the café window to the street, to the faint shine of a silver bumper, parked at a meter. People walking by in blurs.

No, I said.

No?

No.

Why not?

I don't know, I said. I was upset.

Did you look around the room?

No, I said.

Really?

He wasn't in the rest of the room, I said, looking back at him.

How could you tell?

I just could.

I would've looked around the room, said Dad, swallowing his coffee.

Sweet enough? I said.

He lowered his eyebrows. Excuse me?

I heard nothing, I said. He wasn't in the room.

I took a quick look outside the building, George offered, cutting into his steak. Nothing.

So what did you do then? Dad asked.

I crumpled a little, into my corner of the booth. He wasn't there, I said.

I just think it's strange, that you didn't look out the window, Dad said, sitting back and crossing his arms. That's the first thing anyone would do, he said.

Sir, said George.

I looked later, I said.

And?

Zip, I said, wrapping his suit jacket more tightly around me.

Dad peeled the white sandwich paper off into a curl.

No one seemed bothered by the fact that the window was fairly small, and would be very uncomfortable to climb out of. No one seemed to ask questions or take into account the fact that the ivy bushes, below the window, were intact, and did not seem to have taken on the weight of a body. The window was the only possibility, so, according to my father, Joseph had somehow wriggled out the window and floated down, falling gracefully. He had avoided the bushes, or had puffed them back up before he ran off fleet-footed into the night. It was a good image for my brother. A man all in black, a kind of night thief, the type who would jump freight trains and end up on an island somewhere, king.

Dad gave a definitive pat to the curved red sections of the booth vinyl. Then he bit into his sandwich. Okay, he said, chewing. I'll stop. I'm sorry.

I started to shake again. A tremor moved through me, visibly, like an earthquake.

George pushed the mug of tea closer. Hey, he said. Drink more.

He'll be back, Dad said. He touched my hand. He always comes back, he said.

My soup arrived. Crusted with cheese,

golden at the edges. The waiter placed it carefully in front of me, and I broke through the top layer with my spoon and filled it with warm oniony broth, catching bits of soaked bread. The smell took over the table, a warmingness. And because circumstances rarely match, and one afternoon can be a patchwork of both joy and horror, the taste of the soup washed through me. Warm, kind, focused, whole. It was easily, without question, the best soup I had ever had, made by a chef who found true refuge in cooking. I sank into it.

Good, I murmured.

George kept refilling my mug with hot water from the teapot and passing it over.

We ate in silence. After, at the register, my father insisted on paying for George's steak. As we left, the cooks waved thanks from the kitchen, through the flash of a swinging white door.

32

Prospect Avenue was busy by now, night-dark, the half-moon directly above, silvering a sweep of clouds. After George answered a few perfunctory university questions for my father, the three of us walked quietly back to Bedford Gardens, past the coffee shop now milling with people arming up with caffeine to face the evening ahead. Past the rows of houses built in the twenties, with rickety porches and wooden support pillars next to Spanish-tile courtyards and red-tiled roofs. Past the old church on Prospect and Rodney, where sometimes I spied groups huddling on the outside steps with coffee cups. A family of palms: squat, medium and spindly tall. The other trees above us, figs and plums, gleamed in the moonlight, reaching tangled branches up.

At the building, my father gave me a hug. I asked him if he wanted to run up and check out the apartment, but he said no, to my surprise. It's not a hospital, I said, but he just squared his eyes onto George. You'll double-check? he said, and George nodded. We walked him to his car. I told him I'd be home soon. I just have to get my stuff, I said. He shook George's hand firmly. Good, he said, out of nowhere. George and I stood together, watching him go. All around us cars rumbled by, slow, always hunting for parking spots, and as soon as my father's brake lights glowed red, another car clicked on its blinker to claim the space.

George, who had been unusually quiet during the meal, waited for my lead, and after a few minutes we turned from the street and walked into the courtyard area of Bedford Gardens. I couldn't face the stairs yet, so we stopped at the first level, right by the mermaid fountain with its stop-and-start flow of water. The stone mermaid rested on a rock, holding a tilted bucket, and that's what the water came from: a steady stream out of her bucket, back into the sea. The fountain itself, although broken, was framed by a nice stone wall, where we sat down. The stones in the wall were damp, but I didn't mind. The sensation of water creeping into my jeans was uncomfortable but far easier than the whole experience of sitting in that restaurant and trying to describe most of what had happened.

Hey, Rose, George said after a few minutes, pulling a portion off a nearby banana leaf.

Yeah?

He turned to me. The courtyard was dark, except for exterior lamps from a few of the apartments, casting a faint hum of light onto the cement. Heels clicked by, down the sidewalk. With care, George systematically ripped out the green parts of the banana leaf sections, leaving the veins and skeletal structure intact. He worked on it, concentrating. Even with his usual surprised eyebrows, even slightly mussed and tired, he looked almost unbearably handsome to me.

He let out a breath. Nothing, he said. Sorry.

What?

I could see his mind shift over to another subject. When'd you dye your hair? he asked.

I touched an end. It's just an experiment, I said. Last month.

Suits you, he said. How's school?

The usual, I said. You?

It's good, he said. Nodding, to the leaf. I may be going to Boston in the summer, he said.

Boston, I said, vaguely.

MIT, he said.

We faced out, to the entrance. People strode by in hurries. I could feel George's body there, so close to mine, so warm and living, and in a distant way I remembered Eliza's party and realized I'd never told her if I was going to go or not. Something came up, I thought, practicing. George dragged a hand through the fern fronds framing the fountain, the ferns that thrived from the on-and-off drip of the mermaid's bucket.

Thanks for coming today, I said. Really. I can't really thank you enough.

Oh, he said. Please. I'm so glad you called me. And I was glad to hear from you earlier, really —

I reached over to his part of the wall. The stone blocks. Not quite touching, just closer. I wanted to grab on to him desperately, but not in a very good way. More like I wanted to get rid of us both for a couple hours.

We miss you, out there in Pasadena, I said.

He nodded.

We, I said. Me.

—.

So.

So.

Boston, I said.

Can you tell me, he said gently, what you saw?

I lowered my head. No, I said.

Try, he said.

I made faint slashes in the air. I don't know how, I said.

But there's stuff you didn't say, he said.

I kept my eyes on the cement. A cracked fissure began at the base of the fountain wall and then crossed the courtyard like a fixed bolt of lightning.

George peered up, at the apartment. Shadows crossed our feet, bouncing shapes from the movement of the ferns he'd touched. Leafy light frondy patterns, shot through with the upstairs lamplight that sifted through the courtyard.

Should we just check, inside? he said.

I pictured my mother, getting the message in the morning, heading to the airport, a small one in Nova Scotia, blistering with worry, transferring as many times as was necessary.

Why does she have a bucket? I said.

Who?

The mermaid, I said. Does she really need a bucket?

He stood. Come on, he said. Let's go in.

33

At the top of the stairs, we stopped at Joseph's door.

What's this? George asked, pushing on the edge of the bed.

His, I said. It's been out there for weeks. He said he wanted to sleep on the floor.

Huh, George said.

The phone receiver was on the bed. And this?

I put it there, I said. You can see, it's broken.

I hadn't locked Joe's door, so an easy push opened it up, and we stepped inside, into the darkness. Shadows of the furniture in the same places, all things still and inert. The depth of that emptiness. If we'd walked in and found Joseph facedown on the carpet just then, as my mother had discovered him just a couple months earlier, it would've been cause for celebration. But the vacant sound of the place, like it was just waiting to produce an echo, hollowing out, cultivating its hollows, only made me want to turn around and leave.

George brought the phone inside and did the obvious, which I had not even considered, which was to check the base, by the kitchen.

Unplugged, he said. He stuck the cord back into the jack and returned. Took my hand again.

Which way's his room? he said.

He seemed a little nervous, suddenly.

Haven't you been here before? I asked.

He shrank a little, into his shoulders. Early on? he said. But it's been a while, he said.

We walked down the hall, together. Other than the afternoon times with Eddie, I was rarely anywhere alone with a guy, let alone this guy. Something I had wanted for so many years, for my younger self, my current self — this time with George, in an empty apartment, holding my hand! Felt distant now, like something I'd seen in a photograph, or read about in someone else's diary. Instead, it was like we were stepping one foot at a time over the wooden boards of a suspension bridge. He squeezed my hand, and I held on to his tightly.

Joseph's bedroom door was still open at

the end of the hall, so it was just a few steps more to enter, and once inside, to my father's invisible pleasure, George let go of my hand and stepped right up to the open window and looked around and down.

I stayed in the doorway. Looking at the table. The open laptop. The chair.

George closed and opened the window, and then did a full exploration of the room: the closet, with its plaid shirts and boots, the pencils on the nightstand, the page of the New York Times glowing on the laptop, once woken up.

Why'd he give up the bed? he asked, standing in the open rectangular space next to the nightstand.

I don't know, I said. Something about his back.

I wonder if he was sleeping in here at all, he said, pulling on the ponytail holder on his thumb. There's no sign of anyone sleeping on this carpet.

I stepped closer, to George. The room had, in its heavy bareness now, the same full eerie thick feeling I knew so well from years and times earlier.

So, George said. His face was steady, focused, watching mine, trying to ease things for me. Why don't you try to show me, he said.

I shifted, in my spot. Let out a breath. My voice felt too full to use at any length, so I just pointed to the card-table chair, at the desk.

There, I said.

George, watching me carefully, sweet beautiful George, went over to the chair and sat in it. Then he looked up at me, expectantly. What else would a person do? If someone points to a chair and says, There, the general response, like George's, would be to assume that there is something else coming and, in the meantime, sit down. It is something we, people, say: You're going to need to sit down for this one.

So then he sat right on the evidence.

No, sorry, I said, smiling a little. Stand up, I said.

He nodded. Stood. Okay. Yes?

I reached for his arm and pulled him right next to me so that we both faced the desk. I linked my arm with his, close.

There, I said. There.

Is a chair, George said. And a table.

That's what happened, I said.

I don't understand, said George.

I kept pointing. I held on to his sleeve. There, I said.

The chair is somehow connected to Joseph?

Yes.

Can you say more?

No, I said.

Why not?

I put a hand on my forehead. The words lived lower. Below words.

I don't know how to say it, I said. He's gone in, I said.

He's sitting?

No, I said.

He's in a wheelchair?

No, I said.

He's turned into a chair? George said, lavishly.

Ah! I said, and my eyes grew hot and full, and he heard the tears, and glanced over, fast, taking my hands.

Rose? he said, confused.

Just don't move, I said. For a second. Please.

Outside, car locks beeped on, and I closed my eyes and held one of his hands between my own, so warm, his fingers just bigger than mine, that dry warmth I remembered from years before, from our walk to the cookie shop. How his hand had been a lifeline then, too. For many minutes we just stood and breathed next to each other, closer than usual. I could smell that familiar fruit scent of his soap, and his T-shirt, fresh, just recently washed in the laundry.

I don't understand, he whispered.

I laughed a little, under the closed lids.

Me neither, I said. Not at all. Please, I said.

My whole self, calling out: Just now. Just once. Forget all of it. Just now. Don't step back. Please.

Rose — he said.

And he didn't move, closer or farther, and I didn't either, but it was as if a light wind lifted through the window and pushed us just the few extra inches needed. Then the elbows, the shoulders touching, and his arms circled around me, and we held each other close, and I moved my face up to his, my forehead to his cheek, and I was the scared teenager then, and we kissed, a kiss horrible in its pity, or worry, but beautiful because it was George and I'd wanted to kiss him ever since I could remember. Just soft, just lips on lips, just kissing, light. His mouth tasting of sunshine and focus and rumbling adulthood.

It was like we were re-setting the room, together. A room that held nothing inside it now holding two who had known each other through years. It was coaxing and invitation and there was a terrible sweetness to all of it, in the awakeness of my face, and his fingers, and the brushing and gripping of hands on shoulders and faces and backs and in how all the roads had already forked. The surge built and lifted, and I moved into him closer and he pressed into me, and it was turning a corner, heading down new and urgent byways, driving, gravity pulling us lower, but then both of us began to stop it, slowed everything down. Moved our faces apart. Kissing slowly, slower. Pauses. Embellishments. Punctuation. I held on to his arms, tightly. Remember this, I thought. He stayed close, and held my face, and shoulders, and touched the back of my neck, and for what felt like over an hour, we just stood with each other, with hands and lips and skin and quiet.

Thank you, I said. I kept my eyes closed. No one saw that happen, I said. Not even me.

Me, he said.

34

When my mother arrived on Sunday, twelve hours of travel from Nova Scotia to Newark to L.A., we hugged at the door and she kept framing my face in her hands, placing it, as if to make sure it was me. She tried to soften the worry lines pressed into my forehead, but instead, as if drawn by an undetectable marker, they just extended from my forehead onto hers. It bothered her, that I was upset. Usually, like my father, I took Joseph's disappearances in stride and just waited out the time till he returned. Still, she did look rested from her trip, her cheeks red and glistering from the brisk stirrings of winds out east.

We stood facing each other in the front hallway.

Thank you, she said, for checking. She pressed on my shoulders. Her eyes changed. Listen — she said.

I shook my head. No need, I said. There

are bigger things to worry about. I'm not going to say anything.

She kissed my cheek fervently, gratefully, left her tears there. Then picked up her purse and said she was going to drive out quickly to Bedford Gardens to confirm it all.

I listened as her car drove off and then walked around the house. I had trouble standing still. I thought of calling someone — Eliza, even Sherrie — but the only person I really wanted to talk to was George and I already felt like I'd asked too much. I didn't feel like calling Eddie. So while Mom was at Joseph's, and Dad settled down to watch the opening chapter of a Civil War miniseries, I found my way to the kitchen. Windows swiveled open, tabletops clear. A head of garlic was resting alone on the counter, so I dug in my thumb and pulled it into sections. Pressed the heel of my hand on the side of a broad knife to smash down each clove. Peeled papery white layers off the firm yellow centers. Minced.

My mother hadn't seen the bed out on the balcony, and when she came back, she was too agitated to cook, so I said I would do it. I'd already started. As Dad spoke to her in low tones in the next room, I salted a pot of water for spaghetti. I opened a can of good tomatoes, and added it to the chopped garlic and onion sizzling in olive oil. It was the first time I could remember making a whole meal, start to finish. As best I could, I kept focused on the task at hand, and as I chopped parsley into small wet green bits, I just tried to let the ingredients meet each other, as I had tasted in the onion soup.

Dinner's ready, I said, after an hour. My father stepped in, prompt, stretching, and my mother wandered in with weary eyes and set the table. Her shoulders heavy. I placed a bowl of grated Parmesan cheese in the center of the table and served everyone a bowl of spaghetti with marinara sauce. Dad rubbed my hair like I was a little kid; Mom opened a bottle of wine. They picked up their forks and folded into their bowls and ate quietly. I watched them eat for a few minutes, and then my mother asked if I was going to join them, so I felt the narrowness of the corridor and picked up my fork and twirled the pasta around it. The first full meal I'd made on my own. My hand shaking a little as I bit in.

The sauce was good, and simple, and thick.

Sadness, rage, tanks, holes, hope, guilt, tantrums. Nostalgia, like rotting flowers. A factory, cold.

I pressed the napkin to my eyes.

It'll be okay, said Dad, patting my hand.

Once, during the meal, my mother looked up. Her eyes were wet. You made this?

Yes.

It's good, Rose, she said. It's filling. Where did you learn to cook?

Nowhere, I said. I don't know. Watching you?

Have you been practicing?

Not really, I said.

They each had two helpings. I ate four bites of mine.

My father cleared his own dish, rinsed it and left the room.

My mother stayed at the table. Waves of worry about Joseph broke over her as she ran fingertips beneath her eyes.

We sat together, for a while, at our place mats. I tried to stay calm, after those bites. I hardly understood most of it.

When she stood up, moving more slowly than usual, we did the dishes together, washing the red streaks down the drain, spooning leftovers into bowls. I checked the pasta box ingredients to see what factory I'd tasted but nothing seemed to match.

Mom finished rinsing and drying the silverware. The lavender-scented dish soap, a pure clear purple. Outside the kitchen window, lamplight glimpsed off a dog collar as a neighbor toured the sidewalks, pulling the leash.

She squeezed out the sponge to dry and placed it on the aluminum bridge between sink sides. It seemed she'd forgotten I was there.

Where are you? she whispered out the window, into the night.

■ ■ ■ ■

PART FOUR:
HERE

■ ■ ■ ■

35

I lived at home throughout what would've been my college years. I did not go to college. I worked first as a tutor for middle-school kids and then as an administrative assistant at a commercial company that produced cable TV ads. All those smiling people my father and I watched as we sat together paid my bills.

While Eliza and Eddie and Sherrie cycled through the dorms, and the dorm cafeterias, I took down my high-school movie-star posters and replaced them with landscapes and painting prints. I moved the weather-worn marriage stool into the closet and packed my dolls and high-school books in larger boxes and settled those in the garage. It was probably better for me anyway, to go simpler, to avoid the drama of the dorm cafeterias entirely, but mostly I stayed at home because Joseph was gone.

After my visit to his apartment, he did

307

return, one more time. My mother had been driving over every day, several times a day, and on the sixth afternoon she found him facedown again on the floor of his bedroom, starfished. He's back! she sang to us all, on the phone, from his place. He's alive! She sat with him at the hospital, kissing his hands, drenched in reprieve, and my father nodded as if he'd known it all along, and more calls were made and fanfares blown, but I did not feel any relief. Doctors came and tested him extensively and my father called up experts and called in favors, but once Joseph was released he only stayed a few more days. As soon as he had an hour alone in his apartment he disappeared again and did not come back. There wasn't even time to decide if he could stay at Bedford on his own anymore — he went there for a few hours to pack up books for school and Mom had to get groceries for dinner and that was it. To me, this was not a surprise; the act of seeing him there, changing, had been enough to point towards the inevitable future. Whether or not he returned once or twice or three times more, he was headed in, or into, away, and what I'd seen that day was a certain harbinger. The most sobering moment of my life.

When he did return that one time, pasty,

exhausted, more drained and dehydrated than ever, refusing to comment, I went once to the hospital to visit, and that was the last time I saw him.

My mother still drove to his apartment every day, on her way to the studio. To check. He loved this apartment, she said, paying the rent and kissing the envelope fold before dropping it into the mailbox. He will return here, she said, when we drove past. She kept up the lease even though the rows and columns in the red leather ledger advised her otherwise. After six months went by, my father tried to convince her that Joseph knew where we lived — on Willoughby — and that he would come to his primary home first, but she raised her eyebrows when he started talking about it and walked right out of the room. Sometimes in the middle of a conversation about Joseph she would walk out of the room and then out of the house itself and we'd hear her car drive off. I never saw her grab any keys. I think she took to leaving them in the ignition, dangling, like a getaway.

On nights when she was home, in the TV room, huddled close to my father and that red leather ledger, muted television colors making stained-glass shapes on the carpet, he whispered into her hair about investing the rent money for a future day when Joseph would come back and need his savings.

Not yet, she said, sitting straighter. I feel he's returning soon, and he's going to want that place. I felt it strong today, as I was driving home, she said.

She ran her fingertips over the ballpoint-indented numbers, as if they could swirl into a code and tell her where to look.

It was the landlord who finally said no; he wanted to re-do the apartment appliances, and when he found out no one seemed to be living in apartment four at Bedford Gardens, he called up my mother, annoyed. She made up a story about how Joseph was attending graduate school back east in anthropology but that he loved the apartment for his times in L.A. and wasn't it better to have a scarce tenant? The landlord, suspicious about sublets, asked her to move out, and so, on an overcast chilly Monday, I took the morning off work and my mother and I loaded all the items from Joseph's apartment into the same green Ford truck she'd borrowed from the lumberyard long before. There wasn't a lot to pack. Inside, the apartment itself looked just like how I'd seen it last — even the same distant smell of starch still hovering in the kitchenette.

I felt uncomfortable being there, so I kept an eye on his stuff, standing at the edges like a bodyguard, and in each room, my mother wept. She stood at the window in his bedroom, holding the edge for support, like a painting for the neighbors who might look up from their worlds. She stood at his bedroom closet for a while, as if trying to find a secret trapdoor he'd built into the wall leading to a nest he'd made in the insulation of the building. As if he was king of some underground citadel and commanded all the moles and rats.

I had this dream last night, she told me, as we closed the door and walked down the stairs to the full truck. Into clean fresh air. She pocketed the spare key. Downstairs, I'd loaded the folding table and chair into the cab, behind the seats, so they could not be snatched out of the truck bed or fall out on a bumpy turn.

I dreamed he was surfing in Australia, she said, settling into the driver's seat.

She turned on the ignition. Her profile was calm, a little worn, with just the faintest lines at the corners of her mouth pulling down. She faced me. Is it ridiculous? she said.

I pulled Grandma's old bamboo salad bowl into my lap. My other hand behind the seat, holding everything steady.

I bet he'd like it, I said. I heard you can see millions of stars there.

She pulled away from the curb and drove for a while. It felt good, to leave. As she drove down Sunset, I learned the intricacies of the bamboo bowl, which was cracking on the side and had a bump on the uphill northern slant. Boxes slid in the truck bed, to and fro.

At a red light near Western, Mom turned to me. Her face drained of expression.

Rose, she said. Listen. We never finished this discussion. I want you to know. I'll break up with him if you want me to, she said.

With Joseph? I said, tapping the bowl, smiling a little.

Her forehead creased, confused. I feel terrible that you found out about it at all, she said. I've tried to be so discreet —

You've been very discreet, I said.

She bowed her head. More tears leaked from the corners of her eyes and fled past the borders of her sunglasses.

You really don't think your brother left because of this? she said. I can't help but think it. You found out, maybe he found out —

I ran my fingernail along the crack in the bamboo bowl. Mom, I said. It wasn't news. I've known since I was twelve, I said.

She stared at me.

Twelve?

Twelve, I said.

She counted aloud, numbers I didn't understand. But that's the year it started, she said.

I patted the bowl, in agreement.

Did somebody tell you?

No, I said.

Did you overhear something?

No, I said. Just a good guess, I said.

The light turned green.

You were always like that, as a kid, she said wonderingly, pausing. You would come hug me just exactly when I needed a hug. Like magic.

Mom, I said.

I love your father —

Mom, I said. It's okay.

Cars honked behind us. She reached over to my cheek, my ear, touching my hair.

Go! yelled a car.

She moved along. A driver zoomed past and gave us the finger.

Look at you, tough guy, I said.

What a daughter I have, she said, driving. Look at *you*. What an amazing, what a beautiful daughter.

I kept my eyes on the road. Hands in the bowl. It was convenient, how my own survival came across as magnanimous.

It wasn't magic, I said. You always looked like you needed a hug. Hey, Mom, I said. Remember how you said that Joseph would guide you? As a baby?

She gripped the steering wheel. Yes, she said, her voice cracking.

Does he?

She wiped her cheek. What do you mean? Does who?

Larry, I said.

Larry, she repeated. His name new between us.

I watched out the window, waiting. Convenience stores and restaurants and guitar shops passing by.

Not like your brother, she said, slowly. But he has been very helpful.

Then good, I said.

He's a nice man.

I don't want the details, I said. But good.

I know it's wrong, she said, falling back into panic, shoulders rising. I know I should give him up —

No one wants you to give him up, I said.

314

■ ■ ■ ■

At the house, we unloaded the stuff onto the lawn. A few boxes of clothes and science books. The leftover furniture. The salad bowl, and some mismatched silverware and plates.

I lifted a box. Where shall I put it? I said.

His room, Mom said, exhaling. Please.

I stumbled through the front door, arms full. Joseph's room was now Mom's part-time; she slept many nights there, since she said it was a way to feel close to him when she was missing him particularly. The counters were crowded with her things: blouse piles, turquoise bathrobe, jewelry on his desk, makeup on the nightstand.

We marched back and forth, stacking boxes against his wall.

Mom liked to look at his posters, and peer in his desk drawers, but the other unspoken advantage to Joseph's room was that oak side door she herself had installed so many years before. It had its own lock and key, so she could come and go as she pleased, and since she still slept in, I never knew anymore how many nights she spent at home. If my father was troubled by her new level of independence, he did not breathe a word

315

about it. They were kinder with each other than I'd ever seen, talking in lower voices, sitting closer to each other on the sofa, but even so, I often woke up in the morning to find him hunched over, leaving a tray with a cup of tea at the base of Joseph's door.

My father still seemed shockingly unaware of anything that was going on, but based on what I'd tasted, it had occurred to me that inside my mother was some kind of tiny hospital, and my father drove around that one as vigilantly as he drove around the big ones laid out on the map of the city.

He and I hadn't talked anymore about where my brother might have gone. No more theories of windows and checking. No more jovial assurances that we were all over-worriers. He took up jogging to give those restless feet a purpose, and sometimes, a couple hours after dinner, I'd stand at the front door and see my father circling the neighborhood in darkness, in his old raggy Cal T-shirt and shorts. When he ran up the walk, drenched in sweat, in the yellow glow of the porch light I could see a redness around his eyes that was deeper, ruddier, than the redness in his cheeks. He kept a towel outside on the flower-box ledge, and he would wipe down his face and pat his hair neat before he stepped foot back into the house.

When all was unloaded, and the truck was empty, Mom pulled me close and kissed my cheek and flooded me with thank yous so many times and with such elongated emphasis that it only seemed to prove the need for Larry all over again.

I went to work. She drove the truck to the lumberyard. For weeks, Joseph's boxes stayed exactly where we'd placed them against the walls of his room. Mom said she couldn't bear to look inside, so over a series of evenings, daylight extending longer, I finally unpacked them myself. When I found clothing I washed and folded it and put it back into empty drawers; I shelved the books, and the one pot he'd used to cook up ramen joined all our other pots inside the kitchen cabinet. I put a few of Grandma's items — the salad bowl, the movable lamp — back in the side room, where they began. I tossed old sundries, like rice and pasta. I left the Morehead folding chairs and table leaning against the side walls of his closet, and I feared for a day when my father or mother had a spontaneous fit of grief or terror and called up Goodwill to give it all away.

Let me know, I said, rinsing my hands of

dust. If you ever want to give anything away. Just let me know, I said.

I won't give anything away, said my mother.

Because of all this — all the goods crossing the household, all the resettling of room assignments, all the discussions in cars, all the nights of jogging — it wasn't a good time for their only other child to leave home. We needed to be in the same house then, as a kind of checkpoint, or performance of permanence, and if my father didn't actually call roll at the dinner table, ticking off a box for my mother, and then one for myself, it was only because he thought it would make him look like he couldn't count.

All here! he said, on a regular basis, as we passed around the dishes.

36

Shortly after Joseph's final disappearance, George packed up his own things and drove the three thousand miles across valley and slope in his chugging gray VW Bug to Boston. He was starting his graduate program at MIT, and for the first few months, he called at least once a week.

Any news? he always asked at the end, and I always told him no, no news.

We said goodbye, and have a good night, and talk soon.

After summer deepened into fall, after hearing about the mounds of work and lab time he'd been assigned, over the sounds of frantic rummaging at his desk and even, once, an alarm clock ringing, I sank down by the phone base in the kitchen and told him we were fine, that all was fine, in case he was just calling out of obligation.

The rummaging halted.

What do you mean? he said. I call because

I want to.

I lined a pile of yellow phone books into a tower.

I mean, you don't have to take pity on me, I said, getting the phone book corners all matched up. That's gross, I said. You helped me so much, that day. Thank you.

Rose, he said. His voice was tinged with annoyance, and the activity sounds subsided as he settled into a chair. I don't pity you, not at all. What are you talking about?

Outside, our neighbors turned on their sprinklers for a late-afternoon lawn watering. They were trying to grow an avocado tree from a sprouted pit.

Please, I said. George. I never expected anything more than the one time, I said.

Ping, ping, against the side windows.

Why not? he said, after a minute.

Why not what?

Why not expect more than the one time?

Water droplets smeared, on the windows. No one else home yet. I could just picture him sitting in his chair, listening. With his concentrated listening face. With the just-reddening October leaves outside. Elemental in our kiss, for me, had been its property of one-time-ness, which I had told myself even as it was happening: kissing George was a little like rolling in caramel after spending years surviving off rice sticks.

I mean, I said, in a small voice. Right?

Well, he said, louder, it was meaningful to me, he said. Okay? It was not nothing.

No, I said. I pulled the pile of phone books into my lap. For me too. I didn't mean that —

I mean, I'm here, he said. You're there. You should have your own life. I have my own life. That's smart. But you're *Rose,* he said. Okay?

I leaned my cheek on the top phone book. Five-thirty. Water pinging. Parents home soon. It had never felt so wrong to be having such a conversation in their house, an hour away from making dinner for my mother.

George, I said, as softly as I could.

Through the wires, his breathing quieted. For a few minutes, we just stayed there on the phone line, together. Stillness, on his end. I stared at the shelf of cookbooks across from the phone base and mind-moved the black garlic-cookbook to lie on top of the wider-based green pasta-book.

Hey, I said. So. I ate my own spaghetti, I said. I laughed a little. First time I ate anything I made, I said.

And? he said.

Big neon sign in there, I said. Big orange

letters. Saying that I am not ready for George.

No, he said.

Nearly, I said.

That was the first time you ate your own food? he said. In all these years?

First time, I said.

And?

Tastes like a factory, I said, spitting out the word.

From where?

I don't know, I said.

You mean that made the pasta?

I don't think so, I said, mind-sliding the horizontal books shoved into the top of the shelf back into their vertical slots.

Huh, he said, and his voice stretched and moved upwards, as if he were standing. Well, you go figure that out, then, he said. I don't want to call up to have a conversation with a factory. I do that enough with the auto-mated bank guy.

Tall books at the sides, short books in the center. Wide books on the horizontal plane, leaning books straight.

I hate that automated bank guy, he said. *Tioo,* he said. That's how he says *two. Ti-oo.*

You going out?

I guess, he said. There's a study party.

Downward steps of cookbooks, gradated rows.

Okay, I said. Thank you. Good talking to you. Have a good night.

He grunted. Pity you, he said. Ridiculous.

When we hung up, I just sat in the chair for a while with those phone books in my lap. Heavy-weighted paper. All the shelving urgency dissipated. It had felt of utmost importance during the call, this re-shelving, something I was reminding myself to do just as soon as we were off, but now that the phone call was over the urge evaporated. It was comfortable, to sit. Something about being pinned to the chair by all those pages upon pages of phone numbers.

37

That year my brother disappeared, I knew very clearly what I could not do. I could not bear college, the ache packed in the assembly line of trays. I could not yet make the move out of the house. I could not buy a plane ticket to go see George and walk by his side hand in hand against a backdrop of brilliant yellow bursting sugar maples. Could not.

But there were things I could manage, smaller things, and so, on my own, I decided it was time to meet the various cooks of Los Angeles County and to find some useful meals that way. I would eat out as often as possible. This was about all I could handle, and it was the one important thing I figured I could do while living at home. There was a whole lot to consider, and some things need to be considered slowly.

Besides everything else, it had been no small surprise, the Sunday after Joseph disappeared, when I made that spaghetti dinner for my parents and ate it myself. There had been way too much to sort through right away, but I was left with two particularly disturbing first impressions. One was the sickly-sweet nostalgia, in the taste of a tantrum, the longing for an earlier, sweeter time with an aftertaste like a cancer-causing sugar substitute. And the second was that factory.

To taste a factory was not a big deal; I tasted them all the time. I knew them by name and often even by address. But I thought I knew all the factories in America, and the entrance of a new one in that meal had surprised me, a lot.

The day after I made the dinner, while my mother drove back and forth to Joseph's apartment, checking with the police to see if she should file a report, while my father sat on the sofa and insisted aloud, during commercials, that all would be fine-fine-fine, I went to the kitchen cabinet and checked all the pasta boxes. Made in Ames, Iowa, or Fara San Martino, Italy. I knew these places so well — I could name them in a second in any restaurant meal — in the rigatoni, or macaroni, or sheets of lasagna. I reread the ingredients on the slab of Parmesan cheese, which were all fresh, and I walked over to the supermarket and asked at the customer service desk where they got their garlic and onions. I spent an hour in the back room of the market, which smelled of leafy greens and cold cardboard, going over shipping receipts with the customer service representative. She told me how she really wanted to sing in the opera.

At home, I made the same meal again. Both my parents ate it gladly, and as my mother drank her wine and explained how the co-op was being very supportive, I pretended to eat with them by clanking my fork and sipping my water and set aside a bowl for myself for later. When both parents were tucked into their various beds, sleeping, I heated the leftovers on the stove. Sat down at the table, alone.

That same unknown factory, again. Loud and clear, in the food. A machine-tinge I could not identify. Alongside a little-girl voice wanting to go back, to go back to a time with less information. Go back, said the little girl. Blank, said the factory. I steeled myself and sat at the table with a spoonful of pure sauce and tried to move as slowly as I could through all the layers of information, to the point where I thought I was practically feeling the farmer reach his hand down to pick the tomatoes, in Italy; I was nearly hearing church bells ringing through villages in San Marzano, but the tastes of the too sweet nostalgia and stone-cold factory kept returning in a metallic whir, and none of it matched any factory I'd known in my reservoir of factory tastes, which seemed only to indicate that it must've come from the cook.

It was like seeing that photo and not recognizing my own face. It was like lifting my brother's pants and seeing the legs of the chair.

I did not like tasting that, no.

So it wasn't as loud as a neon sign, maybe, telling me I wasn't ready for George, but close.

While Eliza went through school, just as I'd imagined, with keg parties, and virginity losses, and tearful midnight talks with her roommate, and waning updates as the months and years passed, I spent my days working at the office, filing and making copies for other people, and every lunch I scanned the streets and consulted the stacks of those yellow phone-book pages to try out something new.

I started in our neighborhood, buying a pastrami burrito at Oki Dog and a deluxe gardenburger at Astro Burger and matzohball soup at Greenblatt's and some greasy egg rolls at the Formosa. In part funny, and rigid, and sleepy, and angry. People. Then I made concentric circles outward, reaching first to Canter's and Pink's, then rippling farther, tofu at Yabu and *mole* at Alegria and sugok at Marouch; the sweet-corn salad at Casbah in Silver Lake and Rae's char-broiled burgers on Pico and the garlicky hummus at Carousel in Glendale. I ate an enormous range of food, and mood. Many favorites showed up — families who had traveled far and whose dishes were steeped with the trials of passageways. An Iranian café near Ohio and Westwood had such a rich grief in the lamb shank that I could eat it all without doing any of my tricks — side of the mouth, ingredient tracking, fast-chew and swallow. Being there was like having a good cry, the clearing of the air after weight has been held. I asked the waiter if I could thank the chef, and he led me to the back, where a very ordinary-looking woman with gray hair in a practical layered cut tossed translucent onions in a fry pan and shook my hand. Her face was steady, faintly sweaty from the warmth of the kitchen.

Glad you liked it, she said, as she added a pinch of saffron to the pan. Old family recipe, she said.

No trembling in her voice, no tears streaking down her face.

I bowed my head a little. I wasn't sure what else to say. Thanks again, I said.

One of the dim-sum restaurants on Hill Street in Chinatown knew its rage in a real way, and I ate bao after bao and left that one tanked up and energized. An Ethiopian place on Fairfax near Olympic made me laugh, like the chef had a private joke with the food, one that had something to do with trains, and baldness. I didn't even get the joke, but the waitress kept refilling my water and asking if I was okay.

I'm fine, I told her, holding my spongy injera bread packed with red lentils. It's so funny!

She rolled her eyes, and brought me the check early.

My favorite of all was still the place on Vermont, the French café, La Lyonnaise, that had given me the best onion soup on that night with George and my father. The two owners hailed from France, from Lyon, before the city had boomed into a culinary sibling of Paris. Inside, it had only a few tables, and the waiters served everything out of order, and it had a B rating in the window, and they usually sat me right by the swinging kitchen door, but I didn't care about any of it.

There, I ordered chicken Dijon, or beef Bourguignon, or a simple green salad, or a pâté sandwich, and when it came to the table, I melted into whatever arrived. I lavished in a forkful of spinach gratin on the side, at how delighted the chef had clearly been over the balance of spinach and cheese, like she was conducting a meeting of spinach and cheese, like a matchmaker who knew they would shortly fall in love. Sure, there were small distractions and preoccupations in it all, but I could find the food in there, the food was the center, and the person making the food was so connected with the food that I could really, for once, enjoy it. I ate as slowly as I could. The air around me filled with purpose. This was the flora of George's road, and a swinging kitchen door meant nothing. I went over at least once a week, sometimes more, and my time in general was marked by silent sad dinners with my parents and then lunchtime or dinnertime visits to the café as a kind of gateway into the world. It was somehow fitting, that the place had come to my attention first on the night that Joseph left, me sitting across from George, soon to re-set the room with him, wearing my father's suit jacket over my shoulders, shivering, trying to understand what I'd seen. The waiters recognized me on Fridays, when I came in at six. On Sundays, when I went over for lunch, while they served half-glasses of wine for tasting customers lounging at the back counter beneath the gilded chandelier.

I bought very few new clothes, and no new technology, and I paid no rent, and so I spent most of the money I made on meals. I allowed myself the extravagance of leaving a restaurant if I could not bear what I found on my plate, and instead did my father's trick by asking for a to-go box and putting all the food inside it, with a plastic knife and fork, and handing it outside to someone homeless who did not have the luxury of my problem.

38

One afternoon, after a particularly amazing roast chicken, I paid my bill and circled around the outside of La Lyonnaise, finding my way to the kitchen door of the restaurant, a back entrance that opened up into a section of alley that housed a brown Dumpster and a pigeon family. I had the day off from filing. My mother had recently become co-president of the co-op studio, and was busy moving the massive piles of tools into a new loft building off Beverly, close to downtown. Dad at work. He'd gotten so into his jogging that he'd joined a group called Nightrunners that ran exclusively after dark to avoid excess car exhaust. He trained every night at home.

At the back of the restaurant I didn't want to knock on the door; I just felt like standing closer to it, but after ten minutes or so, a small older woman with short dyed blackish hair opened up, holding a white plastic bag of garbage. She stepped out and picked her way carefully on the asphalt in her thin pink satiny slippers. Threw the bag in the Dumpster. Her face looked a little etched and weary, but her eyes were fresh. She stopped when she saw me.

Hello, she said. Delivery?

No, I said. Sorry. I'm just a happy customer.

Ah, she said, pointing. The front is that way.

I nodded. Yes, yes, I said. I know.

She stepped her way back through the alley and returned to the door of the kitchen. Pigeons burbled behind me. She too looked like a regular lady, living in the world — didn't seem particularly with it or excitable or stellar. But that chicken, bathed in thyme and butter — I hadn't ever tasted a chicken that had such a savory warmth to it, a taste I could only suitably identify as the taste of chicken. Somehow, in her hands, food felt recognized. Spinach became spinach — with a good farm's care, salt, the heat and her attention, it seemed to relax into its leafy, broad self. Garlic seized upon its lively nature. Tomatoes tasted as substantive as beef.

At the door, she stood for an extra moment, looking to the side, and she seemed to be watching the squat palm tree in the house across the way as it swayed a little.

Are you Madame Dupont? I said, thinking of the small precise type at the bottom of the menu, with her name and Monsieur Dupont's as owners and co-chefs.

She blinked, yes.

I love your cooking, I said. You make spinach taste like spinach, I said. I stumbled, embarrassed. Sorry, I said. I could go on and on. I don't know how to say it right.

You're saying it fine, she said. Thank you. She fiddled with the doorknob. Why are you in the alley?

I glanced around. Pigeons pecked at the trash. Could I work here, in some way? I asked. On weekends?

She craned her head forward, as if to hear me better. Brushed a little dirt off the step with her slipper.

As a waiter? she said. Waiters apply in front.

I shook my head. No, I said. Not that. Through the back door, I said. Through the food.

Sherrie flashed through my head, years-ago Sherrie, who I'd heard had gone on to sing old standards at piano bars in San Francisco.

Well, I suppose you could take out the

334

trash, she said, reaching back into the kitchen and bringing out another full white bag.

Okay, I said, stepping forward.

Okay? said Madame. She handed it over. Patted her cheek. And we do need a Sunday and Wednesday dishwasher, she said. Our dishwasher just got a job in a movie. Playing a dishwasher.

Please, I said. I walked to the Dumpster and tossed the bag in. I'd love that, I said.

You love washing dishes?

I brushed off my hands. I would here, I said. I do.

39

Grandma died. In Washington. She checked into the hospital, prepared. For her final mailing, she'd given a priority-mail package to the head nurse with careful instructions and our address written on it in big black pen.

To the hospital, she brought a suitcase that contained her nightgown, pills, and pale-blue felt slippers. She died at ninety-one. Mom flew up to the funeral, assumed the ashes would stay in Washington, and arrived home around the same time as the package: pale-blue felt slippers, an empty bottle of pills, and a teak box with carvings of elephants on the rim, inside of which were the soft gray heaps.

Mom ran fingers over the half-circles in the elephant feet. She picked this box? she murmured. I made this box, she said. She turned it over and a few bits of ashes crept out the lid and sifted to the carpet. Sure enough, at the base: L.M.E. carved into a corner. It was the closest I ever got to seeing my grandmother give my mother a hug.

Mom kept herself very busy at the studio, and she did not mention Larry to me again. She made benches, stools, and trunks. Boxes, tables, shelves. No one could take out her splinters like Joseph had, so when Mom came home with clear hands, I never knew if Larry was doing it or if she had just started taking greater care as she worked the planes of wood. I'd never liked seeing my brother take the splinters out of her fingers, nestled up next to her on the couch, side by side, dipping into that bowl of water. For so many years I'd watched the two of them together and I often felt the urge to stay in the living room, like they needed some kind of chaperone. But as I chopped and baked and stirred and walked, they would float in my head, these splinters, new. Joseph had never carved any wood, but he was more connected to things than I'd realized, and by taking the splinters out of her hand, it felt to me now like he'd been almost pulling himself out of her. That at the same time of this very intimate act of concentrating so carefully on the details of our mother's palm and fingertips, he was also removing all traces of any tiny leftover parts, and suddenly a ritual which I'd always found incestuous and gross seemed to me more like a desperate act on Joseph's part to get out, to leave, to extract every little last remnant and bring it into open air.

I found the pair on the shelf of the medicine cabinet, the twelve-dollar tweezers with the angled sharp tips. I cleaned them in peroxide and brought them to a beauty supply shop on Melrose that did makeovers. Just in case you need a spare? I offered. The woman behind the counter eyed me suspiciously, but when she saw how nice the tweezers were, she shrugged and dropped them into her big box of makeup.

40

As my high-school peers went through their later years of college, I worked my free time at the restaurant and days at the cable TV office. Through the subtle shifts of Los Angeles seasons, a movement back and forth through forty degrees, and then through those subtle shifts again. During my free time, I continued to tour the kitchens of L.A. from Artesia to the Palisades. My old rival Eddie Oakley called up out of nowhere one summer evening and we went out a few times, finally having sex on his junior-year college-apartment medium-blue sheets. Cool, he said, patting my arm, afterwards. Full circle, he said.

I slept in his bed for a half-hour, just to try to imagine what it felt like to live there. With car clattering sounds below. With everyone nearby his own age, hollering down the hallways, feet running over a beer-splashed carpet.

On every Sunday morning and Wednesday night, I showed up at La Lyonnaise right on time and I parked myself in front of the sink and cleaned dish after dish after dish. Apparently I was the most grateful dishwasher any of them had ever met. I loved the job; I kept myself focused on clearing the plates, on rinsing the bowls, absorbed in the smells of the kitchen, of piles of chopped onions and rolling pins flattening pastry dough, next to the bubbling pots and sizzling pans, and it was good for me just to be there, to spend as much time there as I could.

At home, my mother no longer woke up in the middle of the night — possibly because she was not in the house at all — and if the living-room light flipped on at 2 a.m. it was my father, up, sometimes having come in from a late-night run. He did not drink tea, but he poured himself a glass of water and then settled into that same orange-striped chair, the vortex of late-night parental thought. I would often hear pages turning of some thickly bound book, and in the muted haze of half-sleep I wondered what he was reading.

George still called once a month or so, and first he had a new girlfriend, who he said was really nice, and then she was his regular girlfriend, and he said she really wanted to meet me, and then he called her his fiancée, and then, in the mail, I received the opalescent envelope invitation, inked in calligraphy. I sent back the little rectangular return card with an attempt at a happy face next to my name: Attending. Steak.

A skinny man at the office, Peter, asked me out. He worked down the hall, in marketing. What? I said, when he asked. I hadn't noticed him much before, with his thick brown eyebrows and earnest voice. He repeated himself. He waited at my desk, squirming slightly, scratching his chin. I wasn't sure what to do, and steely factories flashed through my mouth, uncomprehending, but I bit the side of my cheek and told him sure.

When he asked what I liked for dinner, I countered with a walk.

A walk? he said. Great.

Later that week, after work, we exited the office and walked up Gower together, across Fountain, up Vine to Franklin, crisscrossing past landmarks of Hollywood, churches, stone buildings, miniature landscaped parks. For full sections of the walk we had nothing to say. It wasn't a shocker; at work, once I paid attention, it seemed he could not

341

always maintain eye contact in the general social arena, and when asked about himself would go on about the wrong part of the question without even knowing. He spent the first ten minutes of our walk nervously explaining his latest shoe-purchasing experience to me, and then we just walked. I didn't mind the quiet stretches. It was like we were trying out the idea of being side by side. We stared at the sidewalk as we went, but he did not ridicule me for living at home and not going to college, and when he asked about what I was interested in and I couldn't come up with an easy answer he said it was a far more complicated question than it appeared. Up on Franklin, we had a good conversation about funny grandparents. We stood in the lobby of the Roosevelt Hotel and smelled the old stone pillars. I said it would be nice to see him again. At the end, near my car, I reached out a hand as a thank you, and he stumbled forward to kiss me. His arms pulled me close, and for a second, half a second, all his hitches fell away and he held me with what could only be called confidence. Then we both stammered through a goodbye and fled into the corners.

The next week, at the Lyonnaise café, washing plate after plate clean of the remnants of beautiful food, I finished a big stack and wiped my hands on a dish towel. Leaned against the kitchen door, peeking in the main room of the restaurant. At the bar, people were doing their usual wine tasting. A man had his nose in a glass, and was expounding at length about what he called the edge of leather he'd tasted in a Bordeaux. I listened in the doorway. Monsieur Dupont, a short man with a white mustache, refilled glasses. Do you taste the blackberry? he asked, and the woman with high white heels hanging off the rung of her stool nodded. Blackberry, she said, yes, yes.

41

I missed all the lead-up events and flew in to George's wedding weekend late, on the redeye, ready just in time for the midday ceremony. Before the procession, a woman who knew the order of things pushed me out to sit on the correct side, and I moved down the split between rows of well-dressed people to sit with rows of men I did not recognize. These were new friends George had made since high-school time, wearing a high percentage of joke ties with their fancy suits, and I rested my eyes on bundles of purple and blue flowers as the bride, a red-haired botanist with graceful wrists, walked down the aisle in a dress that highlighted her flowiness, her movements as easy and natural as the ebb and flood of ocean foam.

Her whole face abloom with joy. George, fumbling with his hands, picking at his thumb, nearly dropping the ring.

I do, I do. A kiss.

Dust pollen swirling in the air as the two rushed back up the aisle.

At the luncheon, in a lantern-strewn rhododendron garden, I sat next to Grandma Malcolm, who kept adjusting her fringy yellow shawl and clinking her wine-glass with mine. The band struck up its opening catchy number. I lifted my glass and ate my tiny crab cake and kept an eye on my watch to be sure to leave in due time to catch my night flight home.

Right before dessert, on their tour of the tables, George split from his bride and hur-ried over to me. We hadn't had a chance to talk yet, due to all the flurry.

Look at you! he said, pulling me in for a hug.

It had been at least three years. He looked different, close up: rounder, in a nice way. Like the East Coast agreed with him, gave a little shape and formality to the looseness that was his natural tendency. His wire-rimmed glasses were more oval now, and he wore a belt like it was normal. He'd gained a few good pounds.

I gave him some generic wedding compli-ments, and he held out a hand. Come on, he said, dragging me up. You owe me a dance, he said, tugging me to the dance floor.

The string of outdoor lanterns had dimmed to a muted orange, and tables surrounding erupted in talk and laughter. I held on to his shoulder, stiff. The band singer sidled up to her microphone stand, cooing, and halfway through the song, George drew back and looked into my face.

What? I said.

Remember that cookie shop? he said.

With the clerk and his sandwich? I said. Of course. Remember when you had all-mistakes wallpaper?

He glowed, at me. I'm so glad you're here, he said, squeezing my shoulder. You're the representative, you. He trailed out his arm for a twirl. Still a factory? he said.

I faltered, at the end of his arm. I'd only mentioned it the once.

Getting a little better, I said, winding back in.

He hummed with the trumpet and held me close, and he felt so familiar and not familiar, so mine and not mine.

Hey, he said, remember that time when you came into Joe's room and asked me about the food, what to do about it? he said.

I forget what you said, I said.

I said you might grow into it, he said.

I smelled his shoulder. New tuxedo, perfectly pressed fabric, the same old hint of fruit-scent detergent.

Are you asking if I've grown into it? I said.

I don't know, he said. Have you?

We both laughed, awkward.

I have this job as a dishwasher, I said, feeling the warmth of his hand against mine. At this great place. You know it — remember that place we went to on the night Joe disappeared? With my dad? The French café? You had fries?

You're a dishwasher? he said. Why aren't you tasting stuff for them?

I just like to be there, I said. They give me free meals.

He did a dip. Nothing wrong with washing dishes, he said, bending his knee. It just seems like the wrong job, right? Do they know?

He pulled me up and winked at his bride, who was now dancing with her father across the room.

I watched as she blew a kiss back.

Do they know what? I asked.

He rolled his eyes.

Ugh, you Edelsteins, he said. Come on. It shouldn't be some kind of secret, what you do. I know Joe was working on something, working hard — he showed me a few pages once, years ago, some of the graphs he was making. It was incredible work. Really.

Unbelievable. Now, where does any of that go?

I turned to look at him directly.

Sorry, he said. Sorry. I don't mean to be cold.

It's not cold, I said. It's true.

I mean —

George, I said, holding firmly on to his shoulder. Congratulations to you. Really.

The song was moving into its ending and his eyes split: half melted for me, and he thanked me, but my timing was mostly off and it just sounded like the standard ordinary wedding wish, and most of his thinking was still focused on my brother.

I mean, he's as smart as any of these guys here, he said, waving his arm around the room. His voice curled up, angry.

He should be here, he said.

The band finished up the last notes of the song. Tables clapped, tiredly. Someone called for the cake, and George kissed my cheek and squeezed my hand and thanked me and gave me as much as he could in that moment until time and progress ripped him away and he returned to his bride, who welcomed him in her arms like he'd been at sea for weeks.

42

I arrived home late that night. With a certain quiet, that George was married now. Several hours of the flight I spent at the window, ignoring the movie flashing overhead, my forehead pressed to the glass watching the sun set and re-set over new bunches of clouds as we tracked its movement west. I'd missed the cake-cutting but I'd picked an evening flight so that I could get home in time to go to my Sunday-morning dish-washing, and although it had been impor-tant to go to George's wedding, on the taxi ride to the airport I felt the crumpled paper that had taken the place of my lungs expand as if released from a fist.

When I got home, it was past eleven. Inside, I found my father, awake, sitting up in the orange-striped chair in the dark in his worn Cal T-shirt and running shorts. He held that glass of water in his hand, un-sipped, which only served to reflect the room back to him, cylindrically.

Where's Mom? I said.

Asleep. He waved towards Joseph's bedroom.

You okay?

He didn't really answer, just reached out a hand as a kind of welcome home. I went over to shake it.

How was the wedding?

Fine, I said.

Nice girl?

She seems nice, I said. Pretty, I said. I put down my suitcase and perched on the edge of the red brick fireplace.

In his lap, Dad had opened one of the old photo albums, the heavy pages corresponding to what I'd been hearing from my room. This surprised me; except for the garage sale story, he did not often dip into the past, and that one discovery of *Brigadoon* had been a rare reminder that he'd ever been younger than college.

What are you looking at?

Oh, he said. Just pictures of the family, he said. I couldn't sleep.

I moved closer, to see better. I was glad he was up. I was still wound up from the trip and didn't feel like going to bed yet, and through the dimness of a far outside light we could just barely make out the black-and-white squares of people from my father's childhood. His mother, the dark-haired woman who used all parts of a chicken to feed her family. Uncle Hirsch, holding a football. Grandpa, out and about in town, with some kind of thing on his face.

Was he sick?

Oh, you know, Dad said. The strap.

What strap?

I've told you about the strap, he said.

No, I said. I peered closer. The piece of white cloth looked like it wrapped over the lower half of my grandfather's face and tucked up and away from his mouth.

I used to tell him it looked like he was wearing underwear on his face, Dad said, shaking his head.

For allergies? I said.

I really never told you this?

What?

That he could smell people?

He could what? I said.

You sure?

I coughed, lightly. Um, yes, I said. Very sure.

He touched the photo with gentle fingertips.

My dad, Dad said, would walk into a store and take a whiff and he could tell a lot about whoever was in the store with that whiff. Who was happy, who was unhappy, who was sick, the works. Swear to God. He used to wear that thing on his nose, outside — my dad! Walking down Michigan Avenue with that thing on his face, to get himself a break.

He hit the photo page, as if he couldn't believe there was a photo at all.

He was a good man, Dad said, such a good man. Truly generous. But can you imagine, going shopping with the guy? Once, I told him I didn't want to be seen with him, got locked in my room for two days.

Outside, tree branches rustled in the wind. My throat tightened.

Never said such a thing again, Dad said.

Did he say what he smelled? I asked, very softly.

Pain, he said. He shrugged.

I loved the guy, he said, sitting back. Just loved him, but best when he was not wearing the strap.

I pulled the album closer. Looked at Grandpa, his eyes dark and serious above the cloth. Kind-faced Grandma. Little five-year-old Dad, wearing a bow tie.

He died at fifty-four, said Dad. Smelled death on himself, then he died.

He traced a finger around the square

photo outlines.

I can do that, I said.

Do what?

I smoothed down the page, as if to push it all in.

You can smell people? Dad said.

With food, I said.

You can taste people?

Yeah, I said, not looking at him. Kind of.

He stared at me. No kidding, he said. You never told me that. Is it bad?

I laughed a little. It can be bad, I said.

Dad closed his eyes, rubbed his eyebrows. Huh, he said. Pop hated it too sometimes, he said, remembering. Hated it but also met some good people — we went into Sears one time and he took off the strap to sneeze and caught a whiff of this great guy, just a gem. Irv. Sweetest man, family friend for years. You can taste people? You mean you have to bite a person?

I smiled, down at the page. No, I said. I taste it in the food they make. Whoever cooks the food, like that.

He nodded, though his eyes were still shut and crinkled with puzzlement. He seemed to be churning through various permutations and skipping over a whole range of possible questions.

What a family, he said.

I returned to the photos, for something to do. Tiny Dad, wearing that little polka-dotted bow tie, his hands spread out to the sky.

Cute, I said.

He craned over to see himself. Ach, that tie, he said.

Together, we stared at that polka-dotted tie as if it was the most interesting clothing item in the world.

You know, I have no special skills, he said.

I remember, I said.

He sealed his mouth a little. Nothing like you or Pop, he said.

I turned the page.

I just have this hunch, he said. You know, I saw what it did, over years — that strap! Would you walk around town with a strap on your face all day?

He picked at his sleeve. Dad on Grandpa's shoulders, trying to pluck a plum from the branches of a tree. Smiley little Dad, on a swing.

What's the hunch? I asked.

Just, I imagine, he said, crossing his arms. That I might be able to do something in a hospital. I don't know what. It's too much, right? That if I went into a hospital something might come up, some skill. That's all. Better not to find out, that's what I say.

Keep it simple! Keep things easy!

I didn't move. Held myself very still.

What do you mean, something would *come up?* I said, slowing down my words.

Just, I could do something special, he said. In a hospital.

He pushed his lips together. The moon slipped down into the frame of the window and reached an arm of pure light through the glass.

You have no idea what it is? I said.

Not a clue, he said, evenly.

And it's just a hunch?

Just a pull feeling I get, he said, shifting his seat on the chair. When I see a hospital. A feeling like I should go in. In, in, in.

I dug my hands into the hem of the armrest. My father, out of nowhere, taking shape.

And have you ever? Gone in? I said.

Nah, he said.

Never?

Not interested, he said. I spent time with a sick neighbor once and that was enough for me.

Did he get better?

She was going to get better anyway, Dad said, tapping a hand against his arm.

But did you help her?

I highly doubt it, he said. She was taking

a lot of medicine.

I grabbed his hand. Well, let's go! I said. Let's test it — it's late, so it won't be crowded, and I'll be with you every second, okay? What do you think? This could be great news! I mean, it might help, right? It might be useful information, for the world.

His body grew heavier, gained inertia, the more I pulled.

No, he said. I'm sorry, Rose. I saw what it did to my father. I'm not going in.

But I'll stay right with you, I said, pleading. We'll go in side by side, every second. It's only a test. I won't ever leave your side.

I tugged on his arm, harder.

What if it's amazing? I said.

No, he said. Thank you, but no. His eyes drifted up to mine, stones. He patted my hand and gently extricated his arm from my fingers. His height, still heavying into the seat.

But maybe it could help *me*, I said.

He frowned. I don't see how, he said. Food and hospitals are not the same.

He looked back down at the open book, to steady himself. In a long emphatic stare-down with his baby self. I had to hold myself back from shoving him out of his chair. I wanted to push him in, somehow. To dump him in there, with a crane. To force. It seemed so unbelievably luxurious to me, that he had the option, that he could drive different routes, sit in his seat, thinking, pondering, never know, never have to find out.

Yours is all in the same place, I said, a little helplessly.

And?

I ruffled the weave of the chair arm.

Lucky, I said.

He tightened his lips, and the word *lucky* bounced around us, the wrong word, meaning nothing.

Rose, he said, flatly. I couldn't even go in to see your brother, he said.

And with that, his face locked back into itself.

It was true; when Joseph had been checked into the hospital, Dad had stood outside the electric doors for over an hour, trying to take a step forward. Trying, and trying. I had walked by, on my way to go in. He'd kept a book in his hand to read, so that people passing by would think he had something to do.

You didn't know that was the last time, I said, in a low voice.

But even if I had, Dad said.

For a while, we sat together with the nighttime, undernoted by the distant sound of cars slowing and accelerating, driving the lanes of Santa Monica Boulevard, Saturday night. Moonlight pierced the window. I thought about that trip to the ER, so many years ago, and the doctors standing above, telling me I could not remove my mouth.

I sank my head down on the armrest. I guess if mine were all in one place, I said, I might do the same thing.

He put a hand on my arm. His palm, cool.

Gotta eat, right? he said.

Right, I said.

And just as he said it, like a bird across the sky, my brother flickered through my mind, and although the thought was half formed, it occurred to me that meals were still meals, food still contained with a set beginning and end, and I could pick and choose what I could eat and what I couldn't. And that my father's was a hospital he could drive around entirely, and Grandpa seemed to smell mostly in stores, but what if whatever Joseph had felt every day had no shape like that? Had no way to be avoided or modified? Was constant?

I reached over to touch my father's hand. His eyes found mine.

I'm sorry, he said, his eyes a little stricken.

He gripped my hand back, hard, and the scared light intensified for a second, blazed, then faded from his eyes. He rubbed his free hand over his face. Whew, he said.

Late, he said, in a new voice. He released our grip and clapped a steady hand down on my shoulder.

Time for bed, I said, sitting up on my knees.

He closed the album but he kept his hand on my shoulder and didn't release it, and there were more words in that hand, keeping me there, a little more he wanted to say. It was like once he'd revealed one big thing he thought he might as well tell everything he possibly could. I could see the athlete's urge in it, the sprinter's impulse to throw all things terrifying into one moment and then go to bed and sleep it gone.

Just one more thing, he said.

You saw something that day, didn't you, he said.

The ray of moonlight illuminated his face.

When? I asked, even though I knew.

He didn't answer. I kept my head resting on the arm of the chair.

Yes, I said.

I don't want to know what you saw, he said, placing the album on a side table. I just want to know one thing. Okay?

Okay, I said, in a small voice.

Is he coming back? he asked.

No.

He nodded vigorously, as if he'd prepared himself. He kept nodding, for a while.

That's what I thought, he said. It's been too long.

He pressed down on his forehead, as if to press the thought in there.

Did he say anything? That day in his apartment? Did he ask you for anything? At the hospital?

No, I said.

He wiggled his feet on the carpet. The silver stripes on his running shoes made glinty sparks in the moonlight.

Is he okay? he asked.

I don't know, I said. I don't know how to answer that.

He has some kind of skill? Dad said.

I closed my eyes. Yes, I said. Him too.

For a half-hour or so, my father pressed and wiggled. Shook and tilted. Pushed the news around his body like a pinball had fallen in there and was dodging around his bones and tendons. It was too much for me to watch or think about, so I kept my eyes closed and slept a little.

Finally, I woke up when the moon had lowered enough to send a fresh ray onto the chair and side table, lighting up the gilded print on the front of the photo album, which said *Photo Album.* My father sat alert, still and calm again.

I unwound myself from the floor. Thanked him for the talk. Kissed him good night. I think I'll just take a walk, he said, standing, and he slipped out the front door and into the trail of white that lit his track down the sidewalk.

43

Sunday morning, I walked over to the café for work.

It was a fair May morning, air cleaner than usual, the rugged San Fernando Mountains detailed in the distance as if cars had never been invented. I was early; the doors of La Lyonnaise were still closed.

I walked around the brick wall storefront, watching birds hop on the telephone lines, and knocked at the back until Monsieur turned the knob and let me in.

By ten, about seven or so hungry people had gathered outside the café, and when the door opened, they all headed inside to take their spots for brunch. Outside, a light wind from the ocean blew the air clean, and this was the air that followed them in, washing through the restaurant. I washed dishes for three hours, my head full of my father and George and hospitals and straps, and as the line of silverware eased I asked the main waiter if I could take a half-hour break for lunch. When he said yes, I left the kitchen for a change and headed over to the wine-tasting counter, where I sat myself on one of the stools between a big man with heavy jowls and a petite dark-haired woman wrapped in a red scarf. Monsieur came over from the back room, wiping his cheeks down with the sheet of his hand.

Mimosa? he said, pulling down a champagne glass.

Sure, said the jowly man.

I'd like to try a food tasting, I said.

Monsieur cocked his head. Late-morning wake-up lines still radiated from his eye corners.

A food tasting? he said.

A glass of Chardonnay, please, said the petite woman in the red scarf. Monsieur lifted another glass off the wall, set it upright.

Could I eat my food here, and tell you what I taste in it? I asked, my voice wavering a little.

Monsieur shrugged. I suppose so, he said. Aren't you our dishwasher?

I am, I said.

Good work, said Monsieur.

Sounds fun, said the man. Can I too?

Monsieur popped the cork out of a bottle of white wine, and poured a shimmering glass for the woman.

A quiche, please, I said.

Quiche, echoed the man. Delicious.

The woman with the red scarf spent a few focused minutes with her nose buried in the rim of the wineglass. Madame wandered out from the back, where the smell of caramelizing onions drifted out to us at the counter, like a greeting of midday and sweetness and industry, and she and Monsieur spent a few minutes talking closely, his hand resting easily on the nape of her neck. A waiter ducked into the kitchen and returned with two small plates, holding pie slices of golden-crusted yellow quiche. Monsieur filled another glass of wine for a table, and then brought out the *New York Times* Sunday crossword and a bitten-up pencil. He perched on his stool, behind the counter, and began reading through the clues.

Next to me, the jowly man grabbed his plate. Outside, cars drove up and down Vermont, ducking into parking spots. I looked down at the quiche, with its crisped brown golden edges.

Picked up my fork.

The man next to me ate his mouthful in a rush.

So — we say what we taste in here? he said.

Sure, I said.

Eggs, he said. I taste eggs.

I laughed. Monsieur kept his eyes on his crossword, which was blank.

Yup, Monsieur said, to the page. True, true. There are definitely eggs in quiche.

And this wine has a hint of roses? said the woman next to me.

I took a bite of my quiche, made with such warmth and balance, and swallowed.

I just want to add that the eggs are from Michigan, I said.

The jowly man pursed his lips. We're not talking about location, he said. He took another bite. Cream, he said.

I pulled my stool in closer, to the counter. Madame came over from the kitchen and stood in the door frame.

Yes, she said. There is cream in quiche.

Actually, I think it's half-and-half, I said.

No, she said, but she blushed a little. Ah, she said. It's you. Monsieur glanced up, from his crossword.

I'm on a break, I said.

She nodded, distracted. Her eyes skated up the side wall.

See, there are two different milks, I said, leaning in, on my stool. One is cream, from

Nevada, I think, due to the slightly minty flavor, but then there's regular milk too, from Fresno.

Well, she said. She stepped into the kitchen and I heard her open up the refrigerator, take out a carton.

Monsieur carefully placed four letters into boxes. Quiche Lorraine, he said, to the paper. Named for the Lorraine region of northeastern France, eaten as early as the sixteenth century. German influence.

Ham, said the lady in the red scarf.

I took a sip of water.

Organic pigs, I added. Northern California, I said.

She's making this up, said the jowly man.

Am I right? I said.

Monsieur twirled his pencil, chuckling.

How do you know they're organic? he said.

It's in the aftertaste, I said. Grainier. I'm thinking east of Modesto, I said.

Fresno, said Monsieur, pffing. Same as the milk, he said. There's a farmer we really like. Ben.

The butter is French butter, I said. Not pasteurized. The parsley is from San Diego. The parsley farmer is a jerk.

Ah! said Monsieur, hitting the counter. I don't know why we keep going to him, he said. He is such a jerk.

You can taste that? said the red-scarf woman.

In the way it was picked, I said. He picks it rudely.

Madame stepped back, into the bar area. Nice job with the milk, she said. Did you look in the fridge?

How about nutmeg? said the woman with the red scarf. Madame nodded, and the woman flushed. It's a tricky one, said Madame, dabbing at the corner of her mouth with her apron strap. People never expect it.

Monsieur looked at me directly, waiting.

Far, I said. Indonesia? Standard fare.

Dough, said the big man.

Local, I said. I think you made it yourself.

I made it, said Monsieur. Myself. Last night.

Delicious, I said.

Why are they eating at the wine counter? asked Madame.

Sea salt, said the woman with the red scarf.

You're not even eating, said the jowly man.

It's a food tasting, I said. Instead of a wine tasting.

The crust, mused the man. The crust is —

I took another bite. Let the information rise up, slow. Monsieur had stopped working on the crossword, and I could sense him watching me now. Alert. The sharpened feeling of being paid close attention to.

The cook is a little disillusioned, I said.

Mmm, said Madame, leaning against bottles of wine.

The big man next to me wiped his brow with a napkin. Disillusionment is not an ingredient, he said.

But I had her eyes in mine, and I was keeping them.

But the cook loves to mix, I said. Loves the harmony of putting the right ingredients together. Loves to combine.

That's true, said Monsieur, nodding.

The woman in the red scarf stopped sniffing her glass to listen.

There was also a little hurry during the mixing, I said. It's about eight minutes fast? I said.

The man next to me raised his hand. Or chives? he said.

Eight minutes, I said. Were you rushed?

Maybe four, dismissed Madame.

Monsieur looked up at the ceiling, thinking.

While she was making the quiche, she was planning on calling Édith, he said. Our daughter, he said, looking at me. Remember, Marie?

Behind the counter, Madame was rearranging wine bottles. It looked like she was taking one bottle out, and then trading it with another bottle of the same brand.

It tastes about eight minutes too fast, I said.

Édith was in crisis, Monsieur said. She cannot pass Japanese.

Madame put down a bottle. Not eight minutes, she said, to me.

Eight, I said.

She is bad at writing kanji, said Monsieur.

Five minutes, said Madame.

Monsieur shrugged. A very small smile settled on his lower lip.

There is also a tinge of sadness in the cook, I said.

Now he put down his pencil for good, and folded up the crossword.

In us all, he nodded.

I shifted in my seat. Re-rolled my napkin. It was the first time in a long time that I'd gone full out with my impressions. I had wanted to introduce myself, to people I wanted to meet. That was the whole of it.

On my other side, the woman in the red scarf stared at my plate again.

The pastry crust is made of flour, butter,

and sugar, she said.

Done! said Madame, stepping forward.

The focus broke, and Madame poured the woman a free half-glass of wine, and the man finished his quiche, and talked to Monsieur with great animation about various kinds of bacon. I stayed in my seat. While Monsieur and the man laughed, Madame stepped a little closer to me.

How did you do that? she said, in a low voice.

I don't know, I said. I just can do it.

She reached her arms over the counter. Someone called to both of them from the kitchen, and they spun off to tend to other customers, but I knew I wasn't done. While I waited, the woman with the red scarf tapped me on the shoulder.

She smiled at me.

Hi, she said.

I told her good job, on guessing the dough without even tasting it.

Now, did you know all the food information in advance? she said. She was fumbling in her purse for something. She had an awake face, eyes shining like a small bird's.

No, I said.

You're quite knowledgeable, said the woman, pushing aside gum wrappers and pens. She blinked up at me. The red scarf brought out something in her cheeks, some good kind of redness.

Thanks, I said. I pushed my napkin around the table. It's just this thing, I said.

The woman said aha! and brought out a business card, sliding it over to me across the counter. On it was her name, and a job description for something to do with the schools.

So you can tell things, in the food? she said. Fixing her eyes on me.

I didn't blink. Yes, I said.

Many things?

Yes, I said. Many.

Why don't you give me a call, then, she said, and her giddy guessing self dropped away, and her eyes settled firmly on mine, and she seemed nice, nicer, suddenly. I might be able to use you, she said.

I picked up her card, held it at all four corners.

I work with teenagers, she said.

She turned, and left the room. She didn't look back, but the card was a little rectangular piece of her. I put it in my pocket.

The bar had cleared by then. The jowly man had left, joining the rest of the daily traffic. Monsieur and Madame were busying themselves at the counter, sorting through orders, putting away glasses. Madame still kept her eyes on the tables, check-ing, but the feeling of it had changed. The distance of before was now the discomfort and shyness of going on a first date with someone you think you might like.

Monsieur walked to the front of the bar, from the other side. He held out his hand. We shook.

What's your name again?

Rose, I said. Rose Edelstein.

Well, Rose Edelstein, he said, it looks like we should all go grab some coffee.

44

So you want to become a cook? Madame
said as we walked to their car, together.

I'm not sure yet, I said.

Am I giving you cooking lessons?

Maybe, I said. I just want to be around
while you cook. Is that okay? That's the
main thing, I said.

A food critic?

I just want to learn more about it, I said. I
didn't go to college.

I don't care about that, she said. How old
are you again?

Twenty-two, I said.

Can you chop onions?

I think so, I said.

Well, then, she said, pulling a red net bag
of onions from the trunk of her car. Then
that's where we'll begin.

45

When people asked my mother where Joseph had gone, she said he was on a journey.
It was a word she liked, full of quest and
literature and nobility of spirit. Sometimes
she said he was in the Andes, learning about
ancient cultures. Other times a deep-sea
diver, off a coast in Australia, or else a
surfer; depending on her mood, he either
rode the waves or searched beneath them.
She moved his grandparent fund into a
high-interest low-activity account at the
bank, where the money built upon itself.

She still spent most of her time at the
studio, and for a while, her projects became
very small and intricate: Wooden marbles,
or wooden pillboxes, with embroidered
flowers. Refined wooden tripods, on which
to place small wooden frames. She be-
friended a little girl down the street solely
for the purpose of making an entire fur-
nished dollhouse, but the girl was a tomboy,

and when my mother found her perfect tiny bedroom set smashed by a basketball, she stopped.

Twice a week, I cooked for her. We took out the recipe books together, and she sat and asked about the restaurant and told me about the carpentry innovations while I went through the *Joy of Cooking* systematically. I insisted that she sit, that I didn't need help, that she'd cooked enough for a while. Once again, my salvation looked to any outsider like good and generous daughterliness. For months, we ate only appetizers, and then I moved to soups, and salads, and entrées. I skipped the recipes that sounded too difficult, and my mother picked her favorites and made requests.

She took comfort from what I made. I made it for her. I only ate a little, depending on how much I wanted to bear on any given day. The balances inside were changing, bit by bit, on a daily basis. When her birthday rolled around, I baked her a coconut cake with cream-cheese frosting, and we sat across from each other at the table with big textured slices. Eight, whispered my cake. You still just want to go back to eight, when you didn't know much about anything.

I set a cup of chamomile tea at her place.

She thanked me, still beautiful, with fine lines sunning out now from the creases of her eyelids. We didn't talk about Larry anymore and her constant panic over Joseph had faded a little with time, but I could still see the tightening cross her forehead when she remembered that he was not calling, that it was the call time and the phone was not ringing. Where did he go? tugging at the edges of her eyes, in the tremble of her fork, and all I could give her was that cake: half blank, half filling, full of all my own crap, and there, with bands of sunshine reaching across the table, we ate the slices together.

Your best yet, my mother sighed, licking her fork.

We ate two slices each, that afternoon. Drank more tea. To elongate the time, more than anything.

Neither of us mentioned that we had reached the dessert section of the cookbook, after which was only the index.

After the cake, we cleaned up, as usual. Rinsed the bowls. Stuck the spatula in with the silverware. She said maybe she'd make me a lemon chocolate cake next time, but I put a hand on her shoulder gently and said I didn't really like lemon chocolate cake so much anymore.

But you used to! she said.

I used to, I said. A long time ago.

She ran the sponge along the inside of the sink, to clear it of leftover debris. She did not face me, but I could feel the vibration of tears, a kind of pain hive, rustling inside her. As she resettled the knives and forks in their dishwasher cup. As she squeezed the sponge dry. After a few minutes, she looked up, to watch out the kitchen window.

Sometimes, she said, mostly to herself, I feel I do not know my children.

I stood next to her, as if just listening in. Close. She said it out the window. To the flower boxes, in front of us, full of pansies and daffodils, bowing in at dusk. Where she had directed all her pleas and questions to her missing son, over the last few years. It was a fleeting statement, one I didn't think she'd hold on to; after all, she had birthed us alone, diapered and fed us, helped us with homework, kissed and hugged us, poured her love into us. That she might not actually know us seemed the humblest thing a mother could admit. She wiped her hands on a dish towel, already moving back into the regular world, where such a thought was ridiculous, nonsensical, but I had heard it, standing there, and it was first thing she'd said in a very long time that I could take in whole.

I leaned over, and kissed her cheek.

From us both, I said.

46

On a lunch break at work, I drove over and met the woman who wore the red scarf in an old stone building off Franklin, wedged just to the east of the freeway traffic. She worked with at-risk kids, and she wrote down everything I said on a yellow pad of paper. I wanted to laugh at the officiality of it all, at how earnestly she jotted down *cookies* and *get vanilla* and *feelings in food.* We decided that the following week the kids would make batches of cookies that I would taste. I warned her that it would not be something I could do often. Whenever you can, she said, writing that down too. *Not too often.*

At work, Peter invited me on another walk. We crossed the city in zigzags.

That evening, I drove to the café. Madame and Monsieur were busy figuring out the latest menu plans for the restaurant, and

Madame made me a quick dinner sandwich on a baguette, with pâté and cornichon pickles. The piquant little cornichons, usually a little too acidic for me, were today like tiny exclamation points after the pâté — Pâté! Pâté!

The duck? she said, squinching up her nose.

Great, I said.

Salad?

I ate a forkful of lettuce. Mmm, I said.

Is it organic?

Yes, I said.

Good. She clapped her hands. I wasn't sure if he was telling me the truth, she said. His prices are good.

As I was finishing up, Monsieur came over from the back room with a padlock.

We want you to have a closet, he said. To store your stuff.

You will have supplies, Madame added. And you need to keep an apron here, and a change of clothes in case we go out. Downtown. Markets.

Okay, I said.

He handed the lock to me, fumbling. Along with a little pamphlet with directions.

I forget how it works, he said.

I turned the front dial.

Just pick three numbers you can remember easily, he said. Okay? Good?

I turned it in my hands. A standard pad-lock, with a black face and notched lines in between the numbers.

Can I put other things in the closet? I asked him, fingering the circle on the front.

Ah, he said, raising his shoulders. No matter. Whatever's important, he said. We want you to feel at home.

I went to look in the back. The restaurant itself consisted of three rooms: the main restaurant area, with booths and tables and the wine counter, the kitchen, and a back storage section for the pantry and supplies. In that back section, they'd cleared the small closet for me. It was the size of a standard hall version, with a wooden dowel on top and a small shelf above. The door-knob supported a band of metal where I would hang the padlock. I walked to my car, setting the dial to three numbers. Nine, twelve, seventeen.

At home, at dinner, I explained to my parents that I would be working part-time at the café, learning about cooking in some form or another. That I would have a space to myself. I asked after all the items I wanted. Both of them nodded at me, yes.

It's not moving out yet, I told them. But it's a step.

They helped me pack the car, together. My mother said she wanted to be the first to try the first official meal I cooked outside of the house. We're so proud of you, Mom said, and they stood side by side as I drove away, their smiles sewn up with an edge of fishing line.

As I drove off, I honked the horn, once, and my father raised a hand.

It was easy to unload the car, at the café.

Inside the closet, I put my purse, a white chef's jacket, and a box full of extra kitchen tools and books that I'd bought on my own. Grandma's teak box of ashes. My mother's oak jewelry box. Her apron, with twinned cherries, that she gave me as a prize after I made her a pot roast. A velvet and wicker stool that I did not want to see re-upholstered. A rolled-up poster of a waterfall. A plastic graduation tassel.

In the corner, a folding chair.

47

He returned for two weeks, that same spring I'd found him. Badly dehydrated. Skinnier than ever. With bluish skin, collapsed sheaths under the eyes. Silent, when the doctors probed and pushed.

When Mom discovered him facedown on the floor of his bedroom, it was she who called the ambulance to take him to Cedars-Sinai. The place we'd both been born. For the first few days, he was in intensive care, and when his vital signs stabilized, they moved him to the seventh floor, where he would recover. My father's feet froze at the electric glass entry doors, so he called up all the specialists he knew, former clients, friends of friends, tennis partners, and sent everyone over to find out just what was wrong with his son. On the day I went over, I saw Dad's car parked on one of the side streets just outside the general front area of the hospital. It was empty, and at the entryway he was standing a few yards from the electric doors, absorbed in reading a book. That day, I had my own specific reason for being there. I did not stop and say hello.

The weekend had seemed too busy for a good visit, so I had taken the day off school and walked over, on a weekday, on my own. Just thinking, the whole walk, as I passed the building that had housed the old cookie shop, and Eliza's house, and even the ER where I'd gone years ago when I'd wanted to remove my mouth. Inside the electric lobby doors, I asked the nurse with the giant round glasses Joseph's room number: 714, he said. It was late morning, and the hospital had a low-key feeling, as if it was not a hospital but instead just a place where people do health business. Not a lot of urgency. Slow beeps and clickings. I rode the elevator to the seventh floor with a woman wearing a bright-magenta suit. Her nails, equally magenta, were too long and curved to press the elevator buttons, so she asked me to press hers for her.

Sure, I said.

Six and seven lit up under my fingertips.

On the seventh floor, at the nurse's desk, I

explained that I was there to see my brother. The nurse, a black woman with a perfectly shaped nose and red-tinted hair, said he was getting tested at the moment by a specialist but that I was welcome to wait. She pointed me in the general direction, and I found a seat in the hall outside his door where I waited quietly, watching the nurses busy on their computers, the bulletin board announcing policy changes in red printer ink alongside colorful drawings of families drawn by bored patients. I slept a little, in my seat. Doctors entered and exited Joseph's room. I walked to a nearby window, and sure enough, my father's car was in the choice spot, almost directly below Joseph's room.

My mother came in, kissed me hello, did not scold me for missing school, and went to stand in Joseph's room, listening. Then she bustled out, blew a kiss goodbye. She visited several times a day.

Another hour passed. Morning turned to afternoon. At one, I brought up lunch from the cafeteria, a negligible hamburger grilled by a pothead who wanted to be famous. I ate it in my hallway spot.

When I'd finished, the nurse with the sculptural nose came over.

You know you can always go in when the

doctors are there, she offered. Since you're family.

I shook my head. Soda buzzed in my mouth. Buzz, buzz.

No, thank you, I said. I want my own time with him.

She went back to her desk, to check the schedule. Returned. She had a pretty set of earrings on, lines of twisted gold that moved when she moved, like wind chimes hanging from her ears. She told me that when this current doctor left, no one else was on the schedule for at least a half an hour.

Thank you, I said. I told her I liked her earrings. She handed me a magazine. You're very patient, she said.

I read the fashion magazine cover to cover, and learned about the best way to frame my face, with bangs. How to score high at the workplace by being assertive. The air was warm in the ward — it was a hot May afternoon, dry and grainy with a Santa Ana whisper from the east, and inside, only one rickety fan spun in the corner, recirculating a halfhearted stream of air-conditioning from the vents. I closed my eyes, and practiced hearing all the pinpoints in the room behind me: the nurses, the other patients, tucked into their rooms, the experts, measuring my brother's information.

The cool air, circulating; the fan.

Finally, the latest doctor raised her voice in the tones of goodbye, and her nurse helper left, and when all the various professionals went off to attend to their next patients and the entryway had cleared, I stood and entered Joseph's hospital room. His bed faced west, and through the window at his back, sunlight poured in and glazed the floor. Joseph was facing the other way, but as I pulled a chair near the edge of the bed, he turned his head to see who was next and when he saw it was me, his eyes softened. Nothing I ever expected, in my life. For a while, we sat in silence, together. A plane skirted through the sky outside. Lawn blowers blew leaves around, into the gutters. Cars hummed, at 3rd and San Vicente. At some point I started to fill the space and tell him about all the police write-ups, and about everyone's reactions, and about the group theory of him and the duffel bag and the bushes, and as I was talking, he reached over and took my hand.

His arm was plugged up with tubes. It was the first time I could ever remember him holding my hand, and he held on to it with real focus, with fingers gripping. Those piano fingers, warm, and strong. I edged my seat closer, right to the very end of the bed. He held on tight, and as we spoke, his voice dropped low, to a whisper. It was the kind of conversation you could only hold in whispers.

You're the only one who knows, he said.

In a voice so quiet I had to put my ear right up close to his mouth, so quiet I could hardly hold on to the words, he whispered to me that the chair was his favorite, was the easiest to sustain. That at other times, he had been the bed, the dresser, the table, the nightstand. It took time, it had taken almost constant practice. It was good while he was away, but terribly hard when he returned. I've tried many options, he said. I've tried different choices. But the chair, he said, is the best.

I closed my eyes as he spoke, to hear better. The words, almost ungraspable. Sun on our hands. The sheets, pulled so tight on the hospital bed, sent up a faint smell of brisk laundry detergent bleach.

Does it hurt? I whispered.

No, he said.

His fingers were thin and brittle under mine.

Do you know, while you're away?

No, he said. I don't know anything, while I'm away.

Do you feel the passage of time?

He shook his head. No.

The blanket on his bed grew warm, heated by the slanted ray crossing through the window. Late afternoon Los Angeles hazy sunny sun. I opened my eyes. His skin was still heavy, like it had been before, like more hours had pressed into his face than made sense, like he was a living version of the relativity split between the clock on earth and the one in space. There wasn't much time; soon, a whole new stream of experts sent by our father would be coming in, standing in the doorway with clipboards, and metallic clicking pens, and stethoscopes.

So, I said. Joseph. I have a favor to ask.

Machines whirred beside us. Outside the door, a nurse walked by, soft-footed, on rubber soles.

Joseph squeezed my hand lightly, in response.

You could not usually ask him things, my brother. I had never asked him for anything real. He had sent over George at school that one time, but for so many years I'd begged him to play with me and he'd only do it if my mother offered him a new science book as a bribe. The only time he'd hugged me on impulse was the day, years ago, when I'd come home from the ER after having the fit about my mouth. We did not hang out, or

389

have meals together by choice, or talk on the phone. At times I was sure he forgot my name. But I pressed his hand back, and with my eyes low, pinned to the corner of the pillow, tracing the hemline around the edge, I told him about the line I'd drawn, on the chair. I asked him to only pick that chair, in the future. Not another chair. Not another item. That one. So then, no matter what happened, I would know.

It's just a ballpoint pen line, I said. But it's easy to see. I leaned closer. His heart, on a green circuit, rose and fell on the screen nearby.

Please, I said.

His eyes were still soft, looking to mine.

Do you hear me, Joe? I asked.

Yes.

Does it make sense?

It does.

Will you do it?

He pressed his hand, against mine. Yes, he said.

On the walk home, I passed by my father's car. He was in the driver's seat by then, asleep, his head leaning on his chest, heavy. I picked a camellia flower from a nearby bush, and left it on his windshield.

Headed home, alone.

■ ■ ■ ■

There had been a report in a magazine. About a small island off the coast of central California where only a handful of people lived. At the rim of the island was an abundance of trees with a kind of stretchy, tasty bark, but the birds had taken over those trees and very few were surviving. One in particular fell over — an old elegant palm type, a beauty. It grew closest to the edge of the island, and despite its voracious roots, its enormous trunk, it was no match for the steady impact of beaks and thinner dirt and unprotected weather and the gopher holes that eroded its root system below. It fell all the way over and into the ocean. This was a report about the island. About animals, and tree types, and festivals. I'd read it at the dentist's while waiting for a cleaning.

Many trees in the second ring, up a little higher, had also been overtaken by animals, but some made it through — there, there was enough of a balance of sun and shade, and the roots could dig deeper, and the birds were less crowded, and one of the trees in that area survived, reaching out sideways with tangled branches. It was an interesting tree, one that the islanders com-

391

mented upon. They found it a symbol of survival, in how it leaned so drastically to the side. They held the summer festival under its stretching boughs, and many weddings happened beneath its main branch, the tear-filled vows strewn with messages of reaching.

Twenty yards in? The other trees grew straight up. Plenty of room for elaborate roots. Birds alighted and flew off. Gopher holes made no dents. The trees were strong, functional. They provided shade and oxygen.

Was it so different, the way I still loved to eat the food from factories and vending machines? How once, in junior high, I'd been caught actually kneeling in front of a vending machine, on my actual knees, in prayer position, with bowed head, breathing a thank you into the little metallic grate that received the baggies after they fell down the chute? The security cop, touring the school, had laughed at me. I thought *I* liked Oreos, he chuckled. I love them, I told him solemnly, gripping the bag. I am in love with them, I said. I was around twelve then. I did not know how I would get through the day without that machine at school; I prayed those thank yous to it, and whoever stocked it, and whoever had bought it, every night.

Was it so different than the choice of a card-table chair, except my choice meant I could stay in the world and his didn't?

ACKNOWLEDGMENTS

Many thanks to the Immaculate Heart Center and the Corporation at Yaddo, and for the wisdom and great help of: Bill Thomas, Henry Dunow, Melissa Danaczko, Alice Sebold, Glen Gold, Miranda Jung, Mike Jung, Suzanne Bender, Clifford Johnson, Harold Meltzer, Meri Bender and her dance "Quartet," David Bender, Karen Bender, Brian Albert, Phil Hay, Julie Reed, Lori Yeghiayan, Helen Desmond, and Mark Miller.

ABOUT THE AUTHOR

Aimee Bender is the author of the novel *An Invisible Sign of My Own* and of the collections *The Girl in the Flammable Skirt* and *Willful Creatures*. Her work has been widely anthologized and has been translated into ten languages. She lives in Los Angeles.

The employees of Thorndike Press hope you have enjoyed this Large Print book. All our Thorndike, Wheeler, and Kennebec Large Print titles are designed for easy reading, and all our books are made to last. Other Thorndike Press Large Print books are available at your library, through selected bookstores, or directly from us.

For information about titles, please call:
   (800) 223-1244

or visit our Web site at:
   http://gale.cengage.com/thorndike

To share your comments, please write:
   Publisher
   Thorndike Press
   295 Kennedy Memorial Drive
   Waterville, ME 04901